He was approaching the top of the hill
when a car coming from the other direction roared around a steep curve at high speed and, tires squealing, headed straight for him. "What the hell?"

Adrenaline pumped into his veins. No place to go. A drop-off to the sea on his left, the steep mountainside on his right. He slewed his bike sharply to the right. It skidded on gravel and hit a concrete abutment. He flew airborne over the handlebars onto a bed of rocks, and heard, as from a great distance, the crumple of steel against rock as the car smashed into his Vespa. Heart pounding, he brushed blood away from his left eye with a shaking hand. His head was throbbing, his shoulder hurt and blood seemed to be running down his left leg and into his shoe, but he was alive.

He tried to push himself up. His vision clouded for a moment as a sharp pain shot through his head. What was the car doing? Backing up to try again? Adamo stared in disbelief. He shook his head. He must move quickly. The only escape from the murderous car was by climbing the cliff face. Safety lay in climbing up. He knew how to do that. He stood, weaving, uncertain on his feet. No time to lose. Hands in the crevices. Good. Now get a foothold. Climb!

His toes slipped and lost their grip. He collapsed once again on the side of the road. He raised his head to watch the car that would be the instrument of his death.

Praise for Blair McDowell

"A pulse-racing romance brimming with suspense and intrigue. From bustling New York to beautiful Italy, Blair McDowell paints a picture for the reader that is both breath-taking and evocative. With mystery, danger, true love and hope, *WHERE LEMONS BLOOM* by Blair McDowell has got it all, and I devoured this wonderful story in one sitting."

~Linda Green, Fresh Fiction

~*~

"A non-stop romantic adventure, complete with a dramatic rescue, a romantic cruise, an innocent man trying to clear his name, and his hair-raising confrontation with the ex who did him very, very wrong…All in all, *WHERE LEMONS BLOOM* is romantic suspense where the suspense has the reader frantically flipping pages to make sure everything turns out all right, and the romance is incandescent."

~Marlene Harris, Reading Reality

~*~

"*WHERE LEMONS BLOOM* doesn't take the normal romance route. It gives you more of everything. More fun, more romance, and more acceptance. It should be part of your library. It's a book you'll read and re-read for years to come."

~Melanie Adkins,
haveyouheardbookreview.blogspot.com

Where Lemons Bloom

by

Blair McDowell

Where Lemons Bloom

Cover Art by *RJ Morris*

The Wild Rose Press, Inc.
PO Box 708
Adams Basin, NY 14410-0708
Visit us at www.thewildrosepress.com

Publishing History
First Crimson Rose Edition, 2015
Print ISBN 978-1-5092-0470-0
Digital ISBN 978-1-5092-0471-7

Published in the United States of America

Dedication

To Jeanette

To Gabby
Enjoy This trip to Italy!

Blair McDowell

Acknowledgements

Many thanks to all my Italian friends in Canada and in Italy for their advice and guidance on such things as how the government of Italy works, the Church and the Mafia, and for such inconsequential but important information as how Italians use gesture as a complete second language.

The Amalfi Coast of Italy, the principal setting of *Where Lemons Bloom*, is the home of numerous inns and restaurants. The Albergo de Leone was inspired by a charming inn in Positano, the Casa Teresa. Like Adamo's inn, it is down 110 steps from the road. The restaurant da Salvatore in Ravello is as described, wonderful food in a fantastic cliffside setting, and the delightful Albergo Cesari has been our home in Rome for our many visits to that magnificent city.

To the people who helped me in all these places, thank you.

On the home front, Jeanette Panagapka and Sherry Royal read and reread my manuscript as a work in progress. Their suggestions helped me find my way, more than once, around blind corners.

A good editor is worth her weight in gold, and is as rare as hen's teeth. I had such an editor in Kinan Werdski. *Where Lemons Bloom* is a much better book because of her input and guidance, not to mention her patience. Thank you, Kinan.

And finally, my thanks to Wild Rose Press, a publisher with whom I am proud to be associated.

Know you the land where lemons bloom,
Among dark leaves the golden orange glows,
A soft wind blows from heaven blue,
The myrtle still, and high the laurel stands?
Know you it well?
It's there! It's there
Would I go with you, O my belovéd.
                    ~Johann Wolfgang van Goethe

Chapter One

Fear, stark and vivid, flashed through her. She thrashed in the turbulent water, trying to push herself to the surface. The unyielding riptide pulled her relentlessly down, twisting and turning her body. *Head toward the light*, her instincts screamed as she struggled against the undertow. It was no use. Her lungs were burning, bursting for air. Desperate for breath, she inhaled water.

****

"Come on, damn it. Spit up the water! Breathe!"

Water gushed out. Eve gasped painfully for air. She coughed. More water trickled out. She could breathe again.

Dimly she realized she was lying on her back on the beach. Someone was straddling her and pushing. Rhythmically pushing, pushing.

She lay still for a moment. She was alive. Her lungs and throat burned, but she could breathe. Who was pushing on her? It hurt. Another push. She coughed up more water.

Then it came back. Barbados. She was in Barbados. The undertow…She'd been swimming in the ocean since she was a child, but this time…

She opened her eyes to a frowning face hovering close over her.

"Just stay as you are for a few minutes. I've called

1

for help. But I think you've gotten rid of most of the water you swallowed. How do you feel?" The voice was deep, masculine.

"I've been better." Her throat was raw, her speech, raspy. "I almost drowned, didn't I?"

The man stood and looked down at her. "Yes, you did. Fortunately I saw a rogue wave take you, and I'm a strong swimmer. Didn't you know this stretch of shoreline is unsafe? There are signs posted all along the beach."

"I was just trying to get away from..." What had she been trying to get away from? It was too much effort to remember.

"The hotel pool would have been the safe place to swim." He extended his hand to her. "Do you think you can stand?"

She grasped his hand and tried to pull herself to her feet. Her knees buckled. His arms came around her, scooping her up and holding her effortlessly against him. She was dimly aware of a broad naked chest, of strong arms supporting her.

"It's okay," he said. "I've got you."

Eve started shivering in spite of the heat of the tropical sun.

"Shock," he muttered. "Where are the damn paramedics? I called them ten minutes ago. We need to get you warm."

With her in his arms, he started striding down the beach. Eve was barely conscious of entering one of the beach cottages, of being held under a hot pulsing shower, then gently dried and tucked into a warm bed and cocooned with blankets. Her teeth stopped chattering as her body gradually warmed.

She resurfaced slowly. She wiggled her fingers and toes. She was alive. She remembered her panic in the swirling water. But she was safe, safe and warm now.

He was bending over her. Her eyes focused on his face. Sharply chiseled features. Dark eyes, their expression warm, concerned. His face was unlined, but his short curly hair was a startling silver. She'd seen him earlier, a lone sun worshiper, lying on the beach.

"I see you've decided to rejoin the living." His frown turned to a smile as he spoke.

It was a very nice smile. His rather forbidding face changed when he smiled. She flushed as she realized she was staring at him.

"I don't know what happened to the paramedics," he said. "Would you like me to take you to the hospital? I'd be happy to do so."

"I don't think it will be necessary. I think the worst is over. How could I be so cold in the tropics?"

"Our bodies react strangely to shock. Are you warm enough now?"

A sudden chill shook Eve again.

"Brandy," he said. "As good as a shot of adrenaline."

With the easy grace of a leopard, he walked over to the table and poured amber liquor from an open bottle into a water glass. He looked like a large jungle cat, hard chest, corded arms and legs, all sleek skin and taut muscles.

"Drink," he said. "Think of it as medicine. I think I'll join you. I don't have the excuse of shock, but it's been an eventful afternoon."

He went back to the table, poured himself a generous drink, and returned to stand over her. "It's not every day I pull a mermaid out of the sea."

"Thank you. I'm grateful you were there." She took a sip of the burning liquor. "I don't even know your name."

"What's yours?" he parried.

"Eve."

He laughed. "Then mine must be Adam." He leaned over the bed and touched his glass to hers. "Here's to an afternoon in Paradise."

Eve sat up and realized with a small gasp she was naked under the covers. She pulled the sheet hastily around her. "You undressed me?"

"Forgive the indiscretion. I didn't want to put you in my bed in a wet bathing suit. I might want to sleep in it later. The bed, I mean, not your bathing suit."

"Of course." A flush rose to her cheeks. "I'm sorry to put you out like this."

He gave her a devastating, very masculine grin. "You haven't put me out. In truth, I haven't enjoyed myself so much in years. I can't remember the last time I had a beautiful woman naked in my bed."

"Oh!"

"Sorry. I'll get you something to put on. He turned to a luggage rack and riffled through neatly folded items in his bag. "Here." He held up a large, long-sleeved shirt. "This should be big enough to cover you adequately."

Eve took the garment from him and reached out to take the hand of the man who had saved her life. The shirt dropped unnoticed to the floor as she slid over to make room and pulled him down to sit beside her.

He perched on the edge of the bed, looking distinctly uncomfortable.

Eve smiled at his reticence. She reached up to touch his silver curls. So soft. Without stopping to think, she slid her hand around his neck and brought her lips up to his. He tasted of salt and sun.

He stiffened. Gently he disengaged her arms and stood up, putting distance between them. "If that was thank you, you're welcome. I'll go out on the veranda while you get into the shirt."

She was shocked to hear herself say, "No. Stay. Please stay."

He looked at her, one eyebrow raised in question.

Eve took a quavering breath. She raised her eyes to his and plunged into speech. "Stay. Please. Just lie down with me and hold me." She held up her arms, unconscious of the sheet falling away. "I need to feel human warmth. Just put your arms around me and hold me."

He gazed down at her for a moment, reluctance written in the down-turning of his lips. Then he gave a sigh and disappeared into the bathroom. When he came out he had taken off his wet bathing trunks and put on cut-off denims and a plain white T-shirt.

He lay down beside Eve, carefully keeping the covers between them, and pulled her gently to him so she was cradled in his arms.

She snuggled down, warm, safe, glad to be alive.

Her mind whirled. How had she ended up here, in a strange man's bed? Eve struggled to piece it all together. The flight from Washington...how much champagne had she consumed? Her glass had been refilled several times. On holiday for the first time in years, she'd felt like celebrating. She remembered how her laughter had bubbled up as she'd glimpsed her first sight of Barbados, this emerald green island in a sea so blue it seemed surreal. She'd peered out the window of the plane, craning her neck to keep the scene in view, feasting her eyes on the brilliant colors, sighing as the strain of the past five years faded away.

Her hotel was a delightful surprise. She wasn't sure what she'd expected, but not this exotic setting, a separate cottage with everything so open, so tropical.

Her rescuer's cottage was much like hers. A high mahogany four-poster bed draped in mosquito netting, louvered windows opened to tropical breezes, and a ceiling fan circling lazily. Outside the open door lay a garden lush with hibiscus and oleander and fragrant frangipani. Beyond the flowers, the thin line of the beach and the surf. How beautiful it was. Beautiful, but for her, almost deadly. She shivered.

He brought the covers more tightly around her and pulled her closer. His warmth seeped into her, surrounding her as she lay cradled in his embrace. Tension slowly drained from her body. If she could just stay like this forever, in this place, in this man's strong arms…

She tried to compose her scattered thoughts. How had it happened? She'd wanted a swim. She had put on her bathing suit and stepped out of her cottage. That much she remembered clearly.

Kites. It came flooding back. No, not kites, rectangular parachutes, in every color of the rainbow, at least thirty of them, in wild array, soaring over the sea, moving in breathtaking swoops and swirls and dives, guided by their youthful riders. Eve laughed with the joy of the scene as some of the windsurfers were briefly airborne while others rode the waves, all propelled by the trade winds. They rose and descended with reckless abandon. She gasped as one crashed, but the surfer was up on the board again and back into the fray a moment later. She'd seen pictures of them on the website for the hotel, but nothing had prepared her for this kaleidoscope. How she wished she could join them. They seemed so young, so carefree.

She'd have to walk some distance down the shore to avoid the wind surfers. She stepped out onto the beach and hastily stepped back. The sand was blistering underfoot, and the mid-afternoon sun was still punishingly hot. She went back into her cottage to put on her wide-brimmed hat and slip her thongs on her feet. That's better, she thought.

Giving the colorful parachutes one last look, she walked down the beach to find a place where it might be possible to swim without fear of being hit by a stray surfboard. As she rounded the point, leaving the surfers behind her, Eve saw she was not alone even here. A man was stretched out on a rush mat, his arm thrown over his eyes. Had he been her rescuer?

She'd dropped her towel on the beach at some distance from the solitary sun worshiper, and placed her sunglasses, hat, and thongs on it. Where were those glasses and hat and thongs now? Probably still out there on the beach.

In her mind's eye, she was once again at the edge of the churning white water. The surf was high, but she'd swum in high surf all her life. She'd never been afraid of the ocean. She knew how to dive through the line of breakers. Once past them, she could float on gentle rollers.

Now hip high in the water, she casually studied the

wave pattern. Suddenly, her feet were yanked out from under her as if by some giant hand. She relived her terror as the undercurrent took her and a wall of water crashed over her head.

Eve shivered uncontrollably and moaned, experiencing again that stark moment.

He tightened his strong arms around her. "Hush, you're safe now. Sleep."

Eve came back to the present and nestled down to relax against him. Gradually the all-enveloping warmth from his body seeped through her. She slept.

****

She roused to find her head resting on his broad shoulder, to feel his warm arms encircling her, her leg thrown over his, the covers thrust aside. His eyes were closed, but there was tension in every line of his body. He was not sleeping. She slid her hand under his shirt, splaying her fingertips over the hardness of his chest muscles, threading them through the curls she found. His breath caught, and a muscle clenched along his jaw.

Her hand wandered lower and slid inside his jeans. Ignoring his sharp intake of breath, she touched him gently. He came to life instantly.

She held her breath. What was she doing? She didn't come on to strange men. To any man.

"Don't," he commanded. "I can't do this. You don't know what you're asking. You're experiencing an aftermath of shock. You don't know me from...Adam."

She rushed into speech, afraid if she stopped to think she wouldn't have the courage to continue. "I need to feel alive again. Please."

His hands touched her face gently, and he drew back. "I know you think you want this," he said, his voice hoarse with frustration, "but you won't be happy about it tomorrow."

"If it weren't for you, I wouldn't have any tomorrows. I need this. I need you. I know you want me." Eve touched him intimately again and gave a low laugh. "You can't hide something like that."

He looked at her for a long moment, then stood, stripped off his clothes and moved to his suitcase to retrieve a condom. Back on the bed beside her, he brought his lips gently to hers, just the whisper of a kiss.

Then he was on top of her, his knee pushing between her legs as he kissed her savagely, his tongue assaulting her mouth, then moving down her body tasting and nipping as his busy hands caressed and invaded.

Her soft moan seemed to fuel his attack on her senses. What had she unleashed? Eve was unable to repress her cries as her body arched and responded in dimly remembered ways to the passion coursing through her. It had been so long.

He entered her, and her mind went blank of all but the feeling of climbing, climbing...reaching for...

She convulsed and climaxed in his arms, the sensation prolonged unbearably as he moved in her, drowning her cries with his mouth on hers.

When he collapsed over her, Eve was utterly depleted and complete at the same time. It had never been like this. Never.

Finally her breathing slowed to some semblance of normal. He lay beside her, his arm still under her, holding her close.

"They call it 'the little death,' " he murmured.

"Who...?" Eve had difficulty focusing on his words.

"Poets. John Donne. Shakespeare. Others. The little death. It's as close to paradise as most of us will ever come. So, my Eve, are you satisfied?"

"For the moment."

Her body was still giving her little aftershocks of pleasure. So this was what it's supposed to be like? She'd lived with a man for almost a year, expected to marry him. But she'd never felt anything like this. She'd never experienced anything so all-encompassing, so soul shattering, before. It was incredible.

****

They must have slept. Eve roused sometime after dark to feel his hands gently exploring once again, his lips touching her face with feathery kisses. She slid her hand down his body to find him in throbbing readiness.

He stilled his hands and lips, and, braced above her, asked permission with his eyes.

"Yes, oh yes," she responded to his unspoken plea.

****

She awoke with a start and propped up on her elbow. What time was it? The faint blush of early morning light crept through the louvered windows.

There was something she had to do. What was it? It came rushing back. Of course, the *Wind Surf*. At one p.m. today she was to board a ship for a fourteen-day transatlantic crossing. Her lips curved in a small smile. Fourteen days on a sailing ship and then three months in Europe.

She glanced down at the man sleeping deeply beside her, as memories of the night came flooding back. What had she done? Had sex with a man whose name she didn't even know? What had she been thinking?

Trying to steady her erratic pulse, she slipped out of the bed carefully so as not to waken him. She retrieved the shirt she had dropped so carelessly on the floor the afternoon before and slipped it over her naked body as she crept silently to the door. On the verandah, she looked around to get her bearings. She was in her own hotel complex. Her cottage was just a little way down the beach. She started running and didn't stop until she closed the door behind her, breathless, her heart pounding, safe in her own room.

****

The phone on the bedside table buzzed. Luc Manzel grabbed it, checked to see who was calling, and looked furtively at his sleeping wife. He slipped out of bed, moved quickly and quietly into the bathroom, closing the door behind him. "I've told you never to call this number! What part of 'never' don't you understand, Monica?"

She rushed into speech, her voice shaking. "Adamo is here. I saw him. I saw him today." Her voice rose in panic. "How'd he trace me here? How'd he find me?"

"Take it easy, baby. Did he see you?"

"No. I don't think so. I was just dropping a friend at the airport, and I saw him in my rearview mirror. He was getting into a taxi right behind me. Somehow he's found me." She started to cry.

"Calm down. You don't know he's after you. You don't know anything. But even if he's found you he can't do anything. Did you happen to catch where he was heading?"

"I heard him say 'Surfers' Paradise' as he was

getting into the cab."

"Good girl. I'll have someone check him out. Just stay out of sight for the next couple of days. Chances are he's just taking a vacation in Barbados. Lots of people do. I'll look into it and get back to you. And don't call me at this number again."

Late the next afternoon, in his office on the sixteenth floor of the Conti Building in Manhattan, Luc received the phone call he'd been waiting for.

"He was there all right, boss, right where you said, but he checked out before we got there, shortly before noon. There's no trace of him after he left the hotel. He wasn't on any of the outgoing flights today. He seems to have just disappeared."

There was a moment's silence while Luc stared sightlessly out the window, thinking. "Did you check with the taxi driver who picked him up?"

"Um, no…"

"Do so, and get back to me immediately." He severed the connection. Idiots. He was surrounded by idiots.

Chapter Two

Early in the afternoon, the taxi dropped Eve off at the harbor in Bridgeport. She caught her breath at her first glimpse of the elegant vessel with its brilliant white masts stretching toward the sky. The *Wind Surf.* Her home for the next two weeks.

Immigration was fast and efficient. Surrounded by other passengers, she made her way up the gangplank to the ship. She could hardly believe she was really doing this.

"Welcome aboard, Miss Anderson. You're on deck two, cabin two-thirty-six. Your luggage will be there shortly." The handsome young officer dressed in tropical whites smiled at her. "Enjoy your voyage."

The cabin wasn't large, but there was enough space for everything she'd brought with her. She grinned and bounced on the queen-sized bed. She and her sister Bette always used to check out the beds that way on holidays with their father. The beige and cream linen covers on the bed matched the curtains on two large portholes. Nice! There was a row of cabinets, a desk for her laptop, and a television set. The brochure had said there wouldn't be TV reception, but DVDs would be available in the ship's library. The sun shimmered on the blue Caribbean, through the portholes, reflecting in her mirror. Eve sighed with pleasure. The cabin might be small, but everything in it spoke of comfort.

Someone knocked on her door. She opened it to find a dark-skinned young man there with her bags. She stepped back to let him in.

"My name is Sulu. It is my pleasure to be your cabin steward." He pulled a rack down from the wall, placed her bag on it, and turned to her, smiling. "If you want anything, just call me. My number is there," he said, indicating a card placed next to a bowl of fresh fruit. "The ship will be leaving port at five. You may wish to go up on deck to watch the sails unfurl. Best view is from the Bridge Deck, aft. Will there be anything you need now?"

"No. No thank you." Was she supposed to tip him? No. Her information packet had said tips were added to the bill at the end of the trip.

"Enjoy your voyage," he said, nodding as he left.

Opening her bag, Eve hung her clothes in the narrow closet. Two long skirts with four tops she could mix and match, and one blue silk pants ensemble. Those were all for evenings. The brochure indicated one should dress up a bit for dinner. How had they phrased it? "Casual elegance." She examined her choices critically. Had she bought the right things?

Her slacks and shirts for day wear she put in the closet beside the evening clothes. Shorts and T-shirts she folded and placed in a drawer. The same for her underwear. She had splurged on that. She smiled as she handled the lovely lacy bras and bikini bottoms. And nightgowns, two silk clingy things. Somewhat wasted, sleeping alone. She'd bought two new bathing suits, but she had only one now...

Last night. What had she been thinking? She'd slept with a complete stranger. Her body gave an involuntary jolt at the remembrance of their passion. They'd made love twice, and she didn't even know his name. "Adam," he'd said, jokingly. Adam, to match her Eve. Oh well, she would never see him again. Although it might take a while to erase the memory of his strong dark face with its cap of dense silver curls, or of how gloriously alive she had felt to have him inside her.

Fortunately no one would ever know what she'd done. And now it was over. She was sorry in a way. But she was on a ship bound for Lisbon, and he was in Barbados. She lay down on her bed and stretched like a cat. Life was good.

The speaker erupted. "Good afternoon, ladies and gentlemen. This is Captain Goodwin speaking. The ship will be departing in twenty minutes. There will be complimentary champagne on the Main Deck."

Hastily Eve completed her unpacking, ran a brush through her short brown curls, and, with a last look around, went out to join her fellow passengers. There were reported to be only a hundred and seven on this sailing. She was humming to herself as she left her cabin.

On deck, she accepted a glass of champagne from a waiter and sipped it, leaning over the railing to watch the ship pull out of the harbor at Bridgetown. As green hills and palm trees and colorful houses receded into the horizon, music—soft, insistent, rhythmically throbbing—rose from the ship's speakers. The sails unfurled one by one, as if by magic, while the dramatic and somehow utterly appropriate music swelled. She laughed aloud with joy at the drama of the spectacle. When the last sail was raised and the music had come to its orgasmic finale, she glanced around to study her fellow passengers.

They were of an age. Even the youngest of them appeared to be considerably older than she. And, unfortunately, they seemed all to be in pairs. Adams and Eves, she reflected, a bit regretfully. This could turn out to be a lonely voyage for a single woman of thirty-two. Still, she had her Kindle loaded with books to read, there was a small pool she could swim in, and she could lie in the sun and do absolutely nothing if she chose.

She found a deck chair and watched as the sky slowly darkened and the first stars appeared. A sense of peace enveloped her. Dinner wasn't until eight o'clock. Quite a change for her. Her father used to want his evening meal at five, and even her sister, Bette, with her house full of children, served dinner at six.

****

She was greeted at the door to the dining salon by the chief steward, in tropical whites trimmed with gold braid. "Cabin number? Ah, yes, Miss Anderson. I've placed you at a table for six this evening. Will that be satisfactory?" He motioned to a younger man dressed in formal black. "Miss Anderson, table twenty-one."

Eve followed the waiter to a table in the center of the room. She glanced at her tablemates and stopped, frozen. A flush crept across her features, and her pulse raced as the waiter pulled out her chair. This couldn't be happening. She sat down abruptly, her stomach churning, her legs refusing to support her.

She realized one of the women at the table was speaking to her.

"How're y'all? I'm Betsy Lou Graves. I'm from Atlanta. And this is my husband, Jimmy."

Eve pulled herself together enough to nod acknowledgement. She wasn't sure she could speak, but through a tight throat she managed a terse "Eve Anderson."

The rest of the table followed suit, introducing themselves. Eve waited, her stomach in knots, for him to speak. For it to be his turn.

A knowing smile touched his lips. He nodded gravely to her and said, "Adamo de Leone, New York and Positano."

Adamo? His name was really Adamo? The Italian version of Adam? How utterly absurd.

She clasped her hands in her lap where their shaking wouldn't be visible. He'd be here on this ship for fourteen days. There was nowhere she could go to get away from him. What was he doing here? Going to Lisbon, of course, just as everyone on this ship was. He must be as embarrassed by this unexpected encounter as she was. It was supposed to have been an anonymous one night, and now here they were, incarcerated on a small ship together for the next two weeks.

She put her napkin down on the table and stood. "Excuse me. I'm afraid I'm not very hungry." She turned and made her way blindly through the salon and out to the deck.

She stood at the rail trying to catch her breath. For some idiotic reason she was crying. She sensed him rather than saw him as he came up behind her.

"Please don't cry. I could never stand the sight of a woman's tears. I'm a total coward that way." He leaned on the railing beside her, not touching her. "I did tell you you'd regret it. For what it's worth, I certainly have no regrets." He placed his hand gently under her chin, tilting her head so she had to meet his eyes. "I had no idea you'd be on this ship."

She flinched away from his touch. "I wasn't supposed to see you again. I feel like an utter fool. It won't be easy to avoid each other on a ship this small."

One dark brow rose. "Is that what you want? We should never see each other?"

She looked up at him. He was so utterly handsome. The burnished silver of his hair. His dark eyes burning into her. His long lithe body, as attractive dressed as undressed. He was as seductive as she remembered.

"No," she said. "It's hardly practical to avoid each other for the next two weeks. But I'm not going to sleep with you again."

He grinned, and his face appeared suddenly boyish. "I don't recall we did much sleeping." Then he became serious. "If that's the way you want it, then that's the way it will be. We can't avoid each other easily, so why don't we try to be just friends?"

"Friends?"

"Friends. You know. We talk to each other. We swim together and read together and have our meals together. We get to know one another. Do you really want to spend all your time as a single on this geriatric love-boat?"

Eve laughed. "When you put it like that, no. Friends, then. Shall we shake on it?"

"I don't suppose you'd settle for kissing cousins?"

Eve held out her hand.

He took it and raised it to his lips. "Okay, friends. Now I propose we go back and ask the head steward to find us a table for two. I don't know about you, but I'm hungry."

"Is your name really Adamo?

"The name on my birth certificate and passport is Adamo Francesco de Leone," he said, "In America it got shortened to Adam."

"I think I prefer Adamo. It doesn't seem quite so absurd with Eve."

Eve's tension dissipated as they laughed and chatted about inconsequential things over dinner at a table for two the dining room steward miraculously found for them. At the end of the meal, as they were leaving the dining salon, Adamo stopped to speak to the steward.

"A table for two is ours for the rest of the voyage," he said as he rejoined her. "Now how do you feel about a little stargazing?"

****

Days of white sails and cloudless blue skies followed in a haze of happiness. The shimmering blue sea, the blissful quietude, the magnificent sunsets, were all the stuff dreams are made of. The peace of being under sail, with the only sound the splashing of the sea as the ship plowed through it, seeped into Eve's soul. Time ceased to exist. Life was defined by the sun and the sea and this small ship.

And Adamo.

Eve and Adamo were together from breakfast, taken at a table in the sun on the deck, to candlelit dinners for two under the stars. After dinner Adamo introduced her one by one to the constellations they could almost touch from the bridge at night. Never had Eve seen stars so bright as viewed from the upper decks of this small ship in the middle of a vast dark ocean.

The ship had an open bridge policy, and one day

Captain Goodwin invited Eve, who was a frequent visitor, to take the helm for a few minutes. Adamo laughingly recorded this on his i-Phone. He was always snapping pictures of her—engrossed in a book, splashing in the pool, doing her laps around the small deck, sitting across the table from him at dinner.

"I feel as if we're in some kind of time warp here," he confessed. "The rest of the world has ceased to exist. I know it can't last forever, but if I have pictures they'll prove for a little while there was such a thing as peace."

"Adamo, what happened to you? What destroyed peace in your life to the extent that you have to look for it in pictures? Please talk to me. Tell me what's wrong."

Adamo shrugged his shoulders. "It's not something I can talk about. Just leave it alone, Eve. Please don't ask questions I'm not ready to answer."

Eve wasn't happy about it, but after that, by mutual agreement, they spoke neither of the past nor of the future. They simply enjoyed the golden present. They held hands as they walked the decks, and Adamo kissed her cheek when they parted nights, each to their own cabin. He made no move to break their agreement to be just friends. Was she was relieved or disappointed? She wasn't sure.

One evening they borrowed *Some Like It Hot* and laughed together at the antics of Marilyn Monroe and Tony Curtis and Tony Randall in the old black-and-white movie classic in Adamo's stateroom. Eve was tense with awareness of his closeness as they sat side by side on his bed, propped up against pillows. Would he try to kiss her? But when the film ended he slid off the bed, extended his hand to her, and walked her back to her own stateroom, kissing her goodnight in his usual brotherly fashion, on the cheek.

Eve stood just inside her cabin, leaning against her door. It was she who had insisted on being just friends. She loved being with him the way they were, but...

****

An evening came when there was a chill in the air and the sea was a bit rougher. After dinner they leaned on the rail side by side, looking at the churning wake of the ship. The white sails snapped in the brisk breeze. Eve shivered.

Adamo took off his jacket and slipped it around her shoulders. "We've left the Gulf Stream. It will be colder now. Only two more days to Lisbon."

"I don't want this to end."

"Where will you go?"

"I haven't any real plans. My travel agent booked me into a hotel in Lisbon for two nights. I want to see something of Lisbon. Afterwards...I have three months. I'm not sure where I'll go. Where will you go when we disembark?"

"I'm heading for Rome and then to the Amalfi Coast, but I could be persuaded to spend a couple of days in Lisbon."

An unexpected surge of joy shot through Eve, bringing sudden tears to her eyes. He wasn't ready to leave her. She turned to him, blinking back her tears. "You could?"

He laughed. "I could." He leaned down to kiss her cheek, but she turned toward him so their lips met. His arms came around her as the kiss deepened. When they drew apart Eve was shaken to the core. She stepped back and gazed into the dark pools of his eyes. She was in love with him. When had that happened?

"I'm sorry," he said, his voice hoarse. "I know. Just friends."

"Just friends," she repeated mechanically.

****

They were sailing into Lisbon. Ahead of them they could see the long bridge spanning the Tagus River. It seemed impossible the ship's high masts could sail under it. The same music they had heard when they departed Barbados played over the loudspeakers. As they cleared the bridge, seemingly by inches, the music soared, and the passengers assembled on the deck applauded spontaneously. Then they drifted away to their cabins to finish packing. They would disembark within the hour.

Eve turned to Adamo. "I hate to see it end."

"We have two days in Lisbon."

"I know," Eve replied. "But somehow it feels as if we're ending the fairytale. Once we leave this ship, I'll return to being Cinderella before her fairy godmother intervened, and you will return to…What will you return to, Adamo?"

"Tell me about Cinderella before her fairy godmother," he said.

Eve reached into her purse, pulled out her wallet, extracted a photo, and handed it to Adamo.

He studied it and looked at Eve. "You have an older sister?"

Eve tensed briefly. "Me. Me, just four months ago."

Adamo looked again at the photograph. "I can see you in it now. You look so tired, dispirited, in the picture. What happened?"

"My father died four months ago. He was severely

22

disabled by a stroke, and I spent the last five years looking after him. I don't regret the time with him for a moment, but I guess somehow I lost myself along the way." Eve turned to Adamo. "His death was a shock, even though I'd known it could happen at any time. Somehow my life was defined by caring for him. When he died, it was almost as if I no longer knew who I was."

"Wasn't anyone able to help you with his care?"

"There's only Bette, my sister, and she had two pre-school boys and twins on the way when he had his first stroke. I did what had to be done. We couldn't let him go into a care facility. He was terrified of being left in the care of strangers. 'Storage places for the waiting dead,' he called them."

"I can understand how he felt. You were living at home when he had his first stroke?"

"No. No, I was in Baltimore, attending graduate school. I was in the middle of a Master's program in art history." Eve had a fleeting memory of Alex. Alex she had lived with in another life, when they were both in school, she at Goucher and he in medical school at Johns Hopkins. Alex, who married someone else a year after she withdrew to look after her father.

Adamo's voice brought her back to the present. "Your father was a fortunate man. Not many daughters would have done what you did."

"I just did what I believed was right."

"And after your father died?"

"We sold the house and I went to live with my sister and her husband for a while."

Eve thought back to the months she had spent with Bette and her husband Ed at their home in Silver

23

Springs. "It was strange at first, being in a household so full of life and noise. I must say I was surprised at how easily Bette juggled the needs of her husband and four children all under the age of eight. Not just managed but seemed to enjoy it."

A conversation she'd had with Bette on the subject came flooding back to her. "I don't think I could ever do what you seem to do on a daily basis," she'd confided in one of the rare quiet moments in the household. "How do you manage it all?"

"With a lot of love and an enduring sense of humor," her sister had replied. "You'll see for yourself one day when it happens to you. You're still young enough to have children. You just have to get out there and meet the right man."

The right man. Eve studied Adamo. She was looking at the right man. The man she wanted in her life, to love, to have a family, to grow old with. But he didn't seem inclined to carry their relationship beyond the easy friendship they presently enjoyed. And even that would soon be over. Why had she insisted on keeping the arbitrary line drawn between them? She wanted him as she'd never wanted another man in her life.

His voice interrupted her reflections. "So how did you make the transition from dowdy housewife to goddess? For goddess you surely are." His hand slid tantalizingly down her arm, sending shock waves through her.

She pulled herself together. "Ah, that must remain my secret. But you may have noticed I eat fish when you're having steak. I turn down the pasta and potatoes, and when you're eating sinfully rich chocolate cake,

I'm having a piece of fruit. And I manage somehow to keep up with you each morning in our run around the decks."

"So you do," he concurred. "So how'd you end up on the *Wind Surf?*"

"It was sheer impulse. I had some money from the sale of my father's house, and both Bette and Ed urged me to take a long vacation. One day I found myself lingering in front of a travel agent's window display in the local shopping center. There was this poster of a four-masted sailing ship plowing through an unnamed sea, its sails filled with wind. On impulse I went in and asked about it, and forty minutes later, I walked out of the travel agency with tickets in my hands. Fortunately I already had my passport. I had only five days to get organized, to buy traveling clothes, and to pack. Then I flew to Barbados to spend the night at a hotel before the sailing."

Eve laughed. "The next thing I knew I was being hauled out of the sea by a big brute of a man who then sat on me, swearing."

Adamo joined her laughter. "Luckiest sea catch I ever made."

Eve became serious. "Adamo, this photo is who I am. Underneath these new clothes and this stylish haircut and this newly slim figure, there's a thirty-two-year-old woman deeply afraid of life. I'm a fraud, Adamo. At one time I assumed I had my life all planned. Career, marriage, children. But my father needed me, and somewhere along the way I lost who I was, where I was going. I still don't know everything, but I do know these last two weeks have been the happiest of my life."

Adamo pulled her toward him and held her tight. "We still have Lisbon."

"Yes. We still have Lisbon."

Chapter Three

Eve said her goodbyes to the cabin steward who had looked after her so well, leaving him a generous tip and a note expressing her thanks. Then she went to join the rest of the passengers making their way off the ship and through immigration. A surge of relief swept through her when she caught sight of Adamo in the baggage area.

"Where are you staying?" he asked as he helped the driver load their bags into the back of the taxi.

Eve pulled out the pages her travel agent had given her. "*As Janelas Verdes.* She said it was a nice small hotel close to the harbor."

"I'll see if they have a single available for me."

The hotel was a delight, from the green awnings over its window and the discreet brass plaque beside the door bearing its name to the elegant reception area with an old-fashioned mahogany-fronted desk.

A smiling young woman greeted them and told them she did indeed have one single room left.

"I know we're early," Eve said, "but I wondered if it would be all right to leave our bags here while we go sightseeing."

"As it happens, both your rooms are ready. You can have your keys now. A notation from your travel agent says you're off the *Wind Surf*, Miss Anderson, yes?"

"Yes, we are," Eve replied.

"Then you might enjoy seeing your ship leave Lisbon later this afternoon. There's a lounge on the fifth floor with a patio where you can see the whole harbor and the bridge. You can watch it depart around five."

"Thank you. I'd like that."

Turning to Adamo, Eve said, "Meet you here in fifteen minutes? We only have two days, and I want to make them count. I want to see the Jerónimos Monastery and the Belem Tower and the Explorers Monument and—"

"I'm way ahead of you," Adamo laughed. "I have them all marked on a map, and I know how to get there from here. Meet you in fifteen minutes."

****

Six hours later the two weary tourists stumbled back to their hotel, surfeited with Portuguese art and architecture.

"The Monastery was a revelation to me," Eve said as they climbed marble the steps to the lobby. "I studied the art of the Renaissance for years, and yet I knew nothing about Manueline architecture."

"I liked the giant mosaic map of the world, set in the ground at the foot of the Explorers Monument," Adamo said. "The way it showed the sequence of all the discoveries, with ships marking all the dates and locations where Portuguese explorers first set foot on land. It's hard to imagine the hardships they had to endure, those early sailors."

"Sailors? I almost forgot!" Eve pulled Adamo toward the lift. "We're going to miss the *Wind Surf*'s departure if we don't hurry."

Five minutes later they were on the flower-bedecked balcony on the fifth floor of their hotel, watching their ship sail under the massive bridge over the Tagus, out to sea and into the setting sun. It would be carrying a new coterie of passengers, headed for the Mediterranean. Adamo put his arm around Eve's shoulders and pulled her close. Together they re-entered the lounge.

"Would you like a glass of port?" Adamo indicated the decanter and glasses on a table between two deep leather chairs.

"It seems the right thing to have here," Eve responded.

They sank into the comfortable chairs and sipped the heavy, sweet wine.

Eve paged through a guide book on the table between them. "What do you want to do tomorrow?"

"I think in the morning we might begin with the shopping district, the Baixa. Then we could take a hundred-year-old wrought iron elevator up to the top of the hill for the view. And in the afternoon I'd like to go up to the Castelo de São Jorge."

Eve laughed. "You sound like a guide book."

"Guilty as charged. I brushed up on Lisbon from a book I found in the ship's library."

In the evening, the concierge suggested they try a street of restaurants located under the bridge for dinner.

The waiter seated them on a banquette, side by side, with a view of the water. Eve was uncomfortably conscious of the warmth of Adamo's thigh pressed against hers. Her imagination went on overdrive. She suggested he order for them both.

Their first courses arrived. His consisted of tiny mussels in a white wine sauce, while hers was melon wrapped in the thin-sliced ham of the area. He fed her mussels from his bowl, popping them onto her mouth, watching with pleasure as she enjoyed the succulent sea creatures. She sliced her melon and offered him bits of it. Sharing their food seemed incredibly intimate, almost sexual. Eve shivered briefly at the arousal of feelings she'd been doing her best to suppress.

Adamo poured sparkling Vinho Verde from its distinctive green bottle into their glasses and lifted his in a toast. "To the woman who has made me believe in life again."

Eve was stunned. Could his life have been so terrible before he met her? She plunged into speech. "Adamo, tell me about it. What happened to you? Why are you so unhappy?"

He was still for a long moment. Then he sighed. "I can't talk about it. I'm happy at this moment, here with you. Let's not spoil it." He put his arm around her and gave her a brief hug. "We'll be returning to reality soon enough."

Eve was both puzzled and hurt by his inability to confide in her. Did he have so little trust in her?

The waiter brought their next course, strips of steak with a sauce of peppers and tomatoes, served family style. Eve spooned the spicy mixture onto their plates. Why could he not share his past with her? She had told him everything about herself.

They ate their main course in silence.

The waiter cleared their plates away.

Adamo said, "You must try the dessert. It's a traditional Portuguese sweet made with egg yolks and sugar."

"I couldn't, Adamo. I can't eat another bite."

"Well, I'll order one anyway. You can have some of mine. When you eat someone else's dessert, it has no calories."

Eve laughed, and the tension between them seemed to dissipate. "Is that so?"

"I have it on the best authority!"

****

They walked home, and Adamo saw Eve to her room. There he brushed her hair back from her face, his fingers lingering, tracing the line of her cheek, sending a shiver of desire through her.

"*Mia bella Eve.*" He dropped his hand abruptly. With a brief kiss on her cheek, he said, "See you in the morning," then turned and strode away.

Eve closed the door behind her and walked over to the window. She looked at the view without seeing it. She knew no more about Adamo than she had after their night in Barbados. Why was he so evasive about his past? Whenever she asked him a personal question, he changed the subject. She had told him everything— well, almost everything—about her past. And she knew nothing about his. What wasn't he telling her? Did he have a wife somewhere? Perhaps even children? The possibility filled her with pain. He was clearly well educated, but he never mentioned anything about his work. What did he do for a living? Worst of all, he didn't seem to notice or care their time together was coming to an end. They had just tomorrow. Then he would head for Rome, to do what? While she…

She had a restless night. Melancholy invaded her dreams.

****

Eve was somewhat revived after a brisk shower the

next morning. If this was to be their last day together, she would do her best to ensure it was a happy one.

Now that she could connect to the web again, she sent off a short email to Bette, telling her about the *Wind Surf* and about her experiences in Lisbon. She couldn't bring herself to mention Adamo.

They had breakfast together in the hotel and then hopped on one of Lisbon's yellow streetcars for the short trip to the town center. Together they wandered through the city's most elegant shops, Eve window shopping while Adamo made her laugh aloud with his pithy comments about the haute couture on display.

"You don't care for high fashion?" Eve jibed.

"My ex-wife went in for those kinds of clothes in a big way. And no, I don't care for them. I like the way you dress."

Ex-wife. Eve caught her breath. Not wife, *ex*-wife. He'd never mentioned an ex-wife. Or anything else about his life before he plucked her out of the sea.

"Your ex-wife?"

"I've been divorced for six years."

"Any children?"

"No, none." His voice was flat, closing the subject. "Just look at the mosaics on these sidewalks and the blue-and-white tile murals on the buildings!"

She followed his gaze to the broad sidewalks stretching up the hill as far as the eye could see. They all appeared to be made of small marble stones, a black-and-white mosaic in dizzying wave patterns.

"I've never seen anything like it," she answered mechanically. He had done it again. Avoided telling her anything about himself. Of course it stood to reason a man as attractive as Adamo would have been married somewhere along the way, but why was he so guarded about his past or, for that matter, his present?

"Portugal's an interesting country." Adamo's voice intruded on her dark thoughts. "I wouldn't mind seeing more of it someday. Will you stay on here? See something of the countryside after I leave?"

After he left? Depression settled, cold, on her. The sun no longer seemed so bright, the air no longer so warm on her skin. She shivered. "I don't know. Maybe."

The day passed too quickly. As the shadows grew, Adamo took her hand and said, "We'll have to hurry if we want to catch the sunset. We'd better take a cab up the hill. I want to watch it from the castle, the Castelo São Jorge."

They stood motionless on Lisbon's highest hill, Adamo behind Eve, his arms encircling her as she leaning back against him on the castle ramparts, watching the last rays of the sun turn the puffy clouds on the horizon cotton-candy pink, then mauve. Eve had never been so happy, or so fearful. Would this be the last time she ever felt his arms about her?

Only as the sun settled into the mouth of the river did they turn away.

"Are you up for wandering down a very steep hill, through the Alfama district?" His voice resonated with melancholy. "We'll probably find somewhere along the way for dinner."

"Fine with me." It mattered little to her what they did. She ached with an inner pain. Their time together was coming to an end, and she could see no way to change that. He had made it very clear that these two days would be their last.

The Alfama was unlike any part of Lisbon they had yet seen. Its narrow winding lanes, intersected with steps and sided with small whitewashed houses, looked more North African than European. Doorways were open, and people sat in chairs outside them. Children played chase games up and down the steps, watched over by women, dressed in black, who all seemed to be doing something with their hands as they sat, knitting or needlework or preparing vegetables for their evening meal. There was frequent laughter among them as they called back and forth to each other and to the children. The men smoked their pipes, read their papers, or chatted with their neighbors. There was a sense of community about the Alfama.

Halfway down the hill they found a small local tavern. The doorway, covered by a beaded curtain, led to a dimly lit interior with wooden tables, many already occupied.

"Up for an adventure?" Adamo cocked an eyebrow in challenge.

Eve looked dubiously at the doorway but shrugged her shoulders. "Lead on."

The waiter must have sized them up instantly as tourists because, without asking, he brought them a pitcher of Vinho Verde, two small plates, and a platter containing an assortment of appetizers—sardines and octopus and olives and chunks of cod in a spicy sauce.

"Dolores will be singing soon," he said, as if Dolores singing were all they could possibly be here for.

They looked at each other questioningly. "I suppose we'd better stay long enough to hear Dolores sing," Adamo said, picking up a fried sardine in his fingers, popping it into his mouth, eating it whole, bones and all, washing it down with the tart light wine.

The chatter around them ceased. A tall, gaunt-looking middle-aged woman dressed in unrelieved black walked into the room and perched on a stool. She strummed the first chord on the guitar in her hands and began to sing. Her voice, low and throaty at times, strident and compelling at others, was utterly different from anything Eve had ever heard. Not like the pop singers she had grown up listening to or the classical voices she had come to love later. The songs the woman sang during the next hour were different too. They seemed unutterably sad, filled with longing. They left Eve on the verge of tears.

The singer at last put her guitar down and acknowledged the enthusiastic applause of an audience grown much larger while she was performing.

A man at the table next to theirs leaned over to them. "I see you are strangers here. English?"

"No, American," Eve answered.

"You like our Fado?"

"Fado?"

"Fado, the music you just heard."

"I like it very much, but it seems rather mournful," Eve replied.

"But that's what Fado is," he answered. "Fado is about *saudade*. Longing." He paused. "How to explain in English? Fado is about loss, love, and then love lost forever, followed by a lifetime of sorrow and regret. It is an expression of the Portuguese soul."

The words rang in Eve's ears. Love and love lost, followed by a lifetime of sorrow and regret. Hadn't she set herself up for exactly this? How could she let

Adamo walk away from her? How could she go on living without him? She loved him. He was dark and unfathomable. She knew nothing of his past, nothing of the weeks and years before he pulled her out of the sea on a beach in Barbados. But it didn't matter. She could see into his heart and soul as she knew he saw into hers. And what she saw she loved.

To Eve, Adamo seemed withdrawn as they wound their way down the hillside. He gave her his arm, but appeared to be almost unaware of her beside him as they traversed the steps through the Alfama back to central Lisbon. He looked straight ahead, his expression stony. At the bottom of the hill, he hailed a cab and gave their hotel address. Once there, he followed Eve to her room as he had done the night before and leaned down to kiss her cheek. He had not spoken to her since leaving the tavern.

"No." Eve put her arms around him and kissed him full on the mouth. When she pulled back, shaken, she repeated, "No. We're not going to end it this way. Leave me tomorrow if you must, but stay with me tonight."

Adamo shook his head. "You don't know what you're asking. There is so much about me you don't know, can't know…"

"I don't care. Let tomorrow take care of itself. We have tonight. Are we going to waste it?"

She took his unresisting hand and led him into her room, closing the door behind them.

She was conscious of his small anguished cry as he pulled her to him. There was desperation in his kiss, a kiss that seemed to say "I want you" and "good-bye" at one and the same moment.

Eve broke their embrace and, never taking her eyes off his, stepped back, unzipped her dress and let it fall to the floor. Standing before him in only two sheer scraps of lace, she reached for his belt buckle. Within moments they were on the bed, arms and legs entwined, hands touching, mouths tasting, frantic with repressed desire.

"No. Stop." Eve pulled back, willing her pulse to stop hammering, her breathing to slow. "We're not going to rush this. We'll take it slow and easy. If it's to be our last night together, we'll make it one we'll both remember."

****

Adamo gazed down at the woman sleeping beside him and swore softly. What had he gotten himself into? He'd been sure he had his feelings for her under control. It was supposed to be just a brief fling. And then when he found her on the ship, well, he hadn't wanted to hurt her, so he'd suggested they become friends. And they had. Looking back on the last two weeks, Adamo realized he'd never had a better friend. Not a woman friend, anyway. With women and Adamo, things had always seemed to jump to Plan B, as in Bed, before he really ever got to know them. And that had certainly worked well, he thought bitterly, remembering his ex-wife, Monica.

He'd enjoyed every moment of his time with Eve on the ship. It had been a true voyage of discovery for him. She moved him. He'd found a woman he wanted more from than just sex. A woman to talk to. To share things with. To hold, to protect, to cherish. Yes, that was the word. He wanted to cherish Eve.

He slipped quietly out of the bed and walked over

to the window. *Cherish*? If he truly cherished Eve, he'd get the hell out of her life now. What could he offer her? This trip was just a holiday for her. For him it was a desperate attempt to escape from his old life, and perhaps his last chance to build a new one. How had he ever gotten himself into this mess? He couldn't come to grips with what had happened to him, and he couldn't forgive himself for the damage he'd so unwittingly caused to others.

At one time he'd been worth millions. His had been a name to reckon with in the world of finance. Gone. All gone. Along with his reputation.

He was broke. He had no job. Life as he knew it ended six years ago. His university degrees, his years of owning his own business, they meant nothing now. To say the future was uncertain was optimistic. All he owned was a small inn on the Italian coast and a few thousand euros left to him by his grandfather. He had nothing to offer a woman like Eve.

So why had he suggested staying with her in Lisbon? Prolonging the inevitable? He was going to have to level with her at some point. Tell her the truth. Only what was the truth?

Chapter Four

When Eve awoke the next morning she found Adamo sitting in the armchair by the window, his eyes red-rimmed and hollow.

"Come with me," he said hoarsely. "Come with me to Positano. I can't bear to lose you."

Eve gave a cry of joy and propelled herself into his lap.

He brushed her hair back and caressed her face. "I have nothing to offer you, Eve. I'm pushing forty and I have nothing. But if my wanting you to distraction counts for anything…"

"Oh, Adamo." Eve was laughing and crying at the same time. "It counts for everything." A small voice in Eve's head said, *What aren't you telling me? What happened to you to bring you to this low point in your life?*" She pushed her doubts aside. She loved him. It was as simple as that. Eventually, in his own good time, he would tell her.

Over breakfast Eve asked, "Why Positano? What's there?"

"A small inn, an *albergo*. It was left to me by my grandfather. I hope to make a modest living at it. It's a fresh start for me in any case. It's not much of a future to offer you, but…"

"I'll take my chances on it." Finally, she thought with relief. Finally he's talking to me. "Have you been to Italy often?"

"Not often enough, but I was born there. I didn't come to the States until I was fourteen. I still have family in Positano. An aunt and uncle, cousins. In a way, it's coming home for me, although I haven't been back in several years."

He was silent, seemingly lost in his past.

Eve waited for him to continue. To tell her why he was leaving America to seek a new life back in Italy after so many years away. What had happened to him in the U.S. to make him so desperate to get away?

He pushed himself out of the chair. "I'd better go shower and pack. I'll meet you in the lobby in an hour." He gave Eve a brief kiss and was dressed and out of the door in moments.

Eve looked after him, frustrated. It was like pulling teeth to get information out of Adamo de Leone. But he wanted her with him. It was a first step. She would just have to be patient.

****

In the afternoon they boarded an Alitalia flight and four hours later they were in Rome. They checked into a small hotel, the Albergo Cesári, in the *Centro Storico*, the historic district, near the Pantheon and the Piazza Navona.

"I have things to attend to here in the city," Adamo said. "Do you think you can amuse yourself for a few hours while I see my grandfather's lawyer and take care of some business matters?"

"I should think so," Eve laughed. "I've never been in Rome before. The Colosseum, the whole of the Centro Storico, the museums—I think I can keep myself occupied while you do what you must."

"Good. I'll meet you back here in time for dinner."

Eve stopped at the front desk to pick up a map and some brochures. The hotel was on a pedestrian-only lane. She walked toward the Via del Corso, the street her map showed leading toward the ancient ruins, the Rome of the Caesars. She wove through crowds of pedestrians, nearly all of them talking on cell phones held in one hand while wildly gesticulating with their cigarette-laden other hands. Did Romans all smoke? Apparently so. The only non-smokers she noticed were the camera-draped tourists.

Half an hour later, with the cacophony of twenty-first century Roman traffic at her back, she stood gazing up at the magnificent structure built more than two thousand years ago by an early Roman emperor to keep the populace, some fifty-five thousands of them at a time, entertained and happy. The Colosseum. Paying her twelve euros, she entered and found herself inside the prototype for every stadium she'd ever seen in America. Tier upon tier of seats. And below, instead of football teams, spaces for the animals and the gladiators who fought them for the amusement of the spectators. Her guide book said ninety thousand wild animals had met their death here. Nothing was mentioned about how many gladiators died.

She'd read the rough stone of the exterior was once covered with travertine marble. It had ended up on St. Peter's when Christian pontiffs had succeeded Roman emperors. Somehow Eve found both the setting and its history of bloodshed and mayhem, all for the amusement of ancient Roman audiences, depressing.

She left the monolithic building and crossed to the much quieter center of ancient Rome. Here, broad paths and grassy areas wound through the ruins. She breathed a sigh of relief. The Colosseum had reeked of death. Somehow these ruins spoke more of life. Temples to Venus, to Augustus, to Mars and Saturn, to Castor and Pollux, the mythical founders of Rome. Some had only a column or two left standing, others were almost intact, but all possessed a certain grandeur. She gave up reading about her surroundings and just enjoyed strolling through history.

Her mind turned to Adamo. This was his heritage. Gladiators and warriors and Roman gods. His face and form were reflected everywhere in the marble statues and bas reliefs in the ruins of this ancient city. His ancestors had lived here millennia before hers had settled in America. She paused at the magnificent Arch of Constantine before she left the ancient city and found herself once again in the deafening traffic and carbon monoxide filled air of modern day Rome.

Glancing at her watch, she realized she'd been gone for more than six hours. Adamo would be wondering where she was.

****

In the evening Adamo took her to a small restaurant he knew down a narrow pedestrian-only lane near their hotel. They dined on homemade pasta and drank a local wine served from a ceramic pitcher. Afterwards they strolled to the crowded Piazza Navona. Artists had their work strewn out on the sidewalk in hopes of attracting buyers; musicians played with their cases open in front of them for donations. At one end of the piazza a juggler was performing, and a small crowd had gathered round to enjoy the show.

Adamo stopped before a fountain in the center of

the piazza.

"This has been a favorite of mine since I was a child," he said. "It represents the four great rivers of the world, the Nile, the Danube, the Ganges and the Plate. I think it dates back to the fifteen hundreds."

Four god-like men appeared to be growing out of a massive chunk of marble with water plunging all around them, while below a lion and a horse were emerging from caves. Eve couldn't help noticing how much the faces and forms of the river gods were like Adamo's, from their curly hair to their well-muscled bodies. "I've only seen photographs of this before." She walked slowly around it, studying it from every angle. "I love the reality of it. Somehow it makes me want to climb onto the back of one of those magnificent creatures and ride off into the sunset."

"Sorry, I'm not about to let you do that. Not now that I've found you. Besides, I think that policeman over there might take a pretty dim view of anybody messing around in a Bernini fountain. Italians take their art pretty seriously."

They walked on, holding hands, back toward their hotel, through the balmy evening air and the bustling crowds. Adamo was silent. Twice Eve caught him looking back over his shoulder, apprehensively.

Eve glanced at the distant look, the preoccupied frown on his face. Did he think they were being followed? But why should anyone be following them? What was worrying him? Why couldn't he tell her about it?

"What's wrong, Adamo?" The words were out of her mouth before she could stop them.

With a visible effort, he brought himself back to

the present. Back to her.

"Nothing. Nothing's wrong. Want a gelato?" He pulled her toward a large ice cream counter with about thirty flavors displayed.

"Sure, why not?" Eve laughed in spite of herself. He never ceased to surprise her. One moment he could be dark and moody, the next as light hearted as a young boy.

They continued on their walk a few minutes later, he with his three decker chocolate cone, she with her more modest one dip of strawberry.

"Tomorrow morning after breakfast I must do some banking and then see my grandfather's lawyer again to finalize the transfer of the *albergo*," Adamo said. "You'll have a couple of hours. What would you like to do?"

"Just wander, I think. Absorb Rome."

"The best place for that is the Spanish Steps. Suppose I meet you there at noon."

****

Adamo decided to walk to his lawyer's office. The day was fine, and he needed to think. What was he going to do about Eve? He was going to have to level with her, but how? How could he expect her to understand when he himself had never been able to make sense of it? When she knew about him, he would lose her, and he wasn't sure he could bear that.

Suddenly he had the prickling sensation that someone was following him. The same sensation he had had twice yesterday evening. He stepped and gazed in the window of a stationary shop to see if he his follower would be reflected in the glass. He had to identify whoever it was who seemed to be targeting him.

Nothing. No one. Was he only imagining it?

****

Eve, left to her own devices for the morning, decided to go to the Borghese Gallery. She had a particular fondness for the work of the Baroque sculptor Bernini, and this museum, the former residence of a Borgia Cardinal, held three of the master's works.

She stopped and spoke to the man at the hotel desk for directions as she was leaving.

"You will need to book a time for the Borghese," he said. "They only allow a small number of people into it at one time. Let me call and see what I can do."

A few minutes later, armed with directions and a ten o'clock reservation, Eve made her way out of the hotel to the Via del Corso. She had an hour, more than enough time to walk to the museum.

She strolled through the broad paths of the Borghese Gardens, reliving the past two nights with Adamo. He was a consummate lover. Just thinking about last night made her shiver. She was so in love with him it made her hurt. She wanted to say the words. She wanted to tell him how much she loved him, but something made her stop short of voicing her feelings. It was as if, after his first admission of need, he had put up a wall between them. A wall that said "this far and no further." He held her and caressed her and made passionate love to her, but he did so without words. Not even the meaningless words most men uttered at such moments.

She had seen no more of the vulnerability of the last morning in Lisbon. And yet he had begged her to come with him. He had said he needed her. That must have meant something.

What wasn't he telling her? They had been constantly together for almost three weeks now. He knew all there was to know about her past, and yet she knew nothing of his beyond the fact he had an ex-wife. Anytime she asked even the most casual question, he diverted the conversation in some way.

She looked up to see she'd arrived at the museum. Shaking off her doubts, she took a few minutes to admire the beautiful exterior of the former Borgia cardinal's residence. Then she entered with a small group. Declining the automated tour with headphones, she looked at the brochure she'd picked up at the entrance and strolled to the room containing the first of the works by Bernini. It was his David. Unlike Michelangelo's motionless, awe inspiring, god-like David, Bernini's David was captured at the moment of hurling the stone at Goliath. His body was in motion, tense and straining, his face contorted with effort. Eve decided he was not beautiful in the way the more famous one by Michelangelo was, but somehow he seemed more human, more alive.

She walked on to the room with Bernini's Apollo and Daphne. This was what she'd come to see. She'd fallen in love with this sculpture just from photographs in one of her art history courses, years ago. She walked slowly around it, absorbing it from every angle. Then she sat down and gazed at it. The reality of it was more than she could have imagined.

Eve replayed the Greek legend in her mind. Apollo angered Eros, and, in retaliation, Eros, the Greek predecessor of the Roman Cupid, shot two arrows. The first, a golden one, he shot into Apollo, to make him fall in love with Daphne, and the second, made of lead, he shot into Daphne, to make her despise Apollo.

Bernini's sculpture captured the moment when Apollo, in full pursuit of the fleeing Daphne, almost caught her. According to the legend, Daphne screamed an appeal to her father, the god Peneus, who saved her by turning her into a laurel tree.

In Bernini's rendition of this moment, Daphne's fingertips were sprouting leaves, her toes were turning to roots, and bark was enclosing her torso. But her face, turned upwards, mouth open, what was it expressing? Was it only Eve's impression, or was there regret in it at this last moment? Was Daphne, too late, wondering if carnal love might not have been a preferable alternative?

Eve smiled at her fancy. She was transferring her own feelings into the marble masterpiece before her. She had definitely chosen not to be a laurel tree.

She rose and made her way through the rest of the exhibits perfunctorily, returning for one last moment to Apollo and Daphne before the museum attendants began politely to usher her group out of the museum to make room for the next. She glanced at her watch as she stepped out into a brilliant sunny day. It was almost noon. Adamo would be waiting for her.

She saw him before her saw her. He stood at the foot of the Spanish Steps, looking around and glancing at his watch as she wove her way downwards through the throngs sitting on the steps, toward him. God, he was beautiful. She stood still and studied him for a moment. Even dressed in a city suit and tie, as he was today, he looked leonine, like some misplaced jungle creature. His long lean form, the latent power of his body, could not be disguised by mere clothing. She throbbed in uncontrollable response to his nearness. Would she ever have enough of him?

The frown on his face turned to a smile as he caught sight of her. "I was afraid I was being stood up," he said.

"Sorry. I was delayed by Apollo and Daphne."

"You spent the morning at the Borghese?"

"Yes. And it wasn't nearly enough time. I want to go back."

"We can, any time you like. It's only a few hours by bus from Positano."

Eve experienced a flash of relief. He seemed to take it for granted they would continue to be together. It would have to suffice for the moment.

They had just enough time to grab a quick lunch from a stand near the steps before they collected their bags from the hotel and headed for the bus station.

At the station, Eve saw Adamo go suddenly tense, on full alert, his eyes narrowed, as he carefully scanned the crowd of travelers milling around them.

"Were you expecting to see somebody you know here?"

"No. Not really." He brought his attention abruptly back to Eve. "Here's our bus."

Once the bus pulled away from the terminal, Adamo put his head back and closed his eyes. Eve gazed out the window at the passing countryside. There wasn't much to see except the usual generic surroundings of any superhighway anywhere in the world. Two hours later they arrived at the dingy, smoggy environs of Naples, and the bus crawled through dense traffic, discharging and taking on passengers, until finally they were free of the city. On a long curve, as they approached Sorrento, Eve craned her neck to see the whole of the Bay of Naples displayed behind them. What an incredibly beautiful sight, even encased as it was in its gray-green haze of pollution. The city stretched out in a wide curve, along the waterfront, with Vesuvius, the now dormant volcano that wiped out Pompeii two millennia ago, looming over it. What must it be like to live under such an ever-present menace? Or did people simply not think about it? It was probably no different than living on rivers that flooded annually, or on earthquake fault lines, or in tornado alley, as millions of her fellow Americans did.

Soon after, the bus turned away from Naples and they were on the Amalfi Drive. On Eve's left, the coastal mountain range rose steeply above them while on the right, hair-raising cliffs plunged to the Tyrrhenian Sea far below. Eve had been driving for twenty years, but never had she seen hairpin turns quite like these. Only a low stone wall and a capable driver stood between their bus and disaster. Periodically, tunnels cut through the mountains. When the bus came to one of these, all automobile traffic both ways stopped to allow the bus to proceed through.

As they emerged from one of these tunnels, Adamo roused. "Where are we? Oh, I see. We're almost there."

"What would happen if we met a bus coming the other way?" Eve asked.

Adamo laughed. "We can't. The buses only travel south on this route. There isn't room for two buses to pass each other anywhere on this road."

Their bus pulled over.

"This is our stop," Adamo said, standing and taking their bags down from the overhead rack.

They were barely off the bus before Adamo was engulfed by a laughing, chattering crowd, all speaking at once in Italian, hugging and kissing and touching Adamo as if to reassure themselves of his reality. Eve heard his name repeated over and over, "Adamo, Adamo!"

Adamo returned their embraces. "*Ciao, Zio Valerio, Zia Graziella! Come stai?*"

Finally he broke loose long enough to take Eve's hand and introduce her. "*Questa é la mia amica, Eve.*" He pronounced her name "eh-veh."

"Eve, this is my uncle Valerio, and my aunt Graziella, and these are my cousins, Pietro, Enzio, and Gianni, and this is Gianni's wife, Alicia."

Adamo's relatives crowded around her, hugging and kissing her. "*Piacere! Salve!*" they said to her, and to Adamo, "*Che bella é!*" She was shocked. She wasn't sure what she'd expected, but nothing had prepared her for this cheerful, boisterous family welcome.

"And who is this?" Adamo said, taking a baby out of Alicia's arms. "You didn't tell me about the baby!"

Eve watched Adamo's face soften as he caressed the baby's head.

"He's a very recent arrival on the scene," Gianni said proudly, speaking in English for Eve's benefit. "Giovanni Valerio Adamo de Leone."

"You named him for me?" There was pleasure mixed with astonishment in Adamo's voice.

"*Certo!*"

Grabbing their suitcases, the family pulled them along down a cliff-side path intersected every few feet by steps. Pastel-colored houses, standing tightly against each another, flanked both sides of the walkway.

Adamo's family chattered away in Italian while Eve strained to follow their quick and voluble speech.

The narrow lane seemed to wind and twist forever downward toward the sea. Many steps later, still only halfway down the face of the cliff, they stopped in front of a bright blue doorway. At one side of the door stood a winged marble lion, pitted with age. It reminded her of pictures she had seen of the twelfth-century ones guarding the entrance to the Piazza San Marco in Venice.

Adamo followed her gaze and said, "*Leone,* the Italian word for lion. It was commissioned centuries ago by the de Leone who built this house."

"Oh. Of course."

"Here we are," Gianni said, beaming. "Your aunt has spent the last two days cleaning and scrubbing every inch. And you'll find your *cena,* your supper, all prepared."

Taking Adamo aside, his uncle said, "*Mi dispiace per i tuoi problemi.*"

"*Grazie,*" Adamo answered. "Your belief in me has helped me survive."

Eve gave Adamo a sharp look. "*Tuoi problemi?* Your problem? What problem?"

"Later." Adamo's voice was abrupt.

"Now we leave you to settle in," Adamo's uncle said. "If you need anything, you know we are just down the way." With a mixture of *ciao's* and *arrivaderci's* the family disappeared around the next bend in the lane.

"I guess I should have prepared you for that." Using the large wrought iron key his uncle had pressed into his hand, Adamo unlocked the door. "It didn't occur to me the whole family would be waiting at the bus stop. Although I should have known."

He stepped aside for Eve to enter. "Welcome to the Albergo de Leone."

Eve walked into a large foyer. Blue and white tiles in an antique design of flowers and animals covered the lower half of the walls, while the upper half was painted a soft, creamy white. The glowing rose-colored terracotta floor was also old and beautiful, and very different from the wall-to-wall carpeting Eve had grown up with. Against the wall an antique table topped with a large blue and white ceramic vase was filled with flowers. She walked over to it and, touching the blooms lightly, inhaled their fragrance. "A welcoming bouquet from your aunt?"

"I did call to tell her I was bringing home someone important to me."

The words warmed Eve. He had brought her home to meet his family. "You didn't tell me you had family in Italy."

"Every Italian-American has family in Italy," he quipped. "You didn't tell me you spoke Italian."

"My major field was Renaissance Art. The study of Italian was required. I can read it well, but I haven't had much opportunity to practice speaking it."

"If you can read it, I'm sure you'll pick up the spoken language quickly." Adamo gestured to the right. "Our living quarters are through here. The guest accommodation, nine suites in all, is on the two levels to the left."

Eve turned right as instructed, to a large, high-ceilinged room. Her gaze took in the green painted wooden settee along one wall and the comfortable-looking cushioned chairs on either side. Over a large antique fruitwood table in the center of the room hung a fanciful chandelier, with colorfully painted wrought iron leaves and flowers. "What a lovely room!"

Adamo crossed to the double glass doors on the far side of the room and ushered Eve out to a wide balcony. Far below them, the Tyrrhenian Sea shimmered in the last rays of the setting sun, while, across a ravine, another cluster of houses clung to the next hillside. Lights were coming on here and there, twinkling in the shadows.

They stood together, Adamo's arm around Eve's waist, she leaning against him, watching as twilight turned to darkness.

He sighed. "I'd forgotten how much I loved this place."

"What is that wonderful scent in the air?"

"Lemon blossoms. Lemon trees grow everywhere here."

"It's heavenly." Eve said. "There's a poem by Goethe about lemon trees." She tried to recall the lines. *"Know you the land where lemons bloom…there would I go with you, my belovéd."*

Adamo kissed her, a gentle loving kiss, and hand in hand they moved back into the house.

"You called this 'a defunct inn,'" Eve said. "What I've seen seems to be in beautiful condition. Why did you say 'defunct'?"

"There's nothing basically wrong with the place. My grandfather kept it up. But it hasn't operated as an inn since my grandmother died fifteen years ago. To get it up and running again will take work. We'll need fresh paint, and we'll have to update a number of the furnishings and bathroom fixtures. We'll certainly need all new mattresses and bedding. And then there's the marketing to consider. We'll have to get the word out to the right prospective guests. And I don't have much money with which to do it all."

"But it's beautiful! I can't imagine anyone wouldn't want to stay here."

Adamo shook his head. "Did you count the steps as we walked down here?"

"No. There were a lot of them."

"One hundred and ten to be precise."

"Oh."

"And the usual well-heeled American tourist is retired, over the age of fifty-five, and expects elevators."

Eve nodded. "I can see you've considered this."

"I've had a lot of time to think about it."

"While we're thinking about well-heeled tourists, some of them are likely to arrive by car. Is there a car park anywhere close by?"

"Right at the top of the lane, where we got off the bus. Uncle Valerio keeps his car there."

"We should probably make an arrangement with them for a certain number of spaces on a monthly basis."

"You're right, of course. I hadn't even thought about that." Adamo took a deep breath and continued. "We need to hit the younger, more adventurous tourists. The students, the back-packers, the school teachers, the young couples on their first trip to Europe. We need to be on all the best internet advertising and booking sites."

"You'll need internet access and a good website and maybe you could do on-line booking. I could help set all that up," Eve suggested.

"It's going to take time and money. And in the meantime we aren't going to have much to live on. My grandfather left me thirty thousand euros. I squandered three getting here. I'm going to have to be very careful with the rest."

Eve hesitated only for a moment. "I have about the same. My father left it to me. We could use some of mine."

Adamo stiffened and seemed to draw away. His voice was cold and formal when he responded. "It's kind of you to offer, Eve, but I have to sink or swim on my own. I can't take your money."

Eve wondered why. If they were together, what difference should it make whose money they used? She'd give him some time, but if they needed it…

He took her hand and led her back into the house.

"Our bedroom's through here."

An archway off the living room led to it. Eve stopped in the doorway and caught her breath. It was lovely. Place of honor went to a *letto matrimoniale,* a somewhat narrower Italian version of an American double bed, covered with an embroidered linen spread. A large antique clothes press stood against one wall. What was the Italian word? Oh yes, it was called an *amadio.* A chest of drawers and two chairs were placed against the third wall. The furniture was all painted a light leafy green, floridly decorated with lemon blossoms and fruit. The headboard and the bedside table tops were inlaid with tile, echoing the same lemon design. Glass-paned double doors led to a private balcony.

Adamo put her bag on one of the chairs and rested his bag and backpack on the floor beside it. "I hope you like it."

"Oh, Adamo, it's a fairy tale bedroom."

He laughed. "As befits my fairy tale princess. Suppose I leave you to unpack while I see what Zia Graziella has left in the kitchen for us for dinner."

"Sounds fair to me."

It didn't take long for Eve to unpack her things and store them away in her half of the amadio. She put her panties and bras and nightgowns in two of the four drawers in the chest and left the other two for Adamo. It felt strange, leaving room for his belongings next to hers. Sort of like a commitment. This is what married people did.

Should she unpack his things? Of course. He'd said "unpack."

She put her now empty suitcase out of the way, under the bed, and put his on the chair. When she unzipped it, she noted the care with which he had organized his packing. It was characteristic of him. How could someone so systematic and controlled in his daily life be so savage and uninhibited in bed? She smiled as she unpacked his clothes and placed them in drawers and on hangers.

Now for his back pack. His laptop was there. She took it out of its protective case and placed it on the desk in the corner of the room. Shoes, underwear, socks. Was that all? She unzipped an inside compartment. It seemed to have papers in it. She'd put those on the desk with his laptop. She reached into the compartment and pulled out...

Clippings? Newspaper articles? His picture?

She sat down and began reading.

Adamo came into the bedroom a short time later to find her sitting, frozen, with the clippings in her lap.

White faced, she looked at him. "You're a convicted felon. You spent five years in prison for embezzlement."

Chapter Five

"Yes." Adamo's voice was flat, his expression, stricken. "I was convicted of embezzlement and I spent five years in jail. I'm sorry you found out about it this way. I was going to tell you, but…"

"But what, Adamo? When were you going to tell me? Is this the little *problemi* your uncle mentioned when your family met us at the bus stop? Does everybody know about this but me?"

Adamo held his hand out in supplication. "I'm sorry. I'm so sorry, Eve. I wanted to hold on to you, to what we have together, for just a little while longer. I knew once you found out it would be over." He looked at her, his dark eyes desolate, his voice, defeated.

Eve said nothing.

He took a deep breath, dropped his hand to his side, and, avoiding her gaze, said, "I'll arrange transportation back to Rome for you tomorrow morning. I'll sleep in one of the guest rooms tonight." He shook his head. "I'm sorrier than I can say." His voice broke on the last word.

"I don't believe it."

"What?"

"I don't believe you embezzled eighty million dollars from investors. I don't believe you'd embezzle five cents from anyone."

Adamo looked stunned. "You are singularly alone

58

in your belief. A jury of my peers had no difficulty believing it. The judge believed it. My wife, my friends, all believed it."

"More fools they."

"You've known me for all of three weeks, Eve. How can you be so sure? What makes you so certain of my innocence?"

Eve listened in shock to his words. He expected her to believe these newspaper accounts. He was not even going to try to defend himself. Was he so uncertain of her love for him? Had he been so damaged he couldn't accept her trust in him? Had fear made him hug this ugly secret to himself rather than telling her about it?

She took a deep breath. She had to make him understand. "I know you. Time is irrelevant in this kind of knowing. I know your heart and mind. I know you're incapable of stealing money from people who trust you."

Adamo seemed to cave in. He stooped over and crumpled to a chair, clutching his arms around his body as if in pain. His head dropped down. His voice shook when he spoke. "No one believed me. No one...You're the first."

Eve crossed the room and put her arms around him. He rested his head against her belly, his breath coming in gulps. She held fast to him, cradling his head against her. It was simple, really. She loved him, she believed in him, and he needed her.

Finally he looked up, his eyes red-rimmed. "I kept hoping I'd be able to clear my name. I saved everything the newspapers wrote. They seemed to know more about it than I did. It was like a freight train barreling down on me. It just overtook me. I spent five years in prison and another year on parole. Six years of my life, gone. My wife, my colleagues, my friends, no one believe I wasn't guilty. It was like a bad dream. Only there was no waking from it."

Eve took his hand. "I believe you. Come. Let's have our supper. I think we could both use a glass of grappa. Then if you're up to it you can tell me about it."

After their meal they took their wine out onto the balcony and sat down side by side, facing the sea.

Adamo took her hand and stared into the past. "I met my business partner, Emmett Kenston, when we were undergraduates. He was my roommate. We couldn't have been less alike. I was into everything physical. Swimming, the rowing team, martial arts. Particularly martial arts. I scraped by academically. I was more interested in sports and in having a good time than I was in racking up grades."

He took a sip of his wine. "Emmett was always buried in his books and his computer. He was a complete social washout. But the man was a genius. There was nothing his mind couldn't encompass."

"Didn't you share any interests?

"Not then. I wasn't into academics and any kind of physical exertion was anathema to Emmett."

Eve frowned, puzzled. What could have brought about close friendship between two such diametrically opposite men? She struggled to make sense of what she was hearing. "However did you become friends?"

"I suppose it began as a sort of mutual respect. I was in awe of his intelligence, and he seemed to enjoy my escapades vicariously."

Eve nodded. This she could understand. "Did he have family?"

"Parents both dead. But there is a twin sister, Emma. I've never met her. She lives in some sort of assisted living facility in upstate New York. I think she may be wheelchair-bound. Emmett was devoted to her. He helped support her financially and made the trip to see her regularly."

Eve digested this. "What about women? Was there anyone in his life?"

"No. Never, during all the years I knew him." Adamo seemed to be reaching for words to describe Emmett's reaction to women. "He seemed to be uncomfortable around women. As if they were some sort of foreign species."

They were silent for a few moments as Eve thought about what she was hearing. "Was he gay?"

"I never saw any indication he was. He was sort of, I don't know, uninterested. His mind was full of other things. He was a solitary man, uncomfortable around people, male or female."

"What did he look like? Can you describe him to me?"

"I can do even better. I have an old photo of us together, taken the day we graduated." Adamo went into the house and came back bearing a snapshot a bit battered around the edges. "I'd forgotten I had this. It was in the wallet they returned to me the day I got out of jail."

Eve studied the picture. They were both just boys. Emmett was considerably shorter than Adamo. Thin. A bit stoop-shouldered.

"He looks sort of Woody Allen-ish. Did he really need those thick glasses?"

"Blind as a bat without them."

Adamo put the photograph away. "We were as unalike as two people could possibly be, and yet he became my friend. It was due to his influence I straightened out my life enough to get decent grades and be admitted into the MBA program at Yale. We went on to graduate school together, and, as a result of a course project, we hit on the idea of starting an investment counselling firm. Emmett had an uncanny sense for investing in the right commodities at the right moment, and I had the social contacts and the salesmanship to bring in the clients. From the beginning our partnership was a success. By the time we'd been in business five years we were making more money than we'd ever dreamed of."

Adamo seemed to drift away into his memories.

"You mentioned your wife?" Eve asked, bringing him back. "When did you marry?"

"Right after graduating. She was...dazzling. Vivacious, dark haired, a real beauty. We'd dated on and off all through college. It just seemed the thing to do, getting married. All our friends were doing it."

"Were you happy?"

"For a time. But nothing was ever enough for Monica. She was never satisfied. The apartment in New York, the beach house on Long Island, the cars, the jewelery, the designer clothes...No matter how much she had, she always wanted more. And no matter how much money I made, she managed to spend it all and more. Our credits cards were always maxed out. We were mortgaged to the hilt. We argued about it endlessly."

Adamo took a sip of his wine before continuing. "The real crux of the matter was I wanted a home life and she didn't. What we had wasn't my idea of marriage. For a while I even suspected she might be involved with another man. I'm not proud of the fact I went so far as to hire a detective. All he turned up were some visits to Emmett's apartment. I have no idea why she was going there, but it certainly wasn't an affair. Emmett despised her. I was contemplating asking her for a divorce when my world collapsed. The Securities and Exchange Commission descended on us and found almost eighty million dollars missing from the accounts."

"But wouldn't your investors have tumbled to something like that?"

"Not necessarily. As long as they continued to receive their quarterly interest payments, they wouldn't realize the capital no longer existed. It's called a Ponzi scheme. The original investors are paid 'dividends' from the money coming in from the newer investors, and meanwhile the capital goes missing with none the wiser."

Eve took some time to digest what he had said. "And Emmett?"

The silence was long. Adamo's voice was hoarse when he spoke. "Emmett committed suicide. Emmett's suicide brought the SEC down on us."

"I see. The investigators took your partner's suicide as an admission of guilt and assumed you were complicit in the theft."

"Exactly. And our life style, mine and Monica's, well above our income level, didn't help. Emmett on the other hand, lived frugally. There was no money to speak of even in his bank accounts."

"But what happened to all the money? It must have

ended up someplace. If Emmett didn't have it and you didn't have it, where did it go?"

"Don't you think I've racked my brains these last six years asking myself that question?"

Eve sat silent, pondering what Adamo had told her. "Did your wife stand by you when you were charged?"

"For a while. She even found a lawyer for me. The lawyer for the firm didn't handle criminal cases. Monica was there every day during my trial," he reflected. "But I never laid eyes on her again once I was sentenced. I was served with divorce papers about three months after I went to jail."

Eve hesitated. "Is it possible she was involved in the theft? Could she have gained access to the accounts somehow?"

"I can't begin to imagine how. Emmett would never have allowed her near the books. They barely spoke to one another. And I never bothered with the bookkeeping end of things. I just brought the clients in. Emmett was the financial genius. He was in charge of the accounts."

"But it does seem suspicious she was seen visiting his apartment on more than one occasion. Did you never ask her about it?"

"I intended to, but then everything blew up."

"You've been out of prison for more than a year. Have you tried to contact her? She might know something."

"I have no idea where she is. I tried to locate her once I was released, but she'd moved away with no forwarding address."

"Don't you think that's a little odd?"

"Very, but I don't know what I can do about it."

Adamo stood and walked over to the low terrace wall. He stared sightlessly at the horizon for a few moments. Then he turned and met Eve's clear-eyed gaze.

"You know what bothers me most? All those investors lost their money. People I convinced to place their money in our hands. They lost everything. After all my properties and holdings were sold off, and my debts paid, our investors got pennies on the dollar. That was my fault. I should have been more vigilant. Someone, somehow, got their hands on all that money while I was out playing golf and going to cocktail parties. I can't forgive myself for that."

"Enough. Enough for tonight. We can talk more tomorrow. I think we both need sleep now. Come, love." Eve stood and extended her hand to him.

He grasped it as if it were a life-line.

Over their rolls and coffee the next morning, Eve brought up something in Adamo's story that had nagged at her. "Emmett must have known about the shortfall. You said he was the one who looked after the books."

"There's no question he knew about it. He had to have known, had to have been responsible for it, somehow."

"So, regardless of the fact he had no money when he died, he must have had knowledge as to how the money disappeared and where it went. And he must have known you would be blamed, when you were innocent of any wrongdoing."

"As much as I don't want to believe that, I can't see any alternative."

Eve weighed the possibilities. "But suicides leave notes. Wouldn't he have left a message when he died, explaining what he did and why he did it? Something exonerating you?"

"There was no suicide note."

"That just doesn't make any sense. Not when you were such close friends."

Adamo shrugged his shoulders. "Even the police found it strange. But there was no note. His computer files were wiped clean. I was left holding the proverbial bag."

It hung like a dark shadow between them. The unlikeliness of ever knowing the truth of the matter.

Adamo got up and poured them both a fresh coffee. "I've thought about this for six long years. I don't want to think about it anymore. Thinking about it is destructive. I need to get on with my life."

He contemplated Eve. "I have this beautiful little inn, this piece of heaven on earth. I want to put the rest behind me. I think I can make a go of it here. I'll never be rich, but I've been rich. It isn't all it's cracked up to be. The question is, Eve, are you willing to take on an ex-con and consider living with me here in a country where you hardly even speak the language?"

A surge of happiness washed over Eve. It wasn't exactly a proposal, but he wanted her with him. It was a beginning. She reached over and took his hand. "I'll take my chances."

****

In the afternoon Eve wrote a long email message to Bette, telling her sister about Adamo. Everything about Adamo, including his conviction and her belief in his innocence. She told Bette she was in love with him and intended to stay with him in Positano and help run the little inn he'd inherited.

She hesitated a moment before pressing *send*. She knew it would cause consternation in the Richardson household, but she was going to have to tell Bette and Ed about Adamo at some point. And she might as well tell them everything. Working for the investigative branch of Internal Revenue, Ed had access to private financial information normal citizens didn't. He'd have found out all about Adamo in two shakes, and he'd have told Bette what he knew, and they'd both probably have descended on them here in Positano to save her. Eve didn't want saving. She figured she might as well tackle the problem head on.

After sending her email she went to find Adamo. He was in a little storage shed adjoining the house, stooping down, examining the wheels of a rather old-fashioned motor scooter.

"Look what I found!" he said, pointing to it with pride. "It's a vintage Vespa. A 1968 Vespa 125 Primavera. They're collectors' items, one of the best models Vespa ever made, and this one's in prime condition. My grandfather clearly treasured it. It's going to be our transportation. I was thinking we'd have to look for a small second-hand car, but this is much better."

"You surely don't think I'm going anyplace on the back of that thing?"

"You'll love it. It's perfect for these roads. I'll even teach you how to operate it if you like. You can use it for shopping."

Eve kept her doubts to herself.

In the evening they climbed up the path to Leone's, Adamo's uncle's restaurant, for dinner. It sat just off the main road, across from the bus stop. Zia Graziella had put the "closed" sign on the door. Tonight there would be only family for dinner. In the dining room, ten tables were covered with pristine white tablecloths, but Adamo led Eve through to the terrace, where there was one long family table set up under a grape arbor. Eve heard women's voices raised in laughter coming from the kitchen. She wandered in to find Graziella and Alicia and another woman she hadn't yet met, all chattering and busying themselves around the huge stove and work table.

"Maria, Enzio's *fidanzata*," Graziella introduced a pretty young woman, who looked at her shyly and smiled.

"*Felicitazioni*," Eve said, drawing on her limited Italian vocabulary to congratulate the young woman who was engaged to Adamo's cousin. She seemed young to be contemplating marriage.

Zia Graziella pressed a plate overflowing with pasta into Eve's hands and followed her out to the terrace, carrying a large bowl of tiny local clams cooked in their own broth. Plates of antipasto, sliced tomatoes with mozzarella *da buffa*, carafes of wine, and baskets of crusty bread were already on the long table.

The men, already seated at the table, were laughing at something Zio Valerio had said, as they helped themselves to antipasto.

"My uncle does all the cooking for the restaurant," Adamo explained to Eve. "My aunt cooks on his day off."

Conversation buzzed around Eve as the women joined the men at the table and everyone filled plates. Periodically, Adamo or Uncle Valerio or Aunt Graziella made an effort to include Eve, by speaking more slowly or by translating what was being said into English, but the stream of Italian floated over and around her, inundated her, leaving her hopelessly isolated. She understood about one word in five. The family members were all warm and friendly. They accepted her presence without reservation, but by the time dinner was over, Eve was exhausted with the effort of trying to follow what was being said. Most of it was just inconsequential chatter, but she yearned to be more a part of it.

As they walked back down the hill after dinner, Eve said, "I want to speak Italian better. And I want to do so as quickly as possible."

"They say the best way to learn a language is by taking a lover who speaks it."

Eve laughed. "You never speak to me when we're making love. And if you did, I suspect the words might not be ones I'd have much use for over a family dinner."

"We could start by speaking Italian with each other in our daily life, *cara mia.* You read the language. You just need practice speaking."

"I'd like to try."

As they undressed, Eve commented, "You said no one believed in your innocence. But your family has all rallied round. Clearly they don't believe you're guilty."

"You don't understand the Italian psyche, Eve. I'm family, so they love and support me. It isn't that they believe I'm innocent. It's they don't care whether I'm innocent or guilty. I'm theirs. I'm a de Leone. That's all that matters."

When Eve awoke the next morning Adamo was not in bed beside her. Where was he? She wandered through their rooms looking for him and found him out on the terrace, moving through a set of highly stylized motions, clearly some form of martial arts exercise. She sat quietly watching until he was finished.

Finally he stopped and fell into a chair beside her. "I need a shower."

"What were you doing?"

"Tae kwon do. It's Korean. A combination of kick boxing and karate. I began studying it when I was an undergraduate, and I've continued to use it as a form of exercise ever since. I've gotten out of practice in the last few weeks. It's a discipline. I need to get back to it. It's good for me both physically and mentally. And it stood me in good stead when I was in jail."

"Tell me about it, Adamo. What was it like, being in prison?"

"It's not something I like to talk about. But if you'll go make the coffee while I shower, I'll tell you about it over breakfast."

****

"My 'crime' was considered to be 'non-violent, financially motivated, committed for illegal monetary gain.' As such I should have been eligible for a short stretch in one of the minimum security prison camps. But the prosecution wanted me to turn over the stolen money in exchange for doing my term in minimum security. I couldn't turn over what I didn't have, so I was sent to a maximum security prison."

Adamo lifted his coffee cup absently, then placed it back on the saucer, untouched. "Looking back, I think worst part was the complete lack of privacy and never getting enough sleep…"

Eve raised her eyebrows. "I can understand the

lack of privacy, but sleep…"

"Lights went out at nine, but went on again at midnight, at three a.m. and at five a.m. so the guards could do a head count and verify all the inmates were there. Then at six a.m. we were up and the day began. We worked, of course. I was assigned to the laundry. I made $1.15 an hour. Quite a comedown from my former life."

Adamo stood and walked over to the railing, and stared beyond the distant sea, into the past. "It could have been worse. After one small incident where I… discouraged…my would-be assailants, I wasn't subject to further violence. I stayed to myself as much as possible and practiced a restricted version of tae kwon do daily when we had exercise time in the prison yard. I think that, and perhaps my physical condition and size, kept me safe from further attack."

Eve shuddered.

"After a year, I was transferred to a minimum security prison camp. I have no idea why. Perhaps they just needed space in the high security prison for someone more dangerous. I found myself in a cell more like a basic college dorm room, with only one roommate, not three. I requested outside work on the grounds, mowing, gardening, clearing snow, whatever was needed. Fresh air and hard physical labor saved my sanity. And there was a library. It was pretty minimal, but I read everything in it."

Eve nodded her understanding. Books had saved her during the five years she acted as caregiver for her father. They had been her only escape from the drudgery of her days.

"When I was released from prison, I had no home

left to go to, no friends to turn to, and no money. I got a job as a night clerk in a third rate hotel in Brooklyn. I considered returning home to Italy, but I didn't have the money for a ticket. I was at perhaps the lowest point in my life when my grandfather left me this." He swept his hand to include the whole horizon. "It saved me."

Eve was silent for a long time digesting the bare bones of what Adamo had told her. She was sure it was a highly sanitized version. "But how did you happen to be on Barbados ? And on the Wind Surf?"

"That was sheer indulgence. I saw a brochure advertising the voyage, and I got a very good last minute rate. I desperately wanted to put some time and distance between my past and what I hoped would be my future. I needed time to reinvent myself. I didn't count on meeting you." He looked at her and grinned. "When you pulled me into bed that afternoon…"

"I don't recall you putting up much of a fight."

"I put up a fight, all right. You'll never know the battle I had with myself over it. But I was lost from the start. Have you any idea of the hunger I had for you? Still have for you, *carissima*?"

"No." She walked over to him, fitted her body to his and ran her hands lightly up his arms. "Show me."

****

Luc Manzel answered his phone. "Report."

"Adamo de Leone took a ship to Lisbon. We had someone on the ground when he arrived. He checked into a small hotel near the waterfront. There was some woman with him. Two days later they boarded a plane for Rome. According to our Naples connection, he's in Positano now, with the rest of the de Leone family. The woman's still with him. He's not asking questions. I don't think he poses any threat."

"You're not paid to think." Luc severed the connection.

After five years in jail and a year working in New York, why was Adamo de Leone now moving? First to Barbados. It was an unlikely coincidence that Adamo had chosen the island where the trust was set up and where Monica was now living, just for a vacation. True, he hadn't approached Monica or asked any questions at the bank. Not that he'd have gotten answers if he had. The bank secrecy laws in Barbados concerning off-shore accounts were among the tightest in the world. Nevertheless it was disquieting.

And now he was in Europe, all too close to where the bulk of the money lay hidden. There was no way Adamo could have traced the money, so why was he there? Just to visit family? It seemed unlikely. Where had he gotten the cash to travel with? And for that matter, how had he even managed to get into Barbados or Portugal or Italy? His U.S. passport should have rung alarm bells with the immigration services of those countries. He was a convicted felon. Perhaps he was traveling on an EU passport?

Adamo de Leone was on the move. He was a loose end, and Luc Manzel didn't like loose ends. He picked up the phone again and placed a call to Naples.

Chapter Six

The days took on their own kind of tempo. Eve learned to shop in the local markets and to cook using the somewhat different utensils she found in the inn's kitchen. Everything was metric. The cups and teaspoons and tablespoons she was accustomed to didn't exist here and she found her old recipes were hopeless. But Adamo helped with the cooking, pasta being his specialty, and gradually Eve adapted to the new environment and to a different kind of cuisine.

She'd never realized how many kinds of pasta there were. They bought it in a shop where it was made fresh daily, and occasionally, Zia Graziella brought them some she'd just made. Fish could be bought on the beach from the local fishermen, and there was an abundance of fresh ingredients, tomatoes and peppers and melons. The cheeses were marvelous, everything from the bland mozzarella *da buffa* to pungent gorgonzola. Served at the end of the meal with ripe succulent grapes, they were heavenly. But best of all were the local lemons. They were bigger than oranges, and full of juice. They were used in seasoning many of the dishes and in creating sumptuous desserts.

"Try this," Adamo said one evening after dinner.

Eve took the tiny liquor glass from him and sipped tentatively. The taste on her tongue was a mixture of tart and sweet and, as she swallowed, the scent of lemon blossoms filled her head. "I love it! What is it?"

"It's a liqueur made from the local lemons, limoncello. I thought you'd like it."

Eve's spoken Italian improved rapidly until she was capable of holding her own with shopkeepers, and before long she was able to follow the chatter at the weekly family dinners and contribute volubly. She began to think and even to dream in Italian. It struck her with surprise after one such family dinner, Positano had become home to her, and the de Leones had become her family. She loved Adamo's aunt and uncle. Growing up in a motherless home, with a father who loved her but was usually buried in his books, she had never experienced anything quite like the warmth of this large boisterous clan.

Bette's response to the shock of Eve's initial announcement had been predictable. "Are you out of your mind? What are you doing? What do you really know about this man? This seems a hasty and ill-considered action. Perhaps you should come home, take some time to think it over."

But as time went on and Eve's happiness shone through her messages, Bette and Ed appeared to accept the situation, and even talked about coming to visit them for a holiday.

"Do you realize we've been together for three months, as of today?" Eve said over breakfast one morning.

"Is that so?" Adamo replied. "No, I hadn't realized. But perhaps we should take the day off and celebrate. Go someplace special."

"I can't imagine anyplace more special than this." Eve laughed.

An hour later Eve climbed behind Adamo on the Vespa, remembering with amusement her initial fear of the little motorbike. She scooted all around Positano on it now.

Adamo headed south. A half hour later, in the little town of Amalfi, he turned away from the sea onto a narrow road climbing up the mountainside. Soon the coastal towns looked like toy villages below them. They rode through tunnels, and around twisting switch-back turns, and still they climbed. Finally they were at their destination, a small village perched like an aerie on the mountaintop.

"Ravello," he said as he parked the scooter and helped her off. He led her across the town square and up a winding path to a large old-fashioned hotel with extensive grounds, the Villa Cimbrone. "We used to come up here on Sunday outings when I was a boy," Adamo said. "It seemed like the top of the earth."

They walked hand in hand down a long tree-shaded path to the far edge of the garden. There, overlooking the coastline was a belvedere, paved in marble and surrounded by a formal white marble balustrade adorned with graceful statues. Eve had the sense she might have been in the retreat of some ancient Roman senator. The place seemed ageless in its beauty. The sun was high in the sky and the sea, far below, glittered like diamonds.

"It's lovely. I can see why you wanted to share it with me."

"I've arranged lunch at a place where my family used to come on special occasions."

"Tell me about your family, Adamo. What was it like growing up here? You know everything there is to know about me. I know nothing about your childhood."

"There's not much to tell. I grew up in Positano. I did what all boys do. I fished, I swam, I went to school, and I helped my father out in the restaurant. Leone's originally belonged to my father. We didn't move to the States until I was fourteen. We lived in an apartment in Brooklyn, and I attended the neighborhood school there. I had some problems with English initially, but I picked it up quickly, and I made a few friends. I was good at sports. That made everything else easier. But I missed Italy. I was happiest when my parents sent me back to spend summers with my cousins and my aunt and uncle. Zio Valerio had taken over the restaurant by then. I lived for those summers in Italy."

"Where are your parents now?"

"They died in a crash on the Jersey Turnpike. I had just graduated from high school."

Adamo was silent, his face a mask. Eve thought he would say no more. Then he spoke again.

"I was eighteen. To my shock, my father had taken out a large life insurance policy. Both my mother and my father worked hard all their lives. He must have scrimped and saved to pay the premiums. The money from the insurance saw me through college. But there were no more summers in Italy. I had to work summers to get by. I didn't have enough money to return to Positano until Emmett and I were in business together."

"No brothers or sisters?"

"I had an older sister, Adele, but she died."

Adamo seemed to close down. Eve sensed she would learn no more today.

They walked back through the gardens and down a cobblestone lane, through the massive stone gate in the old town wall. There, suspended out over the cliff, seeming to float over the sea, was a small, charming restaurant, da Salvatore.

The meal was spectacular. Eve had never in her life had anything quite as delicious as the *vitello ai limone,* veal cooked with the wonderful local lemons. It hit her senses on many levels, first the inviting way it looked on the plate, thin slices of veal with lemon slices in a translucent sauce, then the scent, the lovely lemony scent, and finally the melt-in-your-mouth taste.

"I can't continue eating like this," she complained. "I'll gain back all the pounds I worked so hard to lose."

Adamo looked at her critically. "Yes. I can see you're looking more and more like an Italian *casalinga.*"

"An Italian housewife?" Eve laughed. "I don't think I qualify. As far as I've noticed, I'm not a wife of any kind, house or other. I'm not quite sure what the Italian word is for someone in my position, but it's probably not a very polite one."

"I don't think you need worry. No one would dare insult my woman. Now about your weight problem…"

Eve intended to take exception to being referred to as Adamo's "woman," but her attention was diverted by the latter part of his statement. "My weight problem? Do you really think I'm putting on weight?" She looked down at her still slender form to reassure herself. Her clothes weren't in the least too tight.

Adamo's eyes followed hers, sliding down her curves. The soft yellow sundress with its low neckline and short skirt was delightfully revealing.

He grinned. "Obviously running up and down those hundred and ten steps to the road two or three times a day isn't enough exercise. I recommend more time in bed. They say it's marvelous for burning off calories."

"Adamo, I don't think I could survive much more time in bed. In fact I've never in my life spent so much time in bed with so little sleep."

"Clearly you've led a sheltered life," he laughed. "Eve, do you have any idea how happy you make me?"

"No. I think you need to remind me at least once a day." Eve reached across the table to take his hand. This was complete contentment. This was happiness.

They now spent all their waking moments readying the *albergo* to receive guests. The website was up and running and they were listed on the various hotel and small inn sites that might bring them to the attention of travelers. It looked as if they would have at least some guests for their official opening in the spring.

Eve had taken on the task of managing their finances. "I think for the time being we'll have to handle the breakfast service, the room changes, the bookings and the day-to-day dealing with guests ourselves. There's no money for staff. We'll consider getting help later, if and when we can afford it."

"I have a strong back and I don't mind work. But I don't like you having to do it. I didn't ask you here to be a housekeeper."

"Don't be silly, Adamo. We'll do what has to be done, and we'll do it together."

Each of the nine rooms was different. Some were larger, some smaller. Two were suites, complete with sitting room and balcony. All had private ensuite bathrooms and views of the sea. After perusing similar accommodation online, they tried to set their prices competitively, keeping ever in mind the difficulty of getting to their place from the road.

Eve undertook a complete inventory of the rooms. Most of the furniture was old but lovely, some of it antique. But when she tested the beds she found they were uncomfortable, their mattresses hard and lumpy. Of the linens on hand, some were usable, but most were yellowed with age and a bit shabby. Buying beds and bed linens and towels would mean a sizable outlay of their cash, but it was a necessary expenditure. And then there were the cases of soaps and shampoos to be selected and purchased.

"We should go for luxury," Eve suggested. "Good mattresses, top of the line linens and good quality bathroom supplies. They say something about the kind of place we are."

Adamo agreed somewhat reluctantly. "I hope we get some cash flow soon. But you're right. We'll need to spend money to make money. I think we should make a trip to Rome. We'll find a better choice of suppliers there. Maybe tomorrow?"

They took the bus into Rome, and, once settled into the small hotel where they'd stayed on their earlier visit, they began their search for supplies for the inn. The manager of their hotel was helpful in guiding them to good sources.

Two exhausting and expensive days later they had eighteen new twin mattress sets, three dozen sets of Egyptian cotton sheets, four dozen each of thick terry bath towels, hand towels and beach towels, a case of a hundred and forty-four scented bath soaps and facial soaps from a well-known perfumery, and two dozen bathroom glasses. The suppliers promised everything would be shipped to the *albergo* within the next week. They opened accounts so in the future they could simply telephone or email orders.

As they returned to their room at the Cesari, Eve kicked off her shoes and fell on the bed. "To think I used to like shopping. This was a marathon."

"But it's done. Left to my own devices, I'm not sure I'd have chosen the way you did. We spent a lot of money."

"I think it's important we have the best of everything," Eve said. "Particularly beds. Americans expect good beds. We may be small…"

"And hard to get to…" Adamo laughed. He was undressing, heading for the shower, as he spoke.

"But we can build a reputation for offering luxury accommodation. We can be a destination, not just a place to spend a night."

"I hope you're right. The old place never looked so good." He turned back, eyes lingering on Eve sprawled on the bed. "You're tired."

"Never too tired for what I see in your eyes." She was off the bed in one swift motion, putting her arms around him, fitting her body to his in a delightfully familiar way. She gave a low laugh. "You're not too tired, I see."

"We men are at a distinct disadvantage. We can't hide arousal. And when I looked at you on the bed with your hair all mussed and your skirt hiked up…" He reached for the hem of her short skirt, pushed it up and slid her panties down in one swift motion. His hands curved around her buttocks.

"There's a bed right behind us," Eve murmured.

"Beds are overrated. Wrap those gorgeous long

legs around me. I won't let you fall." He backed her against the wall and was inside her and moving.

Eve gave a short gasp and then moved with him. It was fast and furious. And at the end they collapsed on the bed together laughing. How she loved the taste and scent and feel of him. The hardness of his muscles under her hands. And the unexpectedness of his lovemaking.

"I never knew sex could be so much fun," Eve said when she finally caught her breath. "We don't need candlelight and roses and an hour of foreplay."

"Don't knock foreplay." Adamo brought his mouth to her breast and his hand between her legs. "It just doesn't always have to be before. It can be after."

"Not now," Eve said, squirming and pushing him away with laughter. "I'm hungry, and you promised me dinner at Querino's. And this skirt is hopelessly wrinkled now. I have to shower and change."

"We could shower together."

"Not on your life. I remember where that leads. I want dinner. Now."

"You're a witch, you know. When you're near, all I can think of is getting you into bed."

"The bed will still be here after dinner. And besides, you said beds were overrated."

"You`re right. Have you ever tried it in an elevator?"

The next day they took the bus back to Positano. The final preparations were underway for their opening. The first guests were due in two weeks.

The cases of supplies arrived three days after they returned, and the new beds, two days later. Together they set up the rooms. Finally they declared the inn ready for business.

In the evening the whole family gathered for dinner at Leone's. They had closed the restaurant and Zio Valerio left his usual post at the stove to join them at the long table. The prosecco flowed freely.

Enzio leaned toward Eve and in a laughing voice said, "Did Adamo tell you about the time he took the rowboat out and—"

"Watch it, Enzio!" Adamo's voice cut in. "I remember the time you and Alicia—"

"Okay, okay! Truce."

Zia Graziella and Alicia brought the antipasto to the table and everyone filled plates with the cold meats, mozzarella, tomatoes, peppers, and olives

Eve chose one of the tiny black olives and popped it into her mouth. "Come on, Adamo. What happened with the rowboat?"

Zio Valerio gave a deep rumbling laugh. "He was only eight years old. He decided to take the boat out by himself. Without permission, of course. He was well out into the bay when he lost an oar."

Gianni picked up the story. "The story goes he tried to retrieve it using the other oar and lost that one too."

"So then what does he do?" Valerio continued. "He jumps into the water and tries to get both oars back into the boat. Succeeds, too. Only by that time he's so cold he can't climb back into the boat himself. Mind you it was November. Not swimming weather. Lucky for him a couple of returning fishermen found him. Towed the boat in and dropped Adamo off at the restaurant looking like a drowned rat. His father was not pleased."

Adamo joined in the laughter. "He warmed me all

right. Starting with my backside. I couldn't sit down for a week."

As Eve helped Alicia clear away the antipasto plates, she thought about the little boy jumping into the cold water. Adamo hadn't changed much. She had a notion he might still take action without thinking too much about the consequences. He was not a cautious man.

Zia Graziella brought out the pasta, linguini with clam sauce.

"Hey," Adamo said, "I'm not the only one who ever got in trouble. Remember when Pietro and Gianni…"

The stories went on amid laughter and merriment as the main course, veal sautéed with mushrooms and marsala, was polished off.

By the time the dessert arrived, a whole lemon hollowed out and frozen, filled with lemon gelato, Eve was surfeited with both laughter and good food.

Espresso and limoncello signaled the end of the meal

"Now we will see what you've accomplished with the *albergo*," Zio Valerio stated as they pushed their chairs back from the table. "I think we must give it a final inspection before you open."

As they left the restaurant and headed down the path to the inn, Adamo's aunt said, "You said you're expecting your first guests in two weeks?"

"Four rooms booked for the opening," Adamo answered. "A couple from Germany, two women from the United States, school teachers, they said, and two couples traveling together from Britain…More are coming in on the weekend."

"And so it begins," Eve said. "The reservations are trickling in. Most people are booking online. Setting it up was expensive, but it already seems to be paying off."

"I hope so," Adamo countered. "Our capital is seriously depleted."

"What will you serve for breakfast?" Gianni asked.

"We're doing strictly Italian breakfasts," Adamo responded. "We'll offer a selection of coffees or tea, and the usual rolls and *cornetti*. Ruffio's is doing all the breakfast breads for us. He'll have them fresh baked for us every morning. I'll run down on the Vespa at six-thirty to pick them up. We're planning to put a basket of the warm breads and pastries and a plate of fresh fruit on every table. We're serving at individual tables on the terrace rather than in the rooms unless people specifically request otherwise."

Adamo's uncle nodded approvingly. "Ruffio is the best baker on the coast."

Eve laughed. "Ruffio is the only baker in Positano. It's not like we had any choice. But yes, he is very good."

Later, the family members were quiet as they walked through the rooms all newly painted and decorated.

Eve was nervous. Why was no one saying anything?

Back in their sitting room Zio Valerio spoke. "You've done a fine job with the old place. You've managed to keep the original character while making everything fresh and new."

Eve breathed a sigh of relief. They liked what she and Adamo had done.

Alicia added, "I love the fabrics with the lemon designs. They go with the tiles on the tables on the terrace."

"I thought they were a good match," Eve replied.

"Adamo's grandfather had those tiles made to order when they first converted the old house to an inn," Graziella reminisced.

They were taking their breakfast in the kitchen early the next morning when the telephone rang.

Eve answered. "*Albergo de Leone.*"

"Eve." It was Bette's voice. "We're arriving in Rome next Tuesday. Ed has a conference to attend in Geneva on the eighteenth, and we're taking an extra week so we can visit you. Ed's mother is taking the children while we're away. I can't wait. Italy! I'm dying to meet this new man of yours. Ed's arranged for a rental car at Fiumicino. Just send us directions from Rome. Of course Ed has a GPS on his phone, but just in case…We have a whole week free to spend with you. I hope you have room for us."

Finally Eve was able to interrupt the flow. "Of course we have room for you. We're an inn after all. And we're not open to the public yet, so you have your choice of bedrooms. You said Tuesday? That's only five days. Bette, I'm so glad you're coming! I've missed you."

Adamo listened to Eve's side of the conversation with a growing frown. "Your family?" he said, when Eve put the phone down.

"My sister and her husband are coming. Oh, Adamo, I'm so happy. I want them to meet you and to see where and how we're living."

He was still, almost not breathing. He exhaled

audibly. "They're going to try to talk you into leaving me. That's what they're coming for."

"Don't be ridiculous, Adamo. She's my sister. If I'm happy, she'll be happy for me. She just wants to visit. And of course she's curious about you. It's only natural."

He shook his head. "Curious about the ex-con." He got up and walked out to the terrace, staring into the distance, his shoulders slumped in defeat.

Eve followed him. Leaning against him, she put her arms around him and rested her head on his broad back. "I'm a big girl, Adamo. I make my own choices. And I choose to be with you, no matter what anyone may think. But don't prejudge my sister. Give her a chance. I hope she'll see in you the qualities I love, but if she doesn't, it can make no difference to my love for you."

He turned and, pulling her close, buried his face in her hair. "I hope…"

Adamo was quieter than usual during the next days as they chose the room they would put Bette and Ed in and set it up as they would soon for paying guests.

"It will give us a dry run for when we get out first tourists," Eve commented, surveying the room with its fresh flowers and bowl of fruit on the table. Everything sparkled.

Adamo looked around. "I guess it's ready, but it's the innkeeper they're coming to inspect, not the inn."

****

Bette and Ed were expected to arrive in the late afternoon. Eve and Adamo had spent hours in the kitchen planning and preparing their supper. The evenings had turned balmy so Adamo set the table on the terrace. He looked critically at the setting, as if the placement of the knives and forks and wine glasses were of some great import.

"Stop worrying, darling. Everything is perfect. Come, it's time to go meet them."

Hand in hand they climbed the hill to the road. They had reserved a parking place in the garage and explained the arrangement to Ed. They had only minutes to wait before the Hertz rental pulled in and Bette flew out of the car, laughing and crying and hugging Eve.

Ed followed close behind. "Edward Richardson," he said offering his hand to Adamo.

"Adamo de Leone." Adamo looked for signs of antipathy and saw none. Ed's expression was not one of rejection, it was simply noncommittal.

Bette turned to Adamo and to his surprise, hugged him and kissed him on both cheeks. "You're what all the fuss is about!" she accused. "I needed to see firsthand who has turned my usually sensible and literate sister into mush."

In spite of himself, Adamo laughed.

They took the luggage out of the trunk.

"I warned you about heavy bags," Eve said. "It's a long way down."

"Nonsense," Bette replied. "What's the use of having two muscular specimens like we've got if you can't use them to carry bags." Grabbing her small carry on, she started running down the steps.

Eve followed her, laughing, as the men struggled behind, loaded to the gills.

At the inn, Bette looked around their quarters with approval. "You've thought of everything."

"If there's anything we've missed, you must tell us," Eve said. "We open officially a few days after you leave, and we want everything to be perfect. Now unpack and freshen up. We'll meet on the terrace for sunset drinks in half an hour."

Back in their apartment, Eve put her arms around Adamo. "That wasn't so difficult, was it?"

"It was just the first foray; the battle has yet to begin."

Dinner was a festive affair. The food was good, the wine flowed. They might have been any four friends gathered for a convivial evening, except Adamo occasionally sensed Ed contemplating him, as if trying to make up his mind about something.

Finally Adamo could stand it no longer. The tension had been building in him all evening, indeed, for the last several days as he had waited for them to come.

"I think we need to talk about the elephant in the room," he said.

There was a moment's stunned silence.

Then Ed nodded. "In the morning."

Chapter Seven

Adamo slept fitfully. Eve awoke at dawn to find him standing by the window, gazing down at the sea.

"Come to bed," she said, turning the covers back for him beside her. Wordlessly he came to her. She put her arms around him and he fell, finally, into a deep slumber, his head resting on her shoulder. The sun was high in the sky when he awakened.

They came out to the kitchen to discover Bette staring in frustration at the complicated piece of equipment that was their espresso machine. "Does this thing know how to make a simple cup of coffee?"

"One Americano coming up." Adamo laughed.

"Make that two, please." Ed interjected. "I haven't yet acquired the taste for your Italian espresso."

In the warmth of the morning sun, they enjoyed their coffees accompanied by sugary *cornetti,* the Italian versions of croissants, and slices of a delicious, locally grown, pale green melon.

When the Eve stood to clear the table, Ed gestured to Adamo. "Let's take a walk."

The two men went out, Adamo leading the way. He turned left to the path descending to the sea. Ten minutes later they were on the waterfront and a pebbly beach on which a few small fishing boats were pulled up. At this hour they had the place to themselves. They found a bench and sat down.

"Why don't you just tell me what happened to you six years ago," Ed suggested.

"It was a bit like feeling the solid earth disappear from under my feet. I couldn't get a handle on it. One minute I was a partner in a successful investment firm, and the next I was on trial for embezzlement. I don't expect you to believe me, but I simply have no explanation for what happened or how it happened. I only know I never embezzled one red cent from anybody."

"When were you first aware of the shortfall?"

Adam gave a slight shake of his head, trying to remember just how it had all started. "I think it began for me with my partner's suicide. From what emerged later in court, the money was long gone by then, but for me, Emmett's death precipitated everything else."

"I understand you discovered the body?"

"Yes. It was horrible. He'd hung himself."

"How did you happen to be there?"

"The three of us, Emmett, my wife, Monica, and I, were due at a fund-raising event being given by one of our major investors. A gala. Emmett hated those things, but even he knew it was important we be there. It was out in the country and Emmett had no car, so we agreed to pick him up."

Adamo's stomach churned as his mind returned to the past he had tried so hard to forget. "Emmett was supposed to be in the lobby of his building waiting for us. He wasn't there. That's when I began to worry. Emmett was always punctual to the minute. The doorman called through to his apartment, but there was no answer. We couldn't leave the car by the curbside unattended, so Monica told me to wait while she went up to hurry him along. A few minutes later, she was back, crying hysterically, telling me Emmett was dead. To call the police."

"I called 911 and then we both went back up to the eleventh floor." Adamo took a shuddering breath. "The door was standing open. Emmett had hung himself in the bedroom. I think he'd been dead for some time."

Ed interjected, "So you weren't the one to find him. Your wife was. She was there alone in the apartment when she found him."

Adamo frowned. "I suppose so. I went up immediately after calling the police…I tried to calm Monica down while we waited for the police to arrive. She was incoherent."

"How'd she get into the apartment?"

"The police asked us that. Monica said the door was ajar." Adamo shook his head. "It was strange. Emmett was paranoid about his high tech equipment. He had three deadbolts on the door."

"Then what happened?"

"The police questioned us, of course. But we knew nothing."

"There was no suicide note?"

"No. They searched everywhere. There was nothing."

Ed was silent for a moment. "Of course your wife had enough time to remove one."

"What?"

"Do you mean to say the thought never occurred to you?"

Adam shook his head. "Why would she do such a thing? What possible reason could she have? Monica and I didn't have much of a marriage, but surely she wouldn't have stood by and let me go to jail if she had information that could have exonerated me?"

The question hung in the air.

They were silent for a few moments, each with his own thoughts. Then Adamo sighed and continued his narrative.

"Three days later the SEC descended on us to examine the books. It took only a few hours for them to discover we had a shortfall of some eighty million dollars. All that money had been siphoned off in a period of just eight months. Where it went I have no idea."

"How could it have happened without your knowledge?"

"I was unaware because I was a careless idiot who left all the bookkeeping to my partner. I brought in the clients, he invested their money and kept the books. It appears he kept a double set of books. To this day, I can't comprehend how or why Emmett embezzled the money. He never spent a cent on anything except upgrading his equipment. He had a genius for making money, but he lived very simply. I still can't believe he deliberately implicated me in the theft. How could he have killed himself without leaving a message clearing my name?" Adamo's mouth twisted in a bitter expression. "We were friends." He fell silent, his hands locked into fists. He hated dredging it all up.

"You know what I do, what my job is?" Ed asked.

"Eve said you worked for the Internal Revenue Service." Adamo gave a small harsh laugh. "If the IRS wants the taxes on the eighty million they think I have, they're going to have a long wait. My total worth at the moment lies in a small *albergo* in Positano, and what remains of about thirty thousand euros, left to me by my grandfather."

"I'm a lawyer, Adamo. I work in the Investigative Branch of the IRS. We're always interested when money disappears. I requested the transcripts of your trial when we got Eve's first email. Curiosity, I suppose. They made interesting reading."

Adamo nodded. "I can understand your need to find out what you could about me. It must have been a bit if a shock to find your wife's sister involved with an ex-con."

"I expected the worst. But as I read I became increasingly intrigued. The evidence against you was highly circumstantial. The prosecutor implied you had the money stashed away someplace, presumably into off-shore accounts. But he didn't show how it could have happened. He couldn't even show you'd had regular access to the money."

"My lawyer wanted me to admit guilt and go for a plea bargain. I told him I was innocent. I couldn't believe a jury would find me guilty."

"The prosecutor didn't begin to prove your guilt, and yet you went to jail. And you got, not just the short sentence usually meted out in such circumstances, where there is some question of ultimate culpability, but a six year sentence."

"I was in shock at the guilty verdict, and at the sentence."

Ed hesitated, then said, "It seems to me your lawyer was either criminally inept or he was in the pocket of someone who wanted you out of the picture."

Adamo sat frozen, stunned at a possibility he had never even considered. Then he managed, half strangled, "Monica arranged for my lawyer. Our firm lawyer didn't do trial law."

"Interesting. Your wife was alone with the body long enough to destroy a suicide note, if one existed. Your wife arranged for your lawyer. Your wife divorced you as quickly as possible. Then your wife disappeared." Ed looked directly at Adamo. "Could Monica have been involved romantically with Emmett?"

Adamo burst out laughing. "Monica and Emmett? You didn't know Emmett. He had no interest in women. He lived like a monk."

"Monks have been known to fall under the influence of beautiful women."

The enormity of what Ed was suggesting began to sink in. "Five years of my life. Six if you count the year I was required to stay in Brooklyn reporting to a parole officer every week. Monica was sometimes cold and scheming, but was she really capable of something so devious?"

"I don't know Monica, so I can't answer your question. I can only conjecture. If she was involved, she probably had help. It's not all that easy to get eighty million dollars out of the country."

"You sound like you believe me. You're saying you think I'm innocent."

Ed turned to look directly at Adamo. "As it happens, I do. I think you were, to use an old-fashioned word, *railroaded*."

Adamo was too shocked to speak. He had an unlikely ally in Eve's brother-in-law. He'd never expected that.

Almost as if reading his mind, Ed continued, "Of

course you probably know the IRS was interested to see what you would do once you were released from prison. You might have led us directly to the money. But no. You worked nights in a cheap downtown hotel. You lived frugally. When you left for Barbados and then Lisbon, interest was aroused again. But, again, no. You were in Positano, surrounded by family, including, by that time, my sister-in-law. You were making plans to open a nine-room inn. Hardly the behavior of someone who has eighty million dollars stashed away."

Adamo stood and took a deep breath. He wanted to shout with joy. Someone believed him! And not just anyone, but Eve's brother-in-law, someone who had inside knowledge of the world of money. He turned to Ed. "Thank you. I think you just gave me back my life. Even if we never get to the bottom of it, the fact you believe in my innocence means more than I can say."

"Are you going to pursue this?"

Adam hesitated before speaking. Then he shook his head. "No. Frankly, I wouldn't know where to start. I've already spent too much of my life brooding on the past. I've lost six years. I have Eve and I have a chance to build something solid with her here. I don't want more from life than I have at this moment."

****

The week flew by. Adamo enjoyed showing Ed and Bette his world. He began to see Ed as a friend, not as someone to fear. He was no longer anxious that Ed and Bette were here to take Eve away. They had clearly accepted him and his relationship with Eve. Ed had expressed a belief in his innocence. The relief was almost intoxicating.

The two couples spent days exploring the Amalfi

Coast. They visited the little town of Amalfi, and had lunch at da Salvatore in Ravello. They took a day trip down the coast to Paestum too see the magnificently preserved ruins of three ancient Greek temples there. They spent several afternoons lazing on a sandy beach. The June sun was warm, and the water inviting, if a bit chilly.

Most evenings they ate at Leone's, enjoying the different pastas Zio Valerio placed in front of them.

"How can you stay so thin, eating like this every night?" Bette asked Eve.

"You just try running up and down these hundred and ten steps three or four times every day, like I do."

Ed, who was something of a camera buff, took pictures of it all, many stills but some movie shots as well, with his very expensive, state-of-the-art Canon.

"I gave it to him last year, for his thirty-eighth birthday," Bette laughed, "and I've been sorry ever since. He looks at everything through a view finder these days."

One day, toward the end of the week, as the two young women were driving home from a shopping expedition to Sorrento, Bette asked Eve, "What's the island on the horizon?"

"It's Capri."

"Isn't that the island with the famous Blue Grotto?"

"One and the same."

"Do you think we could go there?"

"I'll ask Adamo. I've wanted to go myself, but we never seem to have time."

Adamo spoke to his cousin Gianni, and the next day they all piled into Gianni`s small fishing boat and headed across the bay to Capri. Gianni docked the boat at the town pier and they all scrambled ashore.

Adamo was shocked at the hordes of people milling about on the dock. It hadn't been like this when he was a boy. It used to be a sleepy fishing village. Now, large tour boats from Naples and Sorrento were vying for docking space on which to disgorge their hundreds of day-trippers. The streets of the town were clogged with tourists following guides with hoisted umbrellas. He shook his head. The Capri of today seemed to exist for no purpose other than tourism. He looked in disgust at its streets lined with souvenir shops and over-priced restaurants.

"I haven't been here since I was a kid. It's changed. I'm afraid I don't very much like what's happened to it." Adamo pulled Eve into a doorway as another tour group trooped by.

Eve agreed. "Let's at least see if we can go to the Blue Grotto. That's what Capri is famous for. Can't Gianni take us there?"

"Not really." Gianni shook his head. "There's a tricky entrance to the cave, and it has to be navigated by boats much smaller than mine. But I'll see what I can arrange back at the dock."

Twenty minutes later the two couples and Gianni were ensconced in a rowboat with a small outboard motor. It took longer than they had expected to get to the grotto, and once there, they had to wait in a line of other small boats for their turn to make their way through the small opening. When their turn came, their pilot cut his motor and, using oars, positioned his boat in front of the cave. "Duck down, everybody, and stay down until we're inside," he instructed.

He rested his oars and grabbed a rope suspended over his head. Hand over hand he propelled them through the narrow opening in the wall of the cliff. Suddenly, they were in another world. Iridescent blue water reflected on walls and ceiling of the cave. There were other boats inside. One of the oarsmen was singing, his voice reverberating off the walls of the cave.

No one spoke for a moment. Then Bette broke the silence. "I wouldn't have believed this color, this light, if I hadn't seen it. I'm so glad we came."

Back at the pier an hour later they decided to return to Positano for a late lunch rather than fighting the crowds here. They thanked and paid the guide who had taken them to the grotto and returned to Gianni's boat.

As they were pulling away, a large dinghy off one of the super yachts in the harbor streaked past them too fast and too close for safety, nearly swamping them on its way back to its sleek white floating palace. Gianni shouted at it in irritation as his small boat rocked in its wake.

Adamo jerked his head around to locate the reason for Gianni's stream of creative Italian curses.

"Monica!" His shout echoed over the water. The woman in the dinghy turned and stared, her eyes shielded by sunglasses, before she turned her back.

Without prompting, Ed raised his camera and started shooting the departing dinghy, now weaving its way through the mass of yachts and sailboats moored in the little harbor, coming to rest beside a huge white yacht. The passengers climbed aboard, the woman among them, and disappeared from view.

Ed lowered his camera and turned to Adamo. "Are

you sure?"

"No." Adamo shook his head. "I just got a glimpse. But there was something about her posture, and when she looked at me, I could have sworn…"

"I caught it all. We'll look at it this evening."

"It's probably just wishful thinking on my part," Adamo answered. "I can't seem to get Monica out of my mind since you suggested she might have been the one behind it all. It seems so unlikely, and yet…"

"No other possibility makes sense, does it? If you weren't responsible, someone else was. Emmett had control of the money, but not the means. Someone instigated the scheme, and that someone has to have had the means and opportunity to carry it out. I think the connecting link must have been your wife."

In the evening they looked at Ed's pictures of the incident on his computer. Between the rocking of their boat and the speed of the dinghy, the pictures were fuzzy.

"Can you tell?" Ed asked.

Adamo shook his head. "Not from those photos. I don't know what made me think it was Monica. It was just something about the way she moved, but she was wearing dark glasses and her hair looked different. She could have been anybody."

"Still, she looked directly at you when you shouted her name. Would a stranger have done that?"

"I just don't know."

Ed looked more closely at the shots he'd taken. "At least I can identify the yacht. See there?" He pointed to the screen. "*The Inside Strait II*, registered in the Bahamas. It's an unusual name. I may be able to find out something about it."

Adamo shook his head. "To tell you the truth, I think I was just imagining things. I've been thinking about Monica ever since our conversation about her."

"That's entirely possible."

"I'm beginning to suspect, as you suggested, she set me up. It's an unpleasant feeling. All this time, I was so sure it was Emmett, acting on his own. In any case, I don't want to pursue this. I just want it to go away."

"If it was Monica, and they think you recognized her, you may no longer have any choice."

"They who?"

"Surely you don't think your wife had the connections to pull off this kind of scam by herself?"

"But who…?"

"When I get back to my office, I may be able to track down who owns that yacht."

Chapter Eight

The new website for the *albergo* was up and running. Adamo had placed ads with all the large travel sites, and had contacted several guide books to request inclusion. They had been inspected and approved. They were ready. All they needed was guests.

The opening came off without a hitch. Their first guests seemed to be delighted with their accommodation and their breakfasts, and promised to write reviews. The bookings were coming in steadily now. It looked as if they would be full for most of July and August.

Their days began at six in the morning and often stretched until ten at night when there were late arriving guests. There were beds to make, rooms to change, flowers to arrange, reservations to take, breakfasts to prepare, and laundry, endless laundry to do every day. They were ecstatic over the success of the inn, but they had been six weeks without a single day's break. They were beginning to show signs of exhaustion.

"We need help," Adamo declared as he dragged himself reluctantly out of bed one morning. "We need someone to take over the laundry and we need someone to make up the rooms. And we need to find some way to take a day off now and then."

"Umm," Eve responded from the depths of her pillow. "Go get the breakfast breads. I'll be in the kitchen when you get back."

Later that day, they talked over their problem with Zio Valerio.

"I wondered when you'd get around to asking for our help," he replied. "You should know to look first to your own family. Alicia wants to work. She can do the laundry and have little Giovanni at her side. It's a perfect job for her. Just ask her and you'll see. As for the rooms, Rosa, the sister of Rafaello who waits table at Leone's, is looking for work. I'll speak to him this evening."

A week later the inn was running like clockwork, and Adamo and Eve were able to enjoy being innkeepers without experiencing the exhaustion of those first two hectic months.

****

It was six-thirty on a bright sunny morning. Ruffio was placing still warm rolls and *cornetti* into bags for the *albergo*. Adamo took a deep breath, inhaling the mouth-watering aroma of fresh baked bread. He munched on a sweet roll right out of the oven as the baker put together his order. It was a side benefit to being the one who picked up the breads. It made being up at six o'clock every morning almost worthwhile.

"Two dozen of each," Ruffio said handing the bags to Adamo. "That will be twenty-four euros."

Adamo counted out the bills. "Thanks, Ruff. See you tomorrow morning. *Ciao*."

He placed the bags in the box on the back of the Vespa, climbed on, and headed back up the hill, not hurrying. The sun was still low in the sky, but it bathed the houses and shops in a warm amber light. It promised to be a hot day.

He had a sudden vision of Eve as she looked when he got up, her hair sleep tousled, her face buried in her pillow. A surge of sheer happiness shot through him. A year ago he would not have believed how drastically his life could change. He was content. More than content.

He was approaching the top of the hill when a car coming from the other direction roared around a steep curve at high speed and, tires squealing, headed straight for him. "What the hell?"

Adrenaline pumped into his veins. No place to go. A drop-off to the sea on his left, the steep mountainside on his right. He slewed his bike sharply to the right. It skidded on gravel and hit a concrete abutment. He flew airborne over the handlebars onto a bed of rocks, and heard, as from a great distance, the crumple of steel against rock as the car smashed into his Vespa. Heart pounding, he brushed blood away from his left eye with a shaking hand. His head was throbbing, his shoulder hurt and blood seemed to be running down his left leg and into his shoe, but he was alive.

He tried to push himself up. His vision clouded for a moment as a sharp pain shot through his head. What was the car doing? Backing up to try again? Adamo stared in disbelief. He shook his head. He must move quickly. The only escape from the murderous car was by climbing the cliff face. Safety lay in climbing up. He knew how to do that. He stood, weaving, uncertain on his feet. No time to lose. Hands in the crevices. Good. Now get a foothold. Climb!

His toes slipped and lost their grip. He collapsed once again on the side of the road. He raised his head to watch the car that would be the instrument of his death.

With a squealing of tires, a second car rounded the

bend. Black and white. The police. Thank God.

His world went black.

****

Eve was setting the tables on the terrace with the colorful dishes they had found in a local pottery shop. She placed a sprig of lemon blossom in a small bud vase on each table, and stood back to admire the overall picture. Satisfied, she returned to the kitchen to prepare the melon. Adamo had gone, as usual, to fetch the breakfast breads and pastries from Ruffio's.

She glanced at the clock on the kitchen wall. Where was he? He should have been back by now. As the minutes passed, Eve began to feel a tinge of worry. What could be keeping him? She called Ruffio.

"But Adamo left here an hour ago."

Her worry took on an edge of panic. He was expert at handling the Vespa, but it was a small and vulnerable vehicle and the traffic could be heavy at this hour of the morning. And if he didn't appear with the breads within the next fifteen minutes, what was she going to give the guests for breakfast?

Her phone rang. His first words were "Don't panic. I'm okay."

"Adamo!"

"Call Zia Graziella and ask her to take over the breakfast service. And to bring breads. I'm afraid ours ended up all over the highway."

"What happened? Where are you? I knew that Vespa wasn't safe."

"I'm in the *Pronto Soccorso* at the San Paolo Hospital in Sorrento. In the hospital, the emergency room. But I'm fine. Don't worry. Just ask Zio Valerio to come and get me." The connection was cut.

Graziella had Alicia with her. "Go!" She pushed Eve out of the door. "You'll be of no use here worrying about Adamo. Just go with Valerio."

Eve didn't argue. She and Adamo's uncle raced up the steps to the car park where Zio Valerio's elderly Fiat was housed. They made little conversation as he drove toward Sorrento and the hospital. Eve's lips trembled, and she twisted her fingers in her lap as she fought to contain her rising panic.

She was out of the car and into the emergency entrance before Zia Valerio could lock the car. "Adamo de Leone?" she asked at the desk.

"Fifth bed on the right. But you can't go in there now. The police are with him."

Ignoring the young woman, Eve ran through the double doors and down a bed-lined corridor until she saw Adamo. He was sitting up in bed, his left arm in a sling and a bloody bandage around his head. His bare leg beneath a short hospital gown was also bandaged, with blood seeping through the gauze. His face and arms were scraped and bruised.

Eve burst into tears.

"I'm fine, Eve. It was just a little accident."

The carabinieri officer stared at her for a moment, and then, ignoring her, turned back to Adamo. "You were saying…"

"The car just came from nowhere. Around the curve at very high speed. It swerved toward me. The driver must have lost control of his vehicle. There was a long drop to the sea on my left. I steered sharply right, toward the mountain side of the road and went head over heels off my bike just before the car smashed into it. The driver slammed on his brakes and skidded. Then he backed up. I don't know whether he was stopping to help or trying to take another run at me, but, fortunately, a carabinieri car came around the corner and he sped off."

Adamo looked at the man standing by his bed, taking notes. "Were you one of the officers in the police car? I think I may owe you my life. Anyway, I guess I must have hit my head pretty hard, because I blacked out and the next thing I knew I was in an ambulance on my way here."

The officer placed his notebook back in his jacket pocket. "Tourists don't know how to drive on the Costiera Amalfitana. There's rarely a day without an accident. You were very lucky." He turned to leave.

"That's it?" Eve was incensed. "You're not even going to try to find the car that nearly killed him?"

The officer turned briefly to her. "And you are…?"

"I'm Eve Anderson. And I'm his…"

"Fiancée," Adamo supplied.

"Ah, yes. Fiancée. American?"

"What's that got to do with it?" Eve fought threatening tears.

"This is not an American television police drama. We have no description of the car other than it was a dark sedan. If we had given chase, your…" The pause was long enough to border on insult. "…*fiancé* would still be lying unconscious by the side of the road. By the time the ambulance arrived, the car was long gone."

"Eve." Adamo's voice held a warning note. "Let it rest. I'm fine."

The officer stared at Adamo for a moment, then nodded and left without another word.

The neurosurgeon arrived as the policeman was

leaving. "The CT scan indicated there was no damage to the skull, no blood seepage into the brain," he told them. "But you were, however briefly, unconscious. You'll have to be watchful. It could mean concussion. Lucky you were wearing a helmet."

****

Back at the inn, Eve fussed over him, examining his cuts and scratches and bruises and the place on his left leg that had required stitches.

"Stop it, Eve. I've had worse injuries from a soccer match. I'll live."

She gave into the tears threatening for the last hour. "It wasn't an accident, Adamo. Someone tried to kill you."

"Utter nonsense!" The disclaimer didn't ring true to either of them.

Within four days Adamo was back to his usual activities, although Eve observed he was limping and seemed to be favoring his left shoulder a bit. She saw him wince when he forgot and lifted a case of Pellegrino destined for the kitchen. She said nothing. He was short tempered and abrupt with any suggestion he do less. His leg and shoulder appeared to be healing well, and he had resumed his early morning exercises. Eve watched carefully for any sign of headaches and nausea, the symptoms of concussion, but found none. Thank God he'd been wearing the helmet she'd purchased for him. He hadn't been happy when she insisted he wear it on the Vespa at all times, but he'd complied rather than argue with her about it.

****

They were sitting having a coffee on the terrace after serving breakfast to fifteen guests, when Adamo mentioned the problem created by the destruction of his Vespa. For the moment he was using Valerio's car to make the morning bread pick-up. "We have to get some kind of transportation. We can't keep monopolizing Zio Valerio's car."

"I know. But I'll never feel safe on a motor scooter again. You could have been killed."

"I'm not sure a car would have been much safer under the same circumstances. The question is what can we afford?"

"We're in pretty good shape financially right now. I think we could afford a second hand car. We do need one. Actually I was wondering if we shouldn't get a van. Offer to pick our guests up at the airport or the train station in Naples. We could charge for the service, of course."

Over the next few days Adamo perused the advertisements in the paper and posted at various spots around the town.

"A Mercedes van was advertised on the announcements board near Ruffio's," Adamo told Eve over breakfast one morning. "I called and the owner said we could look at it this afternoon. It's in Amalfi."

"Mercedes is usually expensive. Of course it would lend a touch of class, but wouldn't it be cheaper to get an Italian van?"

"I was hoping for a Fiat, but so far this is the only vehicle I've seen that meets our size requirements and is old enough to be within our budget. Do you want to come with me?"

"I can't, Adamo. One of us needs to be here to greet the arriving guests. You certainly know more about cars than I do. If you test drive it and think it's the right one, go ahead and buy it."

Eve checked in a retired school teacher from Virginia, two backpackers from Sweden, and a Dutch couple on their honeymoon. The honeymoon couple retreated to their suite immediately. How young and sweet they seemed. And so in love.

She sighed. Adamo gave every sign of caring for her, but he had never once said *I love you*. Not once in all the months they'd been together. But if actions truly speak louder than words, he did love her. His love for her was evidenced in a thousand small ways. Why was he so reluctant to admit to it? She was happy with Adamo, but she wanted marriage, a family of their own, while he seemed content just to drift on as they were.

She shrugged her shoulders and went into the kitchen. She had to arrange fresh flowers for the tables on the terrace. Suddenly she caught a whiff of a sour smell, heard the scuff of a shoe. Her spine prickled...

Turning, she suppressed a small scream. A young man with a gun in his hands. A gun leveled directly at her. Her eyes were glued to the small but deadly weapon. For a moment she was unable to speak, her mind rejecting what she saw. Her pulse raced, blood pounding in her head. She grasped her hands tightly together to control their shaking.

Trying to stem her rising hysteria, to keep her voice steady, calm, she said, "What do you want? We don't keep money on the premises."

"Where is he?

"Who?"

"*Il tuo ragazzo*. Your boyfriend, Adamo de Leone." His voice held unconcealed contempt.

"I'm sorry. He's not here at the moment. May I

help you?" She looked into his flat gray eyes, trying to ignore the gun. Her stomach churned. This couldn't be happening to her.

"Wherever he is, call him and tell him to come home. I don't care what reason you give him, but make it convincing. I'll be listening." He spoke in gutter Italian she had some difficulty following, but the threat was clear.

Adamo. He was here to kill Adamo. She had to warn him. Eve picked up the phone and with a shaking hand punched in Adamo's cell number. "Adam." She used the English version of his name. She spoke in Italian but tried to speak it badly, as if new to the language. "Adam, the repair man is here about your motor scooter. I need you to come home now. You can do the rest of the shopping later."

The young man grabbed the phone out of her hand and listened to the response. At first there was silence. Then, "I'll be there in twenty minutes." He clicked the phone off and put it on the counter.

"Now sit down," he ordered. "We wait."

Eve froze, rooted to the spot.

"I said sit down!" he yelled, pushing her roughly into a chair.

Within moments he had her arms strapped behind her, and her feet securely fastened to the legs of the chair with duct tape. Tentacles of fear crept through her as she realized she was helpless. She shivered. Had Adam understood from her strange message that something was seriously wrong? That he should be on his guard? Her eyes were glued to the clock on the wall as the hands moved infinitesimally, minutes seeming like hours. The young man stood alert, listening, his eyes on the door through which Adamo would have to enter. His gun hand was relaxed but poised, ready.

He hadn't gagged her. Why? The answer came to her sickeningly. If she screamed a warning, Adamo would rush toward her, not away from her. It was what the gunman wanted. He wanted her to draw Adamo here. She resolved to be quiet when the front door sounded. Perhaps her very silence would put Adamo on his guard.

She looked again at the clock. Had it really been only ten minutes?

Suddenly, glass shattered and wood splintered, as Adamo hurled himself through the terrace doors behind them. The young man shrieked. With a guttural roar Adamo threw him to the ground, sending his gun skittering across the floor.

The terror Eve had barely been holding in check threatened to consume her. Shuddering, she watched in horror as Adamo knelt over the intruder, planting his knee firmly on the other man's back. She heard the sickening crunch of breaking bone as Adamo twisted the would-be assassin's arm behind him in an impossible angle. The man gave an ear-splitting scream and fainted.

Eve could hear another voice screaming, screaming, without realizing it was hers. Adamo stood, retrieved the gun and swiftly cut Eve's restraints, pulling her into his arms. "It's all right, *carissima.* It's over."

Gradually her breathing slowed and her fear subsided. She was in Adamo's arms. She was safe.

He put his hand under her chin and tilted her head so he could look into her eyes. "Go down to Zia

Graziella's," he ordered. "I'm going to bring him to and question him, and I don't want you here."

"No." Eve took a shuddering breath. "We must call the police."

"I don't want the police involved. We'll never find out who is behind this if we call in the carabinieri. I want to know who sent this thug."

"But…"

"Please, Eve. I don't want you here. I'm going to question him, and you won't like it. You've had enough."

Eve took a shuddering breath. "We're in this together, Adamo. I'm not leaving."

He looked at her long. "Very well."

The man on the floor moaned. Adamo swiftly secured the thug's legs with his own duct tape and pulled him to a semi reclining position against the wall. Then he stalked to the sink and filled a pot with water. He threw it on the intruder.

The man came to, sputtering and moaning. "You broke my arm!"

"Yes, I did. You now have one arm, two legs, and ten fingers unbroken. It's up to you how long they stay that way." Adamo's voice rained icicles, and he looked directly into the man's eyes as he spoke.

Eve drew in a sharp breath and stared at Adamo in shock.

"We'll have your name first."

There was a brief moment's silence.

Adamo took a step toward him.

The man mumbled, "Gino Abruzzo."

"Very good, Gino. So far you only have one broken arm. Who sent you?"

"They'll kill me."

"Possibly."

The ticking of the old fashioned wall clock seemed impossibly loud to Eve. She waited and watched, slightly nauseated.

Adamo cold eyes never left the younger man's. "As I see it you have a choice, Gino. You can answer my questions fully now and I'll see you get to the nearest hospital, no police involved, or I can break your bones, one at a time, and then dump you by the side of the road. You will tell me what I want to know sooner or later." His voice was soft, reasonable, and lethal.

There was only a moment's hesitation before the words started tumbling out. "I work for the Conti Family, Don Alfonso Conti in Napoli. I just do what they tell me. I get a phone call telling me to make sure you can't cause trouble for anyone." He shook his head. "Somebody wants you dead. I don't know who."

"Why?" Adamo seemed genuinely puzzled.

"I follow orders. I don't ask questions."

"What do you know about my accident on the road a few days ago?"

"I don't know nothing about any accident, only they tried to get you once before and failed. And now I've failed. They'll kill me."

"Perhaps, perhaps not, if you help me." Adamo considered the young man. "Where can I find this Alfonso Conti?"

"Are you crazy? You don't want to find him."

Adamo turned to Eve. "You can call for an ambulance now."

When he spoke again to Gino Abruzzo, his voice was cold as ice. "You threatened my woman. If I ever

114

see you again, you're a dead man."

Somehow, in this context, Eve didn't think she minded being referred to as Adamo's "woman."

When it was all over, and Gino Abruzzo had been taken away by paramedics, Eve started shaking again.

Adamo picked her up, carried her to the bedroom and placed her gently on the bed. There he lay down with her, holding her close.

When her teeth finally stopped chattering, Eve asked, "How did you get here so quickly? And how did you get on the balcony? It's a five hundred foot drop to the sea."

"I was already on our path, five minutes from home, when you called. It was clear something was wrong, so I decided to take precautions."

"But how—"

"I went past our place, down to Zio Valerio's. From there I climbed from balcony to balcony, five in all, up the cliff to ours. It's something I used to do as a boy. When I looked in and saw you strapped to a chair, and that young idiot with a gun, I'm afraid I saw red." Adamo thought ruefully about the damage to the doors he'd crashed through. "I guess I'd better call the carpenter. We're going to need new balcony doors."

"But where did you learn how to do that? To injure someone that way?"

"Tae kwon do was developed a long time ago, during the Korean War. It was intended for use in unarmed combat. And I studied under a master." Adamo nuzzled her hair. "I'm sorry. I'm so sorry to have put you in this danger."

"Why? Why are they trying to kill you?"

"I don't know. But I intend to find out."

****

After the restaurant was closed Zio Valerio stopped in to see Adamo. Eve had gone to bed earlier, exhausted.

Valerio walked into the sitting room and settled into a deep cushioned chair with a sigh. "I've been on my feet in the restaurant kitchen for six hours. You left word you wanted to speak with me urgently and privately?"

Adamo described what had happened.

His uncle sat back, clearly shocked.

Adamo paced restlessly. "What do you know about the Contis?"

"The Contis? I know the head of the family, the Capo, Don Alfonso, very well. He's been a good friend to the de Leone's for many years."

"I was under the impression they were a crime family."

His uncle spread his hands in a pure Italian gesture that said, "And so?"

Adamo absorbed this. He stopped in front of his uncle. "How do you come to know him?"

"You've been away too long, Adamo. Have you forgotten how things work here? We don't have one government, we have three. There's the so-called 'elected' government, there's the Church, and then there's the Camorra. Each performs its own functions."

His uncle hesitated, as if seeking the right words. "I wanted to open a restaurant. I could have gone to government officials for the licences, but I'd have needed more money in bribes than I could ever have raised. Sometimes, the Church can pave the way, but not when it comes to something like licences for a restaurant. I suppose I could have prayed for the licences, but I'd have been in heaven before they came."

Adamo shook his head and sat down opposite his uncle. Waiting.

Valerio continued. "Or I could speak to my good friend, Don Alfonso. I could offer him a small piece of the restaurant in return for his protection and help."

"The Conti Family is part owner of Leone's?" Adamo was shocked.

"Twenty percent. Cheap at the price. The licences were issued within a few weeks, and I've been in business now for over twenty years with no trouble from any quarter. It's just the cost of doing business here. It's the system in Campania."

Adamo was silent, thinking. Finally he asked, "Do you think you could get me in to see Don Alfonso?"

"Of course. Nothing simpler. I'll call him in the morning. I can't believe he'd have authorized those attacks on you, Adamo. You're a de Leone. He may not know you personally, but he knows our family. He's always been there for us. Go and see him. Talk to him. But be respectful. Remember, he's a powerful man. You don't want to antagonize him."

"Yes. I understand."

The phone rang just after breakfast. "He can see you at two this afternoon. The address is on the Via del Fontana, in the hills behind Naples. It's not easy to find. I've drawn a map for you. When you come to the gate, there will be a man posted outside. Just give him your name. And when you speak to Don Alfonso, you will refer to him as *Padrino*."

"Godfather. I understand."

"Good. Remember, Don Alfonso has been very good to our family."

At exactly two o'clock Adamo presented himself at the gate to the Conti residence, armed with a gift from his uncle. The man at the gate telephoned through to say he was there, and a second man came to escort him to the garden behind the mansion.

To Adamo's surprise, Don Alfonso was seated in a wheelchair. "Forgive my not standing to greet you."

"Thank you for seeing me, Padrino." Adam inclined his head in a bow. "I understand you have been a friend to my family for many years. I'm very grateful."

The older man coughed and spoke in a hoarse voice. "It has been no hardship to help your uncle. Leone's is a fine restaurant. I used to eat there regularly when my legs could carry me places. Unfortunately, it is not so easy to get around now. But still he occasionally sends me special dishes. His *cannoli al limone* is the best I've ever eaten, anywhere."

"I brought some with me. Your assistant took it to the kitchen."

"Ah. Thank you. Please sit down." He indicated a wicker chair. "I understand from your uncle you have a problem."

Adamo plunged in without preface. "Six years ago I went to prison for a crime I didn't commit. I was accused of embezzlement. I served my time. Now I'm living here, in Positano, trying to put it all behind me. Trying to make a living, running a small inn I inherited from my grandfather."

"I remember your grandfather well. I helped him out from time to time. So what is your problem? Your uncle didn't elaborate."

"Twice in the last two weeks someone has tried to kill me."

The Capo raised his eyebrows. "Have you given any of the other Camorra families in Naples reason to want you dead?"

"No, Padrino. The thing is, the man who was sent to take care of me yesterday was Gino Abruzzo, one of your *soldati.*"

"Ah, Gino. A rather brash young man, but usually effective. How is it you are still alive?"

"He had an unfortunate accident. His gun arm is broken. I believe he'll be out of commission for a while."

The Capo stared at Adamo, silent for a few moments.

Adamo waited.

The older man coughed, and took a sip of water from a glass on the table beside him. "I did not order this. I will need some time to discover who did, and why. I do not care for any of my employees or associates to act without my knowledge. I'll get to the bottom of it and be in touch with you. In the meantime I suggest you take precautions, although you seem well able to take care of yourself."

"Thank you, Padrino."

The old man nodded. The interview was over.

****

Three days later Adamo was summoned to the Conti residence. This time the meeting was in a book lined study with the Capo sitting behind his desk.

"I've spoken with young Gino. He described what happened. If you should ever decide you don't wish to be an innkeeper, I could find a place for you in my organization."

"Thank you, Padrino, but I like being an innkeeper."

"*Che brutto*, too bad." Don Alfonso steepled his hands and looked over them at Adamo. "There seems be some confusion about the two incidents. Gino says the request came to him by telephone from one of my lieutenants. That man, in turn, informed me the original request was from the New York branch of the family. I called my brother Marco, the head of the New York family. As I suspected, he knew nothing about it. He would have called me, not some underling in my organization. He will investigate. Meanwhile I have given those here who need to know, to understand you and all your family are under my protection. I do not believe you will be troubled again."

"You mean to say the order to kill me came from someone inside the Conti organization in New York?"

"It would appear so. But it was done without the knowledge of my brother. He is not pleased about this. I'm sure he will get to the truth of the matter. Someone in America wants you dead. I think I must ask you who would benefit from your death?"

"No one, Padrino. I own nothing but the Albergo de Leone."

"You were convicted of a crime you say you did not commit. If you didn't commit it, someone else did. It appears obvious to me the person actually responsible for the theft is disturbed by a threat from you, real or merely imagined. I suspect you will not be safe until you discover who this person is and"—he hesitated, seeking the right word—"neutralize him."

Adamo nodded his reluctant agreement. "I had hoped to be left in peace to live my life here, but I suspect you're right. Thank you, Padrino, for your help. Would you be willing to give me a letter of introduction to your brother? I may well need his assistance when I return to the States."

"I'll call him. He has already indicated he wishes to speak with you."

Adamo had not discussed his meetings with the Naples crime family head with Eve. He had, in fact, deliberately kept her in the dark. She simply wouldn't understand. The Mafia culture of Italy was incomprehensible to anyone who had not grown up with it. Now there could be no further avoidance of the issue; he would be forced to tell her what he'd learned. The danger was not just to him but, as long as he was with her, to Eve as well. He would have to persuade her to remain in Italy, where she would be under the protection of the Conti family, while he traveled back to the States to try to pick up the trail of a six-year-old crime.

Chapter Nine

Adamo disappeared while Eve was stacking the dishes in the dishwasher. When she finished her chore, she walked out to the terrace where they customarily sat together after dinner. Where was he?

She found him in the bedroom, taking a hand full of shirts out of one of his drawers. His suitcase was open on the bed, and he was methodically packing. His socks and underwear were already neatly folded in the bottom of the case.

He froze momentarily when she came into the room.

"What are you're doing?"

"I have to return to the States for a few days. Some business to attend to. I shouldn't be gone long." He avoided looking at her.

Eve was silent for a long moment. Then she said, "I don't suppose this trip has anything to do with the fact your life has been threatened twice in the last ten days. Or with the two trips you made to Naples this week."

"No. No, of course not. Just some loose ends I have to tie up."

"Adamo, you have to be the worst liar in the world. On that basis alone, the jury should never have convicted you. Now tell me what's going on. You've learned something, and you're trying to keep it from me. You need to return to the U.S. because of it. You went to Naples to see the man Gino Abruzzo mentioned. Conti, I think his name was. What did he tell you?"

"I don't want you involved in this, Eve. I don't want you near me. It could be dangerous."

"I'm already involved, Adamo. I love you, and if you think for one moment I'm going to let you go charging off into danger while I stay here, you have another think coming."

"Eve, be reasonable. Someone's trying to kill me. I can look after myself, but if anything happened to you—"

"You'll just have to see nothing does."

Eve took out her suitcase and tossed clothes haphazardly into it. "Now tell me about it. What did you learn in Naples?"

Adamo sighed and walked over to her. He put his hands on her shoulders and looked into her eyes. "I hoped I could put the past behind me. Start over, here, with you. But it seems my very existence is being viewed by someone as a threat. I need to discover who that someone is and why he or she wants me dead. I need to eliminate the threat, one way or another. And I don't want you anywhere close to me while I'm doing it. Please, Eve, let me do this the way I must. Alone."

"Whoa. Back up, Adamo. Let's start with who you spoke with and what you learned about those two attacks on you."

"Eve, there are things you simply don't have to know. Things you can't begin to comprehend."

"Try me."

Adamo shook his head in defeat. "All right. Come.

123

Let's sit on the balcony for a little while, and I'll tell you what I know. And why it's impossible for me to take you with me on this trip."

Wordlessly, they walked through the kitchen and picked up a bottle of limoncello and two glasses. Adamo poured them each a drink and took a sip of his.

He spoke tentatively. "I don't know what you may have heard, or read, or seen in the movies about the Mafia. But whatever you think you know, it's not even close to the reality."

"The Mafia? I'll admit it wasn't much of an issue on the Eastern Shore of Maryland."

"It's an influence you can't ignore if you live in Italy. Along with the church and the elected government, the 'Families,' the Camorra, control everything that happens here.

Eve shook her head in disbelief. "So you went to the Camorra?"

"Alfonso Conti is the head of one of the largest and most powerful Camorra families in Naples. He's helped my family before.

Eve frowned. "I see."

Adamo shook his head. "No, you don't see. Nothing in your life in America can have prepared you for this. I'm sure it's incomprehensible."

"So help me to understand. What happened when you saw this Alfonso Conti?"

"I told him everything. He has put us under the protection of the Conti Family. That means for the moment, at least, we are out of danger."

"So, if he can actually guarantee our safety here, why are you planning to go back to the States?"

"Don Alfonso strongly advised me to get to the

bottom of this. And he's offered the help of his connections in New York. For our future together, I must find out what occurred six years ago. Who set me up."

Eve reached over to take Adamo's hand. "I've believed for some time we should find out what really happened, but you've always seemed reluctant even to think about it. I agree we'll never be free of it if we don't at least try."

"There is no *we* in this, Eve. I can't allow..."

"*You* can't allow! Just who do you think you are, Adamo de Leone? The last time I looked, you had no legal authority over my actions."

She lifted her chin and ripped out her words. "My life has been threatened; the life of the man I love has been threatened. And you expect me to stay here, serving *cornetti* and cossetting guests, while you put on your armor and run off alone to slay the dragon? You're out of your mind."

Eve's voice had steadily risen. She stood and put her hands on her hips. "And while I'm at it, I'm not your fiancée, as you introduced me to that policeman. I'd have noticed if you'd asked me to marry you. And I'm not your woman! Twice recently you've referred to me as your woman. I'm not anyone's woman but my own. I'll go where I damned well please and do what I damned well please! And I'm coming with you." She stormed over to the balustrade and stood facing the sea, near tears and gulping for breath.

"Feel better now?" His voice was soft. He put a hand on her shoulder, but she shrugged it off. "I won't ask you to marry me as long as this is hanging over our heads. I can't ask you to tie yourself legally to a felon,

Eve. And you are your own woman. I'm well aware of that. I'm sorry if I offended you. I just want to protect you. If anything happened to you, I don't think I could go on living."

Eve turned to him and buried her face against his chest. "And how do you think I feel? No more do I want to live without you. We're in this together, Adamo. Where you go, I go."

Adamo sighed in defeat.

Alicia and Gianni agreed to take over running the inn while they were away, and Zia Graziella offered to help with the breakfasts.

"We've been working with you for months now, Adamo," Gianni reassured them. "We'll manage."

Two days later they were in the Rome Airport. They had their boarding passes. Adamo left Eve in the bag check line while he went to pick up an American newspaper. Ten minutes later he returned to find her no farther ahead than when he left her, at the back of a mob of people clustered around the Alitalia desk. She pushed their suitcases forward a couple of inches with her knees.

"I can't figure out where the end of the line is."

Adamo laughed. "Every Italian is the beginning of another line. Watch. I'll take care of getting our bags checked."

A few moments later Adamo was at the desk, where a smiling attendant checked their two small bags.

"How did you do that?"

"A lifetime of practice."

"So every Italian is the beginning of another line?"

"It's a defining national characteristic. We just don't do lines."

"Hmm. What about Americans and lines?"

"Americans recognize lines. They just figure out ways to push themselves ahead of other people. Canadians, on the other hand, step back and say 'after you.'"

Eve laughed. "Somehow I'd never considered lines a definition of national character. What about other countries?"

"Well, there are the Germans. They have an intense sense of order. No one better try to bull his way ahead in a German line. But the Brits are my favorites. If you put seven Brits together anyplace, they'll queue up. They're pretty much the opposite of us Italians."

Two hours later they were on their way to Dulles, the airport serving the Washington, D.C., area. The Richardsons had suggested using their home in Silver Springs as a base. It was a boon, since they could ill afford lengthy hotel stays. Besides, it would be good to talk with Ed and Bette about their next steps.

After a long, crowded, and uncomfortable flight, the two weary travelers straggled through American immigration and customs and out to the main arrivals level.

The whole family was there to greet them. Eve laughed as Adamo was overrun by four exuberant Richardson boys. Now he knew what she felt like as they descended the bus in Positano to the assembled de Leone clan.

"Bette," Eve scolded, noting her sister's rounded belly, "you didn't tell me you were pregnant again."

"We keep trying for a girl. It's no problem. I'm an old hand at pregnancy now. It's wonderful to have you here."

The next morning after the children had left for school, the two couples sat around the kitchen table and talked.

Adamo told them everything about the attack on Eve and his own two recent escapes from death. He skimmed over his conversations with Don Alfonso Conti. He wasn't sure he could make the role of the Camorra understandable in this very American household.

Ed looked thoughtful. "You do need to get to the bottom of this, but I'm not sure where you should start."

Bette broke in. "I've been thinking…"

They all turned to her.

"Yes?" Adamo said.

"Didn't you say Emmett had a sister?"

"Emma," Adamo said. "She's in some kind of assisted-living care facility in upstate New York. I believe she's pretty much wheelchair-bound. I hadn't planned to talk to her. I don't think she'd be in a position to know anything."

"But didn't Emmett visit her regularly? Perhaps he said something to her." Bette turned to Ed. "Don't you think it's worth checking out? We certainly don't have many other leads."

"Do you know the name of the place?" Ed opened his phone.

"No, but I think it's near Watertown. Emmett used to go there about once a month to visit her, and he flew into the Watertown International Airport."

"That shouldn't be too hard to locate." Ed worked with the device for a few minutes. "There seem to be five possibilities in the area. I guess it's time to make some phone calls."

Twenty minutes later they had an address.

"I'll book the flight," Adamo said. "I guess we'll need to rent a car."

"Get one with a GPS," Ed advised. "It looks like this place is some distance out of town, and it could be hard to find."

The next morning Eve and Adamo flew into Watertown and picked up their Budget rental. They drove for two hours east, through rolling hills and wooded countryside, before coming to ornate gates inscribed with the words *Adirondack Hills*.

A small sign just inside the open gates said *"Visitors are requested to check in at the office."*

"I'm sure this is the place Ed found online," Eve said, "but it doesn't look like any care facility I've ever seen. It looks more like an upscale gated community."

They continued up a winding drive, past several small colonial style brick cottages, no two exactly alike, each with its own grassy front yard and flower beds.

Then at a curve in the drive they saw a large two story Colonial-style brick mansion.

"This has to be the main building," Adamo said, pulling over into a designated parking space.

On the front door there was a sign, *"Please Ring and Enter."*

Pushing the door open they found themselves in a wide entrance hall with doors to the right and left and a massive curving staircase leading to the upper floors.

A severe-looking woman dressed in a navy blue suit appeared from a door on the left. "May I help you?"

Eve responded, "We'd like to see Emma Kenston.

We understand she's a resident here?"

The woman hesitated. "Are you from the press?"

Adamo was momentarily confused. "The press? No, of course not. I'm Adamo de Leone. Miss Kenston is the sister of the man who was my friend and business partner. We just want to talk with her."

"I know your name." The woman peered at him over the top of her glasses. "You're the man who was convicted of embezzlement some years ago. The newspapers were full of it. And there were reporters trying to get to Miss Kenston at the time. We actually had to lock our gates to keep them out. We have to protect our residents. I'm sure you understand."

"We mean her no harm. We just want to talk to her," Adamo said.

"She never believed you did it, you know."

"I beg your pardon?"

"She said her brother had been a fool, and you were innocent. She was shocked when you were convicted. Come into my office, and I'll see if she's available."

Five minutes later they were walking back down the lane to the third cottage on the left. Adamo knocked on the door.

"Come in," a strong feminine voice called.

They opened the door to find themselves facing a woman in a wheelchair. "You're Adamo. I'm so glad to meet you at long last. Emmett spoke of you often." A smile lit her surprisingly beautiful face.

"And he spoke often about you. I'm sorry we never met before," Adamo said. "My friend, Eve Anderson."

Emma took Eve's proffered hand and said, "I have the kettle on for tea. Please come in and sit down. Make yourselves comfortable. I'll be right back. You take milk and sugar?"

"No," they said almost in unison. Eve added, "Black will be fine. Can we help?"

"I have some scones and cookies and some slices of cake on a plate. Adamo can carry the tray if he doesn't mind."

Eve looked around at the room while Adamo and Emma were in the kitchen. It was a large room, furnished comfortably with a flowered chintz upholstered sofa and wing chair and some simple but lovely antique pieces. The windows were curtained in coordinated fabrics. In one corner, a desk held a large screen desktop computer and printer, with papers strewn about it. Against another wall, a Mozart sonata was open on a spinet piano. Fresh flowers were arranged in a low bowl on a round cherry table overlooking the gardens. The place was tastefully and expensively decorated. Eve wondered briefly whether Emma worked and what her financial circumstances were. This facility must be extraordinarily expensive.

A few minutes later the three were seated at the table with a generous selection of cakes and cookies on a large silver tray in front of them.

Emma poured tea from what Eve recognized as a Staffordshire teapot into delicate china cups. "You must forgive me for making such a production of this. I don't have company often, and I do enjoy having someone with whom to share my tea."

"I love it. It takes me back to my childhood. My mother always had her tea and cakes in the afternoon using her best china." Eve examined the woman sitting across from them as she spoke. Other than her hazel eyes, Emma bore no resemblance to the small photograph of Emmett Adamo had shown her. This woman was stunning, with her lovely oval face and her soft dark hair.

"I know what you're thinking. How could we have been twins? Obviously we were not identical. Emmett was born a genius."

"From what Emmett said about you, I think you shared his intelligence," Adamo said.

"Perhaps, although we were very different, even as children. He loved the languages of mathematics and science, while my interests centered more on literature and music. He was very good to me. As soon as he was financially able, he established a lifetime trust for me. I'll never want for anything.

"And he found this place. I could never have afforded it on the small income I make from writing. I love it here. It offers everything I need and still allows me as much independence as I want."

"You're a writer?" Eve was intrigued.

"I have a regular column in the Watertown Express, and I have three novels in print, but I would be hard pressed to live on the income from my writing. Fortunately I don't have to."

"I never had a chance to tell you how sorry I was about Emmett's death. It must have been a great shock to you," Adamo said.

"Yes and no. I was horrified, and deeply saddened, but I wasn't really surprised. He was so conflicted by his situation."

"His situation?" Adamo probed.

"The terrible mess he'd gotten himself into. I wrote to you about it. I was surprised when you didn't answer.

Why didn't you use the information I sent you when you were on trial? I know, second-hand, it would probably have been considered hearsay and not admissible, but it might have helped."

"You had information that might have helped me?" Adamo's voice registered astonishment. "Where did you send it?"

"Why, to your home address, of course. I sent it by post rather than email. I considered it rather too confidential to trust to Internet."

Adamo blanched. "Monica." His hand shook as he placed his cup back on the saucer. "Monica must have gotten it."

Eve drew in her breath sharply. Could Adamo's wife really have been capable of destroying him so completely? Could she have hated him so much she deliberately withheld information that might have mitigated his involvement in the embezzlement?

Adamo's voice was tight with tension. "Emma, please tell us everything you know."

"I know only what Emmett told me. It probably wouldn't have stood up in court. And it's so long ago…"

Eve intervened. "Whatever you know, whatever you suspect, could help us. We can't undo the last six years, but our lives are being threatened."

Emma's eyes widened. "Your lives are at risk?"

Eve told her about the two attacks in Positano.

"But why, after all this time?"

"Obviously someone, for some reason, considers Adamo's continued existence a threat. So you see we really must find out what happened," Eve replied. "We must get to the bottom of this. Anything you remember…"

Emma gazed out the window and sighed. "It all began with a woman."

"A woman? Emmett?" Disbelief rang in Adamo's voice.

"He'd never been in love before, and he was obsessed with her."

Adamo shook his head. "Who was she?"

"He never told me her name. It seems she was married. And he was guilt-ridden over the affair." Emma absently stirred her tea, frowning as she tried to remember the details. "It had been going on for some time before he told me about it. I knew something was wrong, but I had no idea what it was."

"Did he say anything that might help identify her?" Eve pressed.

"No. He said her husband abused and terrorized her. They needed to get far away from him, perhaps even change their identities. It all seemed rather melodramatic to me, but when I tried to suggest less drastic alternatives, police involvement, a restraining order, Emmett said I didn't understand the situation."

They sat in silence for a moment. Emma continued, "It seems she promised to run away with him if he could come up with enough money for them to live on for the rest of their lives in some foreign port. She mentioned the Maldives."

She looked down. "I'm afraid I laughed at the idea. It was so obvious to me she was using him for her own purposes. I said as much to him. He became very angry with me."

"So that's why he embezzled the money." Adamo's eyes narrowed. "He had the money and the woman. If he was planning to run away with her, why didn't he? Why did he commit suicide?"

"The last time I heard from him, he called me to say it had all been for nothing. He was hysterical. He told me she'd lied to him. The money was irretrievably gone, and he'd discovered she was involved with another man. He said he'd been a fool. He sounded...crazed, half out of his mind. I told him he should go to the police. Tell them everything." Emma's voice broke. "But he chose another way. I couldn't believe it when he left you to answer for his crime. How could he have done such a thing to a man he called friend?"

Chapter Ten

The next morning, after breakfast, they reported to Bette and Ed on their visit with Emma Kenston.

"It was Monica," Eve insisted. "I think the woman must have been Monica."

Adamo ran his hand distractedly through his hair. "It can't have been my wife. I never abused or terrorized Monica. That's rubbish. The worst I ever did to her was ignore her."

"Adamo," Bette said, "be reasonable. Do you think a woman who's trying to talk a man into embezzling eighty million dollars would hesitate to lie about her marriage?"

"Look," Adamo said. "I'll give you I was wrong about Emmett. I never suspected he was involved with a woman...any woman. But Monica?"

Ed had been quiet through the exchange. Now he looked directly at Adamo. "Did you notice any change in your relationship with Emmett in the last year of his life?"

Adamo stopped in the act of lifting his coffee mug. He set it back on the table and stared at Ed for a moment. "We were both busy. We saw each other less often. Unless there was some function we had to attend, we transacted most of our business by email." He let out his breath slowly. "Yes. You're right. It was different the last year of his life. We never talked the way we used to. He was…distant."

Adamo turned the possibility over in his mind.

Eve placed her hand on his arm. "What about the detective you hired?"

"Detective?" Ed looked up sharply.

"Our marriage was falling apart. I suspected Monica of having an affair. The detective I hired…" Adamo smiled bitterly.

Eve completed his thought. "The detective you hired discovered she was visiting Emmett's apartment."

"I laughed at him when he reported that to me. I laughed. I didn't ask to see the file, the pictures, or the dates. I just laughed. How could I have been so blind?"

Eve covered his hand with hers. "Not blind, just trusting. He was your friend. She was your wife. What I can't understand is how he could have believed the garbage about your abusing her. Surely he knew you better."

Ed intervened, "Didn't you say you did a lot of martial arts in college?"

"Yes. I still do, but…"

"To someone as introverted as you say Emmett was, your physical prowess might have been enough to make Monica's claims believable. She may have faked a few bruises to make her story more plausible."

Bette had sat silent throughout the exchange. Now she addressed Adamo. "What about the other man? The man Emmett mentioned to his sister. If Monica was the woman, who was the other man?"

"I have no idea," Adamo said. "But then I didn't know much about Monica's life the last year of our marriage."

"It just gets more and more convoluted," Eve

sighed.

"And the money? Where'd it go? We shouldn't lose sight of the money." Ed thought for a moment. "If it remained in the country, the IRS would have found the trail. I'm pretty certain it's stashed in off-shore accounts, where it's untouchable. So who had the expertise to get it out of the country?"

"Emmett never went anywhere, and Monica had never been out of the United States in her entire life." Adamo shook his head. "I can't see either of them knowing how to transfer that much money out of the country."

"There must have been one or more accomplices." Ed took a sip of his now cold coffee. "And why did Emmett commit suicide…that is, if it was suicide."

"What do you mean *if it was suicide*?" Adamo whispered, shock in every syllable.

Ed looked at Adamo and answered calmly. "Emmett Kenston was at the end of his usefulness to whoever was behind this operation. And he may have been threatening to tell all."

"Are you suggesting he may have been murdered?" The enormity of what Ed was implying hit Adamo with the force of a blow.

"It's a possibility. It's an interesting puzzle. And among the more curious pieces of it is the disappearance of your ex-wife. I'd like to know where she is now and what she's living on." Ed paused for a few moments. "What about the detective you hired? Do you think there's any possibility he might still have the file?"

"We can find out with a phone call." Adamo pulled out his phone and looked up the O'Brien Agency in

New York.

Ten minutes later they knew Michael O'Brien kept his records for seven years in case Internal Revenue ever became interested in him. He was just about to destroy the de Leone file along with a number of others from the same period.

"Looks like we'll have to make a trip to New York," Adamo said. "We may as well pay a call on the New York Conti family headquarters while we're at it."

Ed looked up sharply. "Marco Conti? Conti Enterprises in New York?"

"One and the same," Adamo answered. "I've been assured he will see me."

"Why are you going to see him? What's his connection to all this?" Ed asked.

Adamo recounted his experience with Alfonso Conti in Naples.

Ed shook his head in disbelief. "That's an odd coincidence. I tracked down the yacht I photographed in Capri. It belongs to Marco Conti. I couldn't at the time see any possible connection. You seemed uncertain the photograph was actually your ex-wife, so I didn't pursue it."

"Conti? Should I know that name?" Bette looked puzzled.

"Marco Conti is a prominent businessman, long suspected of being the head of one of New York's most powerful crime families. Drugs, prostitution, money laundering…" Ed shook his head. "Nothing has ever been proven. He seems on the surface to be completely legitimate. And he has powerful friends, senators, governors. There are some who say his influence reaches to the White House."

"Did you say money laundering?" Adamo stared at Ed. "Someone in the Conti organization might know how to get eighty million dollars out of the country and into an off-shore account."

"Indeed," Ed agreed. "Adamo, if the woman on the yacht was Monica, then there must be a connection with the Contis."

Adamo sat down abruptly. "You think my wife was involved with the Mafia?"

"I don't know. Maybe you can find some answers in New York."

Two days later Eve and Adamo checked into the hotel in Brooklyn where Adamo had worked for a year as night clerk. Knowing and liking him, the manager gave them the best room in the house. It was small but clean, and was well located for their purposes. Michael O'Brien's office was in Brooklyn.

It was a crisp fall day. Eve, who still had only the summer dresses and slacks she'd taken with her on the *Wind Surf*, realized she'd need some warmer clothes.

"Not a problem," Adamo said. "We're in the land of Macy's and the Garment District. You can go shopping while I see Michael O'Brien."

"Not on your life. I'm going to the detective's with you. But maybe afterwards?"

Two hours later they were seated in O'Brien's office on the fourth floor of a high rise building on Irvington Street.

The detective looked down at some papers on his desk and then up at Adamo. "I pulled out your file to refresh my memory. Yours was a strange case. I got results for you, but you wouldn't even look at them. You laughed at what I found. I wondered whether you'd ever had second thoughts. But then I seem to recall shortly after, you had more to worry about than an unfaithful wife."

"You're right. I was embroiled in an embezzlement trial. I didn't have much time to think about what you'd uncovered. The thought of my wife and my business partner having an affair was ludicrous. Monica would never have been interested in a man whose chief quality was his intelligence, and Emmett was not only uninterested in women, he actively disliked Monica."

O'Brien pushed his chair back and studied Adamo. "So why are you interested now? I seem to recall the man in question committed suicide."

"It's complicated. The short version is I didn't embezzle the money. That means someone else did. And now I'm free, and that particular someone sees my continued existence as a threat. There've been two attempts on my life. The second one endangered Eve."

Adamo took Eve's hand. "It has to stop. And to make it stop, I'm afraid I have to find out what happened six years ago. Emmett is the only one who had access to the money. Somehow, his possible involvement with Monica makes more sense in that light."

The detective slid an envelope across to Adamo. "I pulled out the files after your call."

There were photographs. Emmett and Monica together. Embracing in a doorway.

"No bedroom shots. Couldn't manage those. They didn't go to hotels. But if you look at the dates and hours..." The detective shoved the written report across the desk.

Adamo read them carefully. Over a period of the

three weeks O'Brien had her under surveillance, Monica had been in Emmett's apartment daily, usually for two or three hours.

"How could I have been so blind?"

The detective hesitated. "One other thing. Your wife was also seeing another man. Tall, dark. Well dressed. They were very cagey. I couldn't get a clear shot of them, but I had the impression they knew each other well. With the evidence against her and your partner it didn't seem important at the time."

****

Adamo strode down the street, Eve hurrying after him.

"Slow down. I can't keep up with you!"

"Sorry." He slowed his pace. "Let's get a coffee. I'm still trying to absorb what I've just seen and heard."

They ducked into the next Starbucks. Once seated in low leather chairs with steaming espressos in front of them, Adamo confessed, "I just can't get my head around Monica and Emmett."

"Adamo, there are classic stories about temptresses and men who couldn't initially be tempted. Think of Salome and John the Baptist, of Samson and Delilah. For Emmett to respond to sexual overtures from Monica is not surprising. He was, from what you say, a very repressed man. When a man like Emmett falls, he falls hard. The real question isn't about Emmett. It's about Monica. Why? Why would she have taken the trouble to seduce Emmett? What did she have to gain?"

Adamo gave a short bitter laugh. "Eighty million dollars. But how? She had no resources for hiding that much money."

"We don't know that. Perhaps there was someone

else in her life, someone who did have those resources."

"The other man O'Brien saw her with? A pity he didn't get a picture of that man. Somehow we have to find him. I'm convinced he holds the answers."

"When we find Monica, perhaps she'll lead us to him."

"That's *if* we find Monica. She seems to have done a pretty effective job of disappearing."

Chapter Eleven

Back in their room Adamo placed a call to Marco Conti's New York offices. He had to work his way through several layers of secretaries and assistants, using the name of Alfonso Conti as a reference, but finally he was given an appointment for the next afternoon at two.

In the afternoon Adamo took Eve shopping. "We need a break and you need clothes. What better place than New York for that?"

Back in their hotel room six hours later, with department store bags in a heap on the bed. Eve plopped down in a chair, slipped her shoes off and wiggled her toes. "I think I have enough new clothes to last me for five years!"

"It will be a good thing. We've pretty well exhausted our last month's profits." Adamo took off his jacket and loosened his tie. "All in a good cause."

"Why won't you let me spend any of my own money, Adamo? Don't you realize how ridiculously old-fashioned you're being?"

"The money we spent is not mine, Eve, it's ours. You worked as hard for it as I did. Besides, it gives me pleasure to buy things for you, with you. Now get dressed. We're going someplace nice for dinner."

From her supply of new clothes, Eve slipped on a dress in a soft shade of blue. Sitting at what passed for dressing table in their hotel room, she studied her image in the mirror. She'd been too busy in the last couple of months to notice what she looked like. She looked younger. The lines of worry she had thought permanent were gone. Her face had the soft glow of a woman who was loved.

Picking up her small perfume atomizer, Eve lightly sprayed her neck and wrists.

"I love the way you smell," Adamo said, coming up behind her and nuzzling her neck. "What is it?"

"It's just a little lemon blossom scent I picked up in Positano. It was inexpensive, but I like it."

Adamo grimaced. "Monica paid a fortune for her perfume. She had it custom blended by somebody called Henri of Park Avenue."

Eve turned to him. "Custom blended? You mean it was one-of-a-kind, created just for her?"

"I think so. I only remember it because the bill was so exorbitant. And I didn't even like the smell. It was too heavy."

"But Adamo, if she had it custom made, just for her, she may be still using it. What was the name? Henri? They may have a current address."

They stared at each other. "It might be worth a try," Adamo said. "I could check it out tomorrow morning. My appointment with Marco Conti isn't until two."

"If they have an address for her, I think I might have more luck getting it than you would."

"Why is that?"

"Think about it Adamo. An ex-husband? One who doesn't even know her present whereabouts?"

"When you put it like that. But why should they

trust you? You're a complete stranger."

"They have no way of knowing I'm not a friend." Eve thought for a moment. "What was her maiden name, Adamo?"

"Farrell. Monica Elaine Farrell. Why?"

"Just in case. And she grew up in…?"

"Connecticut. Storrs, Connecticut."

"And her birthday?"

Adamo hesitated. "I think it was…It was October. The thirty-first of October. I remember because of Halloween. She hated having a birthday on Halloween. Good Lord. She'll be forty. That won't sit well." He chuckled.

"I'll need money. You said her perfume was expensive."

"You'd better use a credit card. A place like that would be suspicious of cash."

"Good idea. I'll use my Eve Anderson credit cards instead of the *albergo* one. I even have a platinum one. It should be good enough."

The next morning Eve dressed with care. She had to give the illusion of wealth. She examined the simple navy wool sheath she'd chosen. Jewelry was out of the question. She didn't have any. But a silk scarf and the new cashmere coat she'd found yesterday on sale at Sax would lend a touch of class. And she had her good Florentine leather bag. Those with the gloves and shoes she'd bought in Italy would have to do. Most of it would be attitude. She could manage attitude.

They located the shop with little difficulty. It was on the second floor, over a jeweler's. The discreet brass sign said simply *Henri's*.

"I need to do this alone," Eve said.

"I'll be waiting for you right here."

Eve took the lift to the second floor. The shop, if shop it could be called, looked more like the office of an up-scale medical specialist. She took in the comfortable looking deep leather chairs and the low table with fashion magazines scattered on it. Behind the desk was a shelf with tastefully displayed perfume bottles. The deep velvet curtains to one side presumably led to the laboratory.

An over-coiffed blonde, dressed in unrelieved black and wearing designer glasses embedded with rhinestones, manned the semi-circular mahogany desk.

"May I help you?" The blonde was sizing her up, estimating the cost of her clothes. Eve was glad she'd worn the cashmere coat.

"I certainly hope so." Eve offered her most disarming smile. "It's just so embarrassing. You see we grew up together, and I've never forgotten her birthday before, and now I'm not sure where to send it. She's not at her place in Connecticut, and I'm not sure whether she's at her Florida address or..." Eve left the question dangling and allowed her hands to flutter helplessly.

"I'm sorry. I don't understand." The blonde's voice turned haughty. "We're a *parfumerie*. Did you wish to have something custom blended?"

"No. That is, she already has something custom blended. I just want to send her some for her birthday. It's on October thirty-first."

Understanding dawned. "You want to send one of our clients a birthday present?"

"Yes. That's it." Eve rewarded the woman with glowing smile, as if she'd just solved an earth-shattering problem.

"I'm sure I can help you. The client's name?"

"Monica de Leone."

The woman consulted her computer. When she looked up, her demeanor was frosty. "I'm sorry. We have no one of that name in our files."

"Oh, how silly of me. I forgot she took back her maiden name. It's Farrell. Monica Elaine Farrell, formerly of Storrs, Connecticut. We grew up there."

The woman entered the name in her computer. Then she looked up. "The address I have isn't in Connecticut."

"Of course it isn't. I know that. If it had been I'd just have given her birthday present to her. I wouldn't have to send it to her." Eve hope she wasn't laying it on too thick. "I just don't know whether she's at her house in Florida or…"

The woman frowned at the screen. "The address on her last order was in Barbados, Coral Drive, St. James, Barbados."

"Of course. I should have guessed she'd be there at this time of the year. Now what should I send?"

"We have a lovely presentation bottle. Two ounces. Crystal with a Murano stopper. At six hundred thirty-five dollars." She turned to a shelf behind her desk and placed a small bottle with a blue glass stopper on the counter.

"It's lovely. I'm sure Monica will be delighted with it."

"Very well, madam. An excellent choice. That will be a total of twelve hundred forty-five dollars and sixty-two cents, for the presentation bottle and the custom blended perfume, plus tax." The woman looked expectantly at Eve.

Eve blanched. "Of course." Trying to hide her shock at the price, she pulled out her credit card and proffered it to the woman. She held her breath while it was processed. She hadn't used it in three months and twelve hundred would push her perilously close to her limit. She hoped there wouldn't be any problem.

The woman looked up and gave Eve a practiced, very artificial smile, as she handed her card back. "May we take care of mailing it for you?"

"No, thank you. But perhaps you could gift wrap it?"

"Of course, madam. It will take a little time to blend the perfume. May I offer you a cup of tea or coffee while you wait?"

"No, thank you. I'll just look though *Vanity Fair* while I wait. I haven't seen the October issue yet."

"Very well. I'll be right back." The woman disappeared through the curtained doorway.

Eve grasped the opportunity to walk around the desk and look at the computer screen. Good. She hadn't gone out of the file. There it was. Monica Farrell, 32 Coral Drive, St. James, Barbados. And a phone number. Followed by a series of numbers and letters, presumably the formula for her perfume. Hastily Eve jotted down the address and telephone number.

When the sales woman reappeared fifteen minutes later, Eve was sitting in one of the deep leather chairs, leafing through a fashion magazine.

"Thank you for shopping with us," the woman gushed. "I'm sure your friend will be delighted with her gift."

Eve accepted the small black bag emblazoned in gold with the name *Henri's* and headed for the elevator.

Adamo grabbed her arm the minute she emerged from the doorway. "What took you so long? I was afraid they were going to arrest me for loitering." He laughed. He hurried her down the street and around the first corner. "Were you able to get an address?"

"An address and a phone number. But it cost me twelve hundred dollars. This perfume better be good!"

"Twelve hundred dollars for a bottle of perfume? Good God!" He pulled her into a coffee shop and got them both an espresso. Adamo added two sugars to his and took a sip. "So where is she?"

"She's living in Barbados. In St. James Parish, on Coral Drive." Eve absently sipped her coffee. "It's ironic, isn't it? We were there, both of us, just a few months ago. I wonder if she was there then."

"Possibly. I'm not sure what we should do next. But I'll see if her name and address mean anything to Marco Conti when I see him this afternoon."

Chapter Twelve

At five minutes before the appointed hour, Adamo stood in front of the address he'd been given. The Conti Building rose probably thirty-five stories, a concrete monument to the power and wealth of the Conti family in New York. Adamo entered the vast lobby. It was like any large corporation lobby, with a bank of six elevators and a man sitting behind a desk to direct people to the right floors, to ensure no one got in without proper credentials.

He approached the uniformed man. "Adamo de Leone. I have an appointment with Mr. Conti at two o'clock."

The man consulted a computer screen. "I'll need to see some identification."

Adamo pulled out his driver's licence and passport. The man studied both and looked long at Adamo. Then he handed them back. "You are expected. Take elevator number one."

As Adamo approached the elevator the doors slid open. Although there were several people, probably secretaries and administrative assistants, milling about waiting for elevators, none entered the elevator with him. As the doors closed Adamo realized why. Only one floor was listed. Number thirty-four. The elevator rose swiftly and silently. The doors opened to a large reception room carpeted in burgundy, with a scattering of comfortable chairs and coffee tables. A motherly looking middle-aged woman, dressed in a gray business suit and an incongruous flowered blouse, sat behind a large desk. Her gray hair was pulled back in an old-fashioned bun.

She looked over the top of her bifocal glasses and said, "Good afternoon, Mr. de Leone. Mr. Conti is running a little late. May I offer you some tea or coffee while you wait?"

"No, thank you. I've just had lunch." Adamo had the fleeting notion she looked more like someone's grandmother than the private secretary to one of the most powerful men in America. He took a seat and picked up a copy of the *New York Times* from the nearest table.

It was perhaps twenty minutes later when a young man appeared. "Mr. Conti will see you now." He led Adamo down a long corridor and opened a door, standing back to allow Adamo to enter first. Then he followed and took his place standing with his back to the door.

The man behind the cluttered desk resembled his brother superficially, but where Don Alfonso was physically weak, an old man, Marco Conti radiated vitality. At fifty-something, he was in the prime of life, clearly still a very powerful man. He stood and extended his hand. "Mark Conti. I believe you know my brother."

Adamo shook the proffered hand, absorbing the Anglicisation of the man's first name. "Thank you for seeing me, Mr. Conti. Yes, Don Alfonso said you might be able to help me."

"I've questioned my associates closely. None of

them appear to know anything about the incidents in Italy, the attempts on your life. Not that there's any reason they should."

"And yet the instructions appear to have come from someone in your"—Adamo carefully sought the right word—"your organization."

"Mine is a large and complex conglomerate. We have a hand in many businesses, and it is possible someone here might bear you a grudge, but why, Mr. de Leone? You were found guilty, you served your jail time, and now you are living in Italy. What possible reason could anyone have for wanting to harm you at this late date?"

"It seems someone still perceives me as a threat. Why, I don't know."

"But isn't it clear what happened? You managed to embezzle some millions of dollars from investor's accounts and now someone wants their money back. Perhaps one or more of those investors has connections with criminal elements. I really can't see what I can do to help you. I'm a simple business man."

Adamo took a deep breath. "I wasn't the embezzler. That appears to have been my partner."

"Ah, yes, one Emmett Kenston. He committed suicide, I believe? A convenient person to blame. But you were the one convicted."

Adamo stood, blood suffusing his face. "I'm sorry to have taken your time, Mr. Conti. You are correct. You can't help me. Not if you believe I was guilty."

Mark Conti gestured impatiently with his hand. "Sit down, Adamo. You don't mind if I call you by your first name? I just wondered how you'd react if I assumed your guilt. As a matter of fact, my brother is quite convinced of your innocence, and he has an astute mind. So let's begin again. You are innocent of the crime for which you were sent to jail. It isn't the first time something like that has happened. What do you want to do about it at this late date? And how do you think I can I help?"

Adamo took a deep breath. "It's the money. What happened to it?"

"I think we can safely assume it's stashed in off-shore accounts somewhere."

"But how did it get there? Emmett had no knowledge of such things. And neither did Monica."

"Monica?"

"My ex-wife."

"Perhaps we should begin at the beginning. What do you know, what do you suspect, and what can I do to aid in your investigation?"

For twenty minutes Adamo talked to Mark Conti. He told him everything they had discovered, everything they had inferred from their investigation, right up to and including their morning's adventure at the perfume shop.

"There's just one other thing," Adamo said. "I may have seen my wife on Capri just a couple of months ago."

"Yes?"

"She was in a launch returning to a yacht, the *Inside Strait II*. I believe that yacht belongs to the Conti family?"

Mark Conte's head jerked up. "Is that so? I keep my yacht in Portofino. It is used from time to time by colleagues and members of my family and my firm. If the woman you saw was your wife, it will be interesting to see who she was with." The older man sat quietly for a few moments. He seemed to stare into space. Then he spoke.

"Barbados is one of the top off-shore money havens in the world. Doesn't it seem just a little too much of a coincidence that your wife is living there?"

"I don't know anything about off-shore tax havens. But I know you can't take eighty million dollars out of the country in a suitcase. Someone with knowledge about off-shore trusts has to have first set up accounts and then arranged for electronic transfer of the funds. I'm quite sure neither Monica nor Emmett had the knowledge necessary for setting up trust accounts on Barbados or anyplace else. The question is, who was that someone?"

There was silence in the office for several minutes. Mark Conti stared into space, seemingly deep in thought. Adamo was about to thank him and leave when the older man spoke again. "Why don't you ask your former wife?"

"Ask her?"

"Yes. Just take out your phone and call her. You said you have her number."

Adamo laughed out loud at the idea. "Good lord, that's a direct approach." He brushed his hand absently though his silver curls. "I don't know. I wouldn't know where to begin a telephone conversation with her. There are so many questions." He stood and paced.

"You'll never know the truth of the matter if you don't ask her, Adamo. Maybe she won't have the answers. Or maybe she'll lie. But at least you'll have had the satisfaction of asking the question."

Adamo stopped pacing and looked directly at the

older man. "You really think I should?"

"Yes, I do. And I think you should think about what you want to say. Be prepared."

Adamo was silent for a few minutes. Then he said, "May as well get it over with." He moved over to the window, his back to Mark Conti. He couldn't do this under the other man's scrutiny.

The phone was answered on the second ring. "Farrell residence." The voice was a woman's, strongly Barbadian in accent.

"May I speak with Miss Farrell please? Just tell her it's an old acquaintance."

He waited, his anxiety increasing by the moment. When he heard her low, well-modulated voice, "This is Monica Farrell," everything he'd planned to say seemed to vanish except, "Why?"

He didn't realize immediately he had voiced the thought.

"Who is this? What do you want?" Her voice was shrill.

"It's Adamo, Monica. I just want to know why—"

"How did you get this number?"

"I just want to know why you did it, Monica. Did you hate me so much?"

"Hate you?" She hissed the words. "You weren't around enough for me to hate."

"I know I share the blame for the deterioration of our marriage, but really, Monica, Emmett? You got poor Emmett into your bed. You seduced him, you probably fucked his brains out until he'd do anything you told him to do."

"You must be joking!"

"I have a detective's report of the dates and hours.

At the time I was too blind to understand, but in hindsight...You got him to embezzle the funds, didn't you?"

"You'll never prove it."

"How did you get the money out of the country, Monica? You had to have help."

"I don't know what you're talking about."

"Did you enjoy Capri? The Conti Family owns the yacht you were on. I've spoken to Mark Conti. They knew you only as a one more convenient party girl along on the trip. They're not sure who invited you. Exactly who were you sleeping with on that little jaunt? I expect Mr. Conti would be interested to know."

"I'm living outside U.S. jurisdiction, and this conversation's over."

There was the dead space of a disconnected call.

"That went well." Adamo turned back to Mark Conti with a wry smile.

"Actually, I think it did just what it needed to do. It rattled her cage. I think she'll be nervous about what your next step will be. And that's a good thing."

"She sounded terrified when she realized it was me on the phone. She has no reason to fear me unless she was really implicated in the disappearance of the money. She didn't even try to claim her innocence. So in a way, we know now. I'm not sure it's better than not knowing. I hate to think she conspired in the theft. That she may have driven poor Emmett to suicide. But it's now her problem, not mine. So what do you suggest I do next?"

"We must somehow to lure your ex-wife back to the States. We need to know the identity of the man with whom she was involved. Perhaps we can persuade her to reveal who he is. It only makes sense he was the one with the financial connections, the one who directed the transactions. And I'm beginning to suspect he could be a member of my organization. That possibility does not please me. I'll do some further investigation among my own staff and get back to you. Please don't take any further action without conferring with me."

Adamo stood to leave. "Of course, *Padrino*. Thank you."

Mark Conti slammed his hand down on his desk so hard the pile of papers beside his computer scattered and fell to the floor. "Don't call me that!" His voice was harsh, his eyes cold and flinty. "I'm not your Godfather or anyone else's."

Adamo flinched at the older man's response to a common Mafia courtesy.

"Please," Mark Conti continued in a calmer voice. "I am not Mafia, and *Padrino* is not a word we use in my corporation. I run a legitimate business. Mining operations, real estate, hotels, casinos…"

Adamo responded, skepticism clear in his voice, "Prostitution, drugs, money laundering…"

Mark Conti sighed. "Ah well, we can't always control what goes on in our individual establishments, but I've worked all my adult life to make and keep the Conti Corporation legitimate. Sit down, Adamo. If we're to work together on this you must understand one thing. I left all that behind me thirty years ago when I first came to the States. My older brother, yes. He's Capo of a Camorra family. I left Italy because I wanted to get away from everything that entails. And I left with my brother's consent, approval, and support."

Adamo hesitated briefly and then resumed his seat. "Sorry, but when your brother said you'd help me, I assumed—"

"Unfortunately you're not alone in that assumption. I've been fighting the Mafia label since the day I opened my first hotel. It's true my brother backed my first hotel venture to get me going, but since then, I have accomplished everything without resorting to organized crime or Mafia money. I now have controlling interests in shipping, in telecommunications, in mining, and in hotels and casinos. These business interests are legitimate. I know, because of my family background, I'm suspect; I know the IRS looks at all my accounts more carefully than at some others. My corporation has been the target of their investigations more than once. But I will brook no connections with organized crime knowingly."

"I'm sorry. I didn't know."

Mark Conti settled back in his chair and took a deep breath. "No, I suppose not. How could you? My brother sent you to me. It was an obvious assumption."

"What is your connection with the Naples family, then? Clearly Don Alfonso believed you could help me."

"Alfonso was the eldest of us. I was the youngest. We were separated in age by twenty years. When I expressed an interest in emigrating to the U.S., he encouraged me. He helped me get started and he respected my wish to make my way on my own in the world of legitimate business. But a Camorra background is hard to shake off. It has made me suspect and has forced me to be doubly vigilant. If Alfonso believes in your innocence, so do I. And if there is a

159

Mafia connection with anyone in my employ, I need to know who that someone is. Particularly if he or she has been using my business to move money around illegally into off-shore accounts. You may rest assured I'll do my best to discover the truth."

****

Luc Manzel was about to step into the elevator that would take him to his eighteenth floor office when he caught a glimpse of Adamo emerging from Mark Conti's private elevator. Quickly he turned his back. What business could de Leone possibly have with Conti? A shiver of apprehension ran down his back. He was going to have to do something about that damned Italian. Why couldn't he just let matters rest?

Chapter Thirteen

When Adamo rejoined Eve in their hotel room, he recounted his conversation with Mark Conti, omitting nothing. He paced restlessly as he talked.

Eve listened without interruption or comment.

At the end of his tale, Adamo stopped and stared at Eve intently. "He isn't through investigating. But if the person who ordered these attacks is in his organization, it's not someone obvious."

"So Mr. Conti suggested we should try to lure Monica back to the States somehow? He says she needs to be on American soil where she will be subject to U.S. laws and where we could pressure her for a name?"

"That's about it. But I don't see how we can do it. What leverage do we have?" Adamo paced restlessly around their small room. "I'm afraid we're not very much better off than we were before."

"We should go back to Silver Springs and talk this over with Ed and Bette. Don't forget, you have a powerful ally in Mark Conti. He said he'll get back to you, and he will."

The next morning, sitting around the kitchen table in the house in Silver Springs, they brought Ed and Bette up to date on their adventures in New York.

"Mark Conti suggested we should try to get Monica to return to the States. He said we'd have a better chance of learning the truth if she were back on home turf. But considering the way she responded to my phone call, I'm not sure how we can make that happen. How are we to induce Monica to leave her safe haven?" Adamo shook his head. "It's pretty clear we can't touch her there."

Ed stood and refilled their coffee cups. "It's true you can't touch her over the money. But perhaps we can find some other way to lure her back to the States."

"I don't see how." Adamo put his cup down. "If we had anything concrete on her…"

Bette gave a crooked smile. "Why don't you just lie?"

"Lie?" Adamo turned his full attention on Bette.

"Lie. Tell her you have new evidence about Emmett's suicide. Evidence that implicates her. And you're willing to give it to her, rather than turning it over to the police, for a large cash settlement. Maybe a letter you've just discovered, I don't know. Just make up something."

Adamo grinned but shook his head. "It wouldn't work. She'd be suspicious of anything from me, especially after my call."

"Emma," Eve interrupted. "If Emma were to contact her and read her an excerpt from Emmett's 'last letter' to her…" Eve laughed aloud. "I'll bet Emma would love to help."

"But Emmett didn't leave any letters. He didn't leave any written trail."

"Monica doesn't know that. It's worth another trip to Watertown, don't you agree?" Eve looked around the table.

"Maybe," Adamo said. "But we can't do this

without letting Mark Conti know what we're planning. I promised not to take any action without consulting him."

"Call him," Eve replied. "You have his number. See what he says."

This time Adamo was put through to Mark Conti's personal line immediately. He explained what they were contemplating.

The others could hear Mark Conti's laugh booming over the phone in response to their plan. "Delightfully devious," he said. "I think I'd like to join you on this little excursion. I'd like to meet your Eve and this sister of your partner's. Emma you said? She lives in upstate New York? I believe there's an airport at Watertown. We'll take my plane. I'll pick you up at Dulles tomorrow morning at eight."

They called Emma to let her know they were coming, and, the next morning, Adamo and Eve found themselves once again on the way to Watertown, this time in the comfortable cabin of a private jet, in the company of Mark Conti and the silent man who was always by his side. Mark Conti introduced him briefly. "My assistant, James Conroy."

With Eve he took more time. He took her hand and held it, studying her face. "I can see why Adamo is in love with you. You are charming, my dear."

Eve blushed. Adamo had never once used the word "love" to her, not even in their most intimate moments.

"She's lovely," he said to Adamo as if Eve were not present. "I suggest you not waste any time in pinning her down legally. You don't want one like this to slip through your fingers."

Eve turned to Adamo to see how he would respond

to this direct challenge.

Adamo answered with stony silence.

****

A limousine with a uniformed driver awaited them at the Watertown airport.

"You know it's a really harebrained scheme, don't you? Don't be surprised if Emma laughs us right out the door," Adamo said as they headed out of Watertown, toward the mountains and the Adirondack Hills complex.

"I think she'll love it," Eve replied. "And I know she'll want to have a part in uncovering the truth about her brother's death."

"You said she's wheelchair-bound?" Mark Conti asked.

"Since she was a child. But she leads an active life. She's amazingly independent, really," Eve answered.

In the parking lot of the Adirondack Hills complex, Mark Conti instructed the driver to wait for them. The four of them checked in at the main house and then walked to Emma's cottage. When Emma opened the door to greet them, Adamo and Eve entered, followed by Mark Conti. James Conroy nodded a greeting but remained outside, back to the door.

"So you're Miss Kenston," Mark Conti said, taking both her hands in his. "I've been looking forward to meeting you."

"And I, you, Mr. Conti."

Their eyes held each other's for a long moment, as if they were the only people in the room.

"Please call me Mark."

"And I'm Emma. I've heard quite a bit about you from Adamo. I'm very glad you've decided to help us.

It has seemed unresolved for so long. My brother's death..." Tears glistened in her eyes.

"We will get to the truth of the matter, I assure you, Emma. We may never be able to make the truth known publically, but we will have the truth. That I promise you."

Emma wiped her eyes. "I believe you. And I promise I'll be satisfied if I know what really happened. Not knowing is a terrible thing."

She looked at Adamo and Eve as if just realizing they were in the room. "It's good to see you both again. Please"—she gestured gracefully to the chairs around the cherry table—"sit down." Turning back to Mark she said, "Would you like to come with me into my kitchen, Mark? You can help me take the tea things to the table."

Adamo observed Emma and Mark disappear into the kitchen with some amusement. "He has never yet suggested I call him Mark," he murmured to Eve.

"You're the wrong gender, and you haven't got those stunning hazel eyes and beautiful face and glorious dark hair." Eve laughed softly.

A few minutes later the four of them were seated around the cherry table in the front room of the little brick cottage, with cups of Earl Gray, small cucumber sandwiches, and slices of cake on their plates.

Abruptly Mark Conti asked the question that had been in the back of Eve's mind since first meeting Emma. "What happened to leave you like this, in a wheelchair?"

"Polio," she answered without hesitation. "I contracted polio when I was eight years old. I lived, but I'll never have full use of my legs."

Eve looked at her in shock. "I thought polio was eradicated by the Salk vaccine."

"No. It was brought under control, but never eradicated. My father was on a diplomatic mission in India, and we, my mother and Emmett and I, that is, went with him. India is one of the nations that resists, even today, requiring the Salk vaccine."

"That's appalling," Mark interjected.

Emma continued. "In 1988, after I contracted the disease, world leaders set the year 2000 as the date for completely eradicating polio world-wide. They later changed the date to 2005, then to 2012, and now the date they project is 2020. I seriously doubt it will ever be completely eradicated. It's not just India. There are several other countries where they still resist, or even disallow the vaccine. And an infected traveler from any of those countries can carry the disease to anywhere in the world."

"You've made quite a study of this," Mark said.

"I'm an active member of the Polio Survivors Association. We do what we can to keep the public informed. As long as one country doesn't accept its role in eradicating polio, the disease will flourish. The number of polio victims is actually on the rise today."

"I had no idea," Eve said.

Emma took a deep breath. "But that's not what you're here to talk about. How can I help you?"

Adamo told Emma everything they had discovered. "It's not much, but we thought you'd like to be brought up-to-date."

"It's quite a lot, actually. You now know where your ex-wife is. She may lead us to the person behind all this. But there must be more to it than that." Emma stirred her tea absently. "You're here for a reason. You have a plan, haven't you? Some way of getting to the truth of the matter?"

Adamo and Eve looked at each other, grinning.

"You promise you won't laugh?" Eve said.

"I'm not sure I can promise that."

"We decided since there's no evidence, we might just create some," Eve said. "Perhaps a letter from Emmett to you."

Emma's eyebrows rose. "The missing suicide note. What a clever idea. Emmett left no paper trail. He never committed anything to paper. But Monica wouldn't know that, would she? Of course it wouldn't hold up in court—"

"But it doesn't have to," Mark interjected. "That's the beauty of the plan. It just needs to be convincing enough to get Monica briefly back to the States, to pay a blackmailer and retrieve the damaging 'evidence.' Once we have her in our hands, I believe we can get the truth out of her, one way or another."

"And you propose I should be the blackmailer, the one to whom the letter was addressed." Emma's mouth curved upwards at the corners.

Adamo said. "Monica wouldn't trust anything coming from me. Of course we don't expect you actually to meet with Monica. Eve can play your part. I take it Monica's never met you?"

"No. I'm not sure Emmett even told her much about me. I don't think theirs was that kind of relationship." She bristled. "But if you think I'm going to let anyone 'play my part' you are very much mistaken. It will give me the greatest pleasure to meet the woman who destroyed my brother."

"Somehow, I was certain that would be your response," Mark said. "Now I've met you, I'm sure your presence on the scene will be an asset."

"Now where did I put my box of writing paper? Oh yes, in the desk drawer, of course." Emma wheeled across the room and returned to the table with a box of note paper and a pen.

"Use plain computer paper for the note." Mark walked over to her desk and took a piece from her printer. "From what I've heard of your brother, I don't think he'd be likely to use that very pretty floral paper you have in your hand.

Emma laughed. "No, of course not."

Emma sat at the table, her pen poised. "My handwriting is rather illegible, but then so was Emmett's. I don't suppose it will be put to any handwriting tests in any case. It just has to sound convincing when we contact Monica. And perhaps look old enough when we meet her. What should I say?"

Adamo's mind raced through possibilities. "I think we should keep it short and sweet. If we get too wordy, Monica will smell a rat."

Dear Emma, Emmett's sister wrote. She held the pen poised above the paper. "How should I phrase it? It's his last communication with me. It's his suicide letter."

"No." Mark shook his head. "Why would Monica care about a simple suicide note? It would simply confirm what the police have already decided. It has to say more. The letter must suggest Emmett was going to the police. He was going to confess to his part in the embezzlement. That should shake the ex-Mrs. de Leone up."

Adamo agreed. "It's chancy, but what have we got to lose?"

Emma tried again.

My dearest sister,

By the time you receive this I will be gone. I have made a dreadful shambles of everything. I've been involved for the last year with my best friend's wife, Monica de Leone. I think I must have been somewhat out of my mind. I can't explain my despicable actions any other way. Because of her I embezzled a large sum of money from the firm. And now I've discovered she was playing me for a fool. She and her lover, the man who arranged the off-shore trust accounts for her, have simply used me. It's as if I've just awakened from a nightmare. I now see everything for what it really was.

Eve leaned over to see what Emma had written. "That's great. If what we've surmised is accurate, this letter should terrify her. But now you need to add something about Emmett planning to confess to his involvement in the embezzlement to the police."

Emma nodded and picked up her pen once more.

I will write a letter confessing everything to the police, and then end it all. I have nothing left to live for. I am so sorry, my dear.

> *All my love,*
> *Emmett*

Eve shook her head. "You have a real talent for fiction, Emma. No wonder you choose to write novels."

"Novels?" Mark looked at Emma in open admiration. "I'd like to read them."

Emma gazed up into his face. "I'll happily give you copies before you leave. But I must warn you they haven't had great literary success."

Adamo looked over Emma's shoulder and read again what she had written. Something about it bothered him. "Why is the letter only now coming to light?"

"Good point." Emma inserted a sentence.

I have a feeling I am being watched whenever I leave the building, so I will hand this letter to the doorman to mail.

"There. That does it." Emma gave a satisfied sigh. "You know it feels almost as if Emmett did write it. I think it may be what he would have written if he'd had the chance. All we need now is an old enough envelope addressed to me. Good thing I never throw correspondence away."

"But why would you be threatening Monica after all this time?" Adamo absently put his tea cup down. "Why would you not have done so at the time? Or simply have gone to the police with it seven years ago?"

Eve and Emma looked at each other. Emma grinned. "He was so sorry. The doorman, that is. He put Emmett's letter in a drawer and forgot all about it. When he retired this year, he cleaned out all his belongings and came across this letter. He knew about Emmett and me and thought I would want to have it, even after all this time. He was very apologetic in the note he enclosed."

Adamo laughed. "A little weak, but possible. Perhaps the very existence of such a letter will be so frightening Monica won't think to ask that question."

"So when will we call her?" Emma took a sip of her tea.

Adamo stood and went to the window. The leaves

on the maple trees lining the drive were turning scarlet. It was seven years since he had last seen maples in their fall splendor. Seven years, all because of Monica's greed, Monica's treachery. He turned back to his three confederates. "We can't approach her by telephone. She'll suspect it all comes back to me. And she'll just hang up. Perhaps I shouldn't have made that impulsive call."

Mark Conti disagreed. "The call was useful. Your ex-wife will be rattled as a result of it. Another threat will add to her unrest. But a phone call isn't the best way to handle this. She will have to see the physical evidence if she's to be convinced of the danger."

"How do you propose we do that?" Emma asked.

All four were silent. Then Eve suggested tentatively, "We could send her a photocopy of the letter by mail, and enclose a note saying it recently fell into your hands and the original is available for...I don't know, perhaps a hundred thousand dollars? And someone will contact her by telephone with a time and place for the meeting."

Adamo nodded slowly. "It might work. But I think Emma could ask for considerably more than a hundred thousand. If we're correct in our assumptions, Monica has millions at her disposal. Maybe Emma should demand half of what she stole, say forty million."

"No." Mark was emphatic. "No. You should ask for a low enough payment she'll think it a small price to pay for her safety. An amount she can carry into the country in a suitcase. Our objective, after all, is to get her on American soil."

"Agreed, then," Adamo said. "A hundred thousand dollars, to be personally delivered to Emma by Monica at a place and time yet to be revealed."

Mark Conti read the letter carefully once more. "You know, this is not bad for an improvised plan. Although has it not struck anyone we might be endangering Emma?"

Adamo's head jerked up. "Good Lord, no. No, I hadn't even considered that. You're right, of course."

"I'm not worried about my safety," Emma said.

"But I am," Adamo said. "How can I have been so thoughtless? Isn't it enough my life and Eve's had been threatened? Now we've involved you in the danger. I can't do that, Emma."

Emma bridled. "I know what you're thinking, Adamo. *Emma, who is tied to a wheelchair!* I won't have it. I won't have this plan that might lead us to the truth derailed because of some unlikely but theoretically possible danger to me."

There was silence in the room for a few moments. Then Mark commented, "Does the communication with your ex-wife have to suggest to her the blackmailer is Emma?"

"No." Adamo's eyebrows rose as he realized the implication of Mark's comment. "The original letter is supposed to have come to Emma, but we could add a covering note, perhaps typed, in which the writer says it only recently came into his hands and he is willing to sell it. The person who writes the blackmail note won't identify himself."

Mark agreed. "It's a reasonable precaution. Nevertheless, I believe I'll arrange some protection for you, Emma. If not for yours, for my own peace of mind."

"Thank you, Mark. I really don't think it will be

necessary, but if you wish to do so, I won't object."
Emma smiled sweetly up at Mark Conti.

Soon after, with both Emmett's suicide note and
the covering letter from the supposed blackmailer in
their hands, Adamo, Eve, and Mark Conti took their
leave. James Conroy, silent as always, accompanied
them.

On board the plane, Mark Conti picked up his cell
phone and gave a few cryptic instructions.

After the brief call he turned to Adamo. "We'll
have someone keeping round-the-clock watch over
Emma Kenston within the hour. Lovely woman, isn't
she?"

Then he opened the first of the three novels Emma
had given him on their departure.

Chapter Fourteen

It was done, for better or worse. A copy of Emmett's "suicide letter" and a covering letter from the supposed blackmailer were in the mail to Monica. Now there was nothing to do but wait. Wait for Monica to receive the letters. Wait to make the phone call setting up time and place for the meet. Wait for her to react. Wait for the next call from Mark Conti. The tension in the Richardson household was evident.

"I think we should get away for a few days," Eve suggested. "Give Bette and Ed some space. We've been underfoot for the best part of a month, during which time Bette's been coping with morning sickness and Ed's been working long hours."

"Where would you like to go?"

"Let's go to the Eastern Shore, where I grew up. I'd like to show you St. Michael's and Ocean City, and the house in Shoreport where I lived for so many years."

"Sounds good to me. I'll see if I can get a good price on a rental car. Do we need to make hotel reservations?"

"I'll book us into a B&B I know in St. Michael's for three days. We can make side trips from there. And at Ocean City it will be well out of season and we'll be able to find inexpensive hotel accommodation once we get there. Have you ever had steamed crabs?"

"Not that I recall."

"You haven't lived until you've had steamed crabs caught in the morning, hot from the steamer, covered with Old Bay seasoning and served on newspapers, outside at picnic tables."

That evening they checked into a restored brick colonial with fourteen guest rooms and extensive grounds, on the outskirts of St. Michael's. Their room was at the very top of the house, under the eaves, with a corner view over the Chesapeake Bay.

After watching from Adirondack chairs in the garden as the sun set over the bay, they dined in a restaurant on the harbor. Eve ordered for them. "After all, fair's fair. You always order for us in Italy. Now we're on my turf."

They feasted on she-crab soup, followed by shad roe with bacon, accompanied by shoe-peg corn. As they ended their meal with peach cobbler, Adamo commented, "If this is an example of Eastern Shore cooking, I'm happy to let you order for the rest of the week. I've never had anything like it, either in New York or in Italy."

Back in their room, Adamo nuzzled her neck. "Do you know how hard it's been these last weeks, staying at your sister's, trying not to let anyone hear us making love?"

"You never say anything when we're making love, anyway."

"Inside I'm shouting. I just swallow it. It adds to my pleasure to hold it all inside. But you're not so quiet. Your sounds drive me wild."

"Like this?" Eve gave a low laugh and then moaned.

"No. More like this." Adamo's hand slid down to plunge between her legs.

Eve couldn't repress her yelp.

Adamo's dark eyes went opaque. He pulled her close and buried his tongue in her mouth, invading, tasting. Then slowly he caressed her, kissing her wrist, the inside of her elbow, the hollow at the base of her throat, his hands busy touching, inviting, arousing.

Eve threaded her hands through his hair, then reached inside his shirt and twisted her fingers through the curls on his chest.

She stepped back and slipped her dress off, letting it drop in a puddle on the floor, standing before him clad in only her bikini. He tucked his thumb under the waist band and eased the scrap of lace down, while his mouth followed, leaving Eve gasping. Scooping her up, he placed her gently on their bed and stood simply staring at her for a moment. Then stripping off his clothes he joined her, covering her body with his. "*Mia bella Eve…*"

They were the last words he spoke as he led her, sensation by sensation, to the place where she was spiraling out of control, out of mind, out of body to a final aching cry and her slow descent back to earth, to the sheets, now rumpled and twisted beneath them. Her breathing was jagged, her body still somewhere on another plane, one where only pleasure existed.

When her heart stopped hammering and her breathing returned to some semblance of normal, Eve said, "I need a shower."

His eyes followed her as she slipped out of the bed and crossed the room, unaware of how seductively her buttocks swayed. Of how, even after what had just passed between them, he still wanted more. He could already feel the fresh stirrings of desire.

In the bathroom Eve took a deep, shuddering breath. How could he do this to her, again and again? Shouldn't their lovemaking begin to feel more routine, more comfortable? They'd been together for six months now, and still he was capable of shaking her to her very core. Would it always be like this? A small voice said *I hope so.*

She stepped into the shower and turned the water on full blast. Her body was still pulsing with the aftershocks of her orgasm. She leaned against the marble of the shower stall, the warm water cascading over her. Her hands touched her erect nipples, her still sensitive mons in wonder. Small ripples of pleasure almost painful in their intensity followed where she touched.

"Let me do that." He stepped in with her.

Sometime later she was conscious of him drying her gently and carrying her to back to the bed. "Insatiable," she said as she drifted off to sleep, her head on his shoulder, her leg thrown across his.

"Yes," he murmured into her hair. "Aren't we lucky to have found each other?"

The next morning, as the first light began to filter into their room, Eve shook Adamo awake. "I want to take a walk."

"Wake me when you come back."

"Get up, Adamo. This can't wait. You can crawl back into bed later if you want. Hurry. Just throw on some clothes and come with me."

As the sky began to take on the rosy hue that precedes sunrise, Eve led Adamo down a winding sandy path between high sea oats on one side and wild marsh grasses on the other, to a place she knew well. As they stepped out to a cove, she motioned to him to move quietly. Before them were what seemed to be thousands of birds—mallards, with their brilliant green neck bands; brown and white Canada geese; swans, both white and black; and smaller water birds of varieties Adamo couldn't begin to identify. Some floated on the quiet water, some fed in the shallows, still others were flying in or out. As Eve and Adamo stood, holding hands, a flock of geese took off, shaking the water from their wings and falling into their age old V-formation.

"It's a major resting point for them on the way south in their annual migration," Eve said. "This used to be one of my favorite outings every year. Dad would bring us up here, Bette and me, just to see this. I was so hoping we were at the right time of the fall and they'd still be here."

"Tell me about your dad."

"He was wonderful. My mom died when we were young, and Dad pretty much raised us on his own. He was a history professor at a small community college, and he loved his work. He was a highly literate man. Our friends grew up with Snow White and Cinderella. Bette and I grew up with *The Iliad* and *The Odyssey*. His idea of a bedtime story was *The Tempest.*"

Adamo laughed. "That explains a quite bit about you. I think I would have liked him."

"I think he'd have liked you."

"I'm not so sure. I may have two university degrees, but I'm not what you'd call a cultured man. When your father was reading Greek sagas and

Shakespeare to you, I was reading Batman comic books."

"Don't denigrate yourself, Adamo. You quote Donne and Shakespeare to me. I see the books you read. Chinese philosophers, Dante, books on art…"

"Ah, you've caught me out. It's just so I'll know what you're taking about when you're nattering on about Donatello and Caravaggio."

Eve laughed. "You're incorrigible."

They spent the afternoon wandering through the quaint shops lining St. Michael's main street, and then dined on large succulent oysters on the half shell, and steamed crabs, in a restaurant on the boat harbor.

The next morning, they headed for Ocean City. Once settled in their beach-front hotel, Eve took Adamo by the hand and led him down to the old boardwalk.

On one side, a wide beach of golden sand the width of a city block extended north and south as far as the eye could see. Foaming breakers, row upon row, marched and retreated, leaving dark wet sand in their path.

Eve sat down on a bench, took off her shoes, and rolled up her pants. "I want to walk on the beach."

Adamo noticed with a frown a man in a dark suit sitting on a near-by bench, ostensibly reading a newspaper. He didn't look like he was dressed for a day at the beach. Adamo shook off his unease. Surely no one would be following them on a beach holiday. He said nothing to Eve about his suspicions.

"Come on, Adamo. Just leave your shoes here. No one will take them."

Hand in hand, they trudged through ankle-deep sand, to the surf. There they walked along at the water's edge where the icy foam could wash over their feet. Once they misjudged their distance, and water splashed over their knees, wetting their pants legs. Laughing they wandered back to the boardwalk and rolled their pants legs down to dry in the sun and breeze.

"I grew up swimming here. I never thought of the ocean as something to be afraid of, not until Barbados. Of course we knew enough not to go in when the seas were stormy or the waves were too high, but I had no idea the sea could look so inviting and be so treacherous…"

"I sat up to watch you that afternoon. It never occurred to me you intended to try to swim there. There are some great swimming beaches in Barbados, but that isn't one of them."

"Lucky for me you were watching."

"Lucky for me. Look what it got me." He laughed and pulled her close.

"Oh! There! That sign!"

"What?"

"I haven't done that in years." Eve grabbed Adamo's hand and pulled him across the boardwalk and down a side street. In front of an old brown shingled building, bicycles stood lined up in a rack. A hand lettered sign advertised "Bicycles for rent."

"Can we?" Eve led him through the doorway.

The portly man behind the counter appeared to be sizing them up. "You want two bikes or a tandem?" he asked.

"Two bikes," Eve said firmly.

"You sure you don't want a tandem?" he asked. "Costs less."

"No," Eve said firmly. "Two bikes."

"Very well. If that's what you want." He heaved his bulk out of the chair and ambled toward the door.

Once outside he pulled the first two bikes out of the rack.

"I'll choose my own," Eve said, moving down the rack until she found what she wanted. "This one." She pulled out a Trek Pure.

"That one'll cost you more."

"You've had that bike here for at least fifteen years. I rented it that long ago. It should cost less than those." She pointed disdainfully to the sleek racing-style bicycles farther up the rack.

The proprietor gave up and turned to Adamo. "And you, sir. What will you have?"

"I'm not much of a cyclist. What do you say, Eve?"

"The hybrid. It'll be more comfortable than those racing bikes. We're going on an outing, not a race."

They pedaled the length of the board walk at a leisurely pace and then cut over to the road heading north. Eve breathed deeply as the familiar fragrance of the long needle pines and the salt scent of the ocean hit her. She could see the sea intermittently through sandy dunes covered with wild oats. How she loved this wild stretch of road between Ocean City and Rehoboth Beach. She had pedaled it often with Bette when they were teenagers. The weather-beaten cottages she remembered still dotted the landscape, but she noted they were increasingly interspersed with more modern condo developments and high rise hotels. She sighed.

"What's wrong?"

"When I was a child, none of this development was here. There were a few cottages, and a wonderful old light house station, but nothing else. I can't say I think this is an improvement."

They found a beach shack restaurant and had cold beer and fried clams on thick fresh rolls for lunch.

Adamo took a bite of his overstuffed sandwich. "I've enjoyed this morning. I must confess I've never been on a bike before. I was a little hesitant."

Eve looked at him in astonishment. "Never been on a bike!"

"Nope. Row boats, sailboats, motorcycles, and motorbikes, but never a bicycle. I like it. It's quiet. And slow enough for us to enjoy the passing scene."

Pedaling back they passed a lone biker coming the other way. He was dressed in a dark business suit, and he was wobbling uncertainly on his racing bike. As they passed him, Adamo heard him uttering a stream of inventive curses under his breath.

They were being followed. Not very effectively, but someone was following them.

The next morning they checked out of their hotel and drove down to Shoreport, the small town where Eve had grown up. It was fifty miles south and a short distance inland from the sea.

As Eve drove, Adamo kept a wary eye out for any vehicle that might be on their tail. It was easy to spot him. The gray Ford stayed just far enough behind to be inconspicuous, but on this winding, sparsely traveled country road, any car keeping pace with them, speeding up and slowing down as they did, had to be following them. Adamo chose not to mention his suspicions to Eve.

He studied the shady lanes and neat small houses as Eve turned off the main road, into the town of

Shoreport. They approached a small strip mall. "Pull in here," Adamo said. "Do it quickly. Drive around in back, to the delivery area."

Eve did as instructed, bringing the car a halt behind the stores. "What's the matter? Why are we doing this?"

"I think someone may have planted a homing device in our car," he said, reaching around under the dashboard.

"Who..."

Adamo opened the compartment and felt around. Then he stepped outside the car and reached under the front and back bumpers. It was there, tucked below the licence plate. He held it up for Eve to see.

She drew in her breath sharply. How could this be happening?

"Stay here. I'll only be a moment."

Adamo disappeared around the corner of the strip mall, moving stealthily, hugging the wall.

The gray Ford pull into the shopping center lot, and the man he had last seen on a bicycle near Ocean City got out and looked around.

Adamo returned to their car a few minutes later, he said. "I'll drive."

Eve walked around the car, and slid into the passenger seat. "Are you going to tell me what's going on?

"Lucky thing Toyota produced so many models in the same silver-gray as ours. I hope our tail will be following someone else for a little while, before he discovers his mistake."

"You mean to tell me someone was following us?" Eve tried to repress her sudden tremble. "Why would anyone do that? We're just taking a little holiday."

He started the engine and drove out the side road rather than though the shopping center parking lot. "You know a back way to your house?"

"Sure. Just keep on this road for five blocks and then turn left, past the college."

"How did this town come to be named 'Shoreport' when the water's a good ten miles from here?"

"Just one of life's mysteries. It may have to do with the crab cannery on the other end of town. The college and the cannery are the town's two principal employers." Eve turned toward Adamo. "Why are we being followed?"

"For the same reason someone tried to kill me in Positano. They think I pose a danger. We won't be free until we've found out who that person is and in some way…the word Don Alfonso used was 'neutralize' him."

Eve shivered. "I hate it. I hate that someone we don't know wants to harm us for some reason we can't comprehend. Why can't they just leave us alone?" She sat forward. "Turn here. It's the third house on the left."

He pulled the car over to the curb and turned off the motor.

She sighed. "There it is. That's the house I grew up in. I see the new owners have painted it. Good. I'm glad it went to someone who will care for it."

Her thoughts turned to the day her father died. "It's funny how unimportant details stay in your mind," she said. "It was bitterly cold that day. I remember the frost had turned the grass to silver. I was coming back from marketing, and the apples fell out of the top of my grocery bag and rolled all over the porch as I was fumbling for the front door key. I had to scoop them up and put them back in the bag. When I got inside, I called up the stairs to let Dad know I was back."

Her eyes burned with threatening tears. "He was gone. In spite of all my care, he was alone when the second stroke took him. I'll regret that as long as I live." She wiped her eyes and blew her nose. "Sorry. Maybe this wasn't such a good idea after all."

Adamo gathered her into his arms. "It can be painful to go home again."

"No," she said, "I needed to do this so I can move on."

Adamo squeezed her hand. "I know all too well about the difficulties of moving on."

He started the car. "We'd better get out of this town. I'm afraid the man who was following us will be searching for us once he realizes he's been tricked. And if he's reporting in to someone, he may well know by now you once lived here. Where do you want to go next?"

"We may as well head back to Silver Springs. I'm glad we did this trip into my past, but we should get back to today. We have things to do."

They were approaching the Chesapeake Bay Bridge when Adamo's phone vibrated. He pulled over and listened intently for a few moments. "Understood. I'll be there."

He turned to Eve. "Mark Conti will be in Washington tomorrow on business. He wants me to meet him at the Willard Hotel in the afternoon."

****

"Son of a bitch lost me. I was certain they didn't know they were under surveillance, but it seems I underestimated de Leone. He stuck the damned homing device on another car. I followed it for forty minutes before I realized what he'd done. And I ache all over from a twenty mile bike ride, trying to follow them yesterday. Christ, I haven't been on a bike since I was fifteen. They seem to be taking a vacation. There's no other reason for where they are or what they're doing. Walking on the beach, bicycling, revisiting her home town."

Luc considered what he was being told. Could it really be that simple? Was he only imagining a threat where none existed? But if so, what had de Leone been doing in Mark Conti's office?

The man continued. "Why am I doing this, Luc? Do you want them taken out? I could have done that any number of times in the last three days. Couple of shots on a deserted road. There'd be no connection back to you. What do you want me to do?"

Luc hesitated. The Italian was potentially a threat, but it would be considerably harder to arrange an undetected accident for him here than in Italy. And a gangland style hit was not on. The police would be swarming all over everything, and if they located the hit man, it could lead straight back to him. He'd just have to wait a bit longer and see what Adamo de Leone was up to.

"Do nothing for the moment. Just keep him in your sights."

Chapter Fifteen

Adamo went into Washington with Ed as he drove to work on Monday morning. His appointment with Mark Conti wasn't until two, but he figured he could find something to do until then. He'd spend the morning in the History of Flight Museum at the Smithsonian Institution. Or maybe just walking on the Mall. He hadn't been in Washington since he was a boy. He could amuse himself there for a few hours.

As he wandered under the suspended Wilbur and Orville Wright plane in the Smithsonian, he felt the hairs on the back of his neck bristle. He had the eerie feeling he was being observed. He looked carefully around him. No one seemed to be paying him any particular attention. Still...

He continued on through the museum. The sense of being watched and followed grew stronger. He tried to identify his stalker, but in the crowded museum it was impossible.

Perhaps outside his follower would be easier to make. As Adamo walked down the museum steps he saw a tour bus at the curb, and a group milling about, beginning to board. Moving quickly, he inserted himself into the middle of the group, and began a conversation with an elderly lady from Wisconsin. "Yes, it was wonderful A great museum. Did you see the space exhibits?"

They climbed aboard together, and Adamo took an inside seat near the rear of the bus. Under the seat in front of him, someone had stashed a tote bag with a baseball cap poking out of the top.

As the bus pulled over at the Jefferson Memorial, Adamo removed his jacket and tie, and with a silent apology to the owner, stuffed them into the tote, leaving the original contents of the bag neatly folded on the seat beside him. Putting the pilfered baseball cap low over his all-too identifiable silver hair and carrying the tote, he infiltrated himself into the middle of the group trooping off the bus.

Once inside the monument, he slipped behind a pillar. Was his follower still with him? He hunched his shoulders to disguise his height and ambled down the steps, over to a taxi stand. He slid into the back seat of the first cab in the line. "The Willard," he instructed the driver.

He glanced out the back window. No one seemed to be following, but in this traffic it was hard to tell. As the taxi threaded its way down Constitution Avenue, he called the hotel.

Fortunately Mark Conti was in. "I'm being followed. Eve and I were followed when we were on the Eastern Shore this past weekend, and I'm pretty sure I'm being followed now, although I've tried to shake him."

"That's very interesting."

"Do you still want me to come to the Willard?"

"Where are you now?"

"In a taxi somewhere on Constitution."

There was a moment's silence. Then, "Have him drop you off at Palmer's Steak House on Constitution.

Take a menu and look at it, briefly. Get up and walk toward the back of the restaurant as if you're going to the men's room. Walk through and out the kitchen door. My driver will meet you there and ensure you're alone."

Fifteen minutes later, after following Mark Conti's instructions to the letter, Adamo stepped out of the black limousine at the service entrance to the Willard. Conti's assistant, James Conroy, was there to greet him.

"Mr. Conti is waiting for you." They took the service elevator to the twelfth floor. From there, Adamo followed the stony-faced, black-suited man to the stairwell, and they took the stairs down one flight to the eleventh.

"I don't believe you were followed here," Conroy said, "but just in case."

Hastily donning his jacket and tie, Adamo followed the man into Mark Conti's suite. There, Conroy took up his usual position just inside the door.

"Please join me." The older man rose briefly and indicated a chair across from him at a room service table set for two, complete with white linens and silver tableware. "I spent the morning in the Senate offices and I haven't yet had lunch." He poured a glass of wine for Adamo. "I never talk business over meals."

Adamo gratefully accepted the proffered glass and took a sip. "Thank you, sir." He helped himself to some of the smoked salmon and arugula salad. He realized he was hungry. Breakfast had been a number of hours ago.

"So tell me about Eve." The look Mark Conti gave Adamo reminded him of the one his father had given him when he'd been caught smoking at the age of twelve. "You're staying with her family, so I take it your interest in her is more than casual."

Adamo laughed. "It's not casual, no."

"Then…"

"I love her." Adamo realized he had not spoken those words before. Not to Eve. Not even to himself. What was it about this man that made it so easy to admit the truth to him? A truth he'd fought to ignore, even to reject.

"What are you going to do about it?"

"Do?" Adamo ran his hand distractedly through his hair. "I can't marry Eve. I haven't got a very good track record where marriage is concerned." He paused. "I can't tie her to me while all this is hanging over my head. I'm a convicted felon. My whole future is tied up in a small inn in Positano. I have nothing to offer a woman like Eve. She deserves better."

"I see. And have you discussed this with her? Have you told her how you feel? How you're willing to sacrifice your own happiness so she can have 'better'? Has she indicated she wants or needs this 'better' you say you want for her?"

"I suppose not, not in so many words. She knows I care for her."

"Care for her?" Mark Conti shook his head. "That's a rather insipid expression. A moment ago you said *love*. You said you loved her. Which is it? They're not the same."

Adamo began to feel under siege. "I love her, but I just can't. I can't tie her to a jailbird."

"Nonsense. When happiness is offered to you, grab it with both hands. Don't ask whether you're worthy. We're rarely worthy of the women we love. A happy marriage is the greatest gift a man can have in life. I know. I was happily married for twenty-two years to one woman. I lost her to cancer."

Mark Conti pushed his chair back from the table, signaling lunch was over, took his coffee cup with him and walked across the room to the sofa. "Come." He indicated a chair. "Sit and tell me what you've discovered."

Adamo was relieved at the cessation of personal questions. The same questions he asked himself a hundred times a day. Always with the same answer. It wouldn't be fair to Eve.

Mark Conti took a sip of his now cold coffee and made a grimace of distaste. "I've never been able to accustom myself to American coffee." He put the cup down on the coffee table. "You've heard nothing more from your ex-wife?"

"No. It's been only a few days…One of us will call her with instructions when we're sure she's had time to get the blackmail letter. Perhaps we should have Ed make the phone call?"

"I think it might be best. A man's voice, one she won't recognize. Keep me informed. I will want to be involved in any arrangements you make to meet with her.

"Of course." Adamo scanned Conti's face. Should he ask the question burning in him? He took a deep breath. "Have you any further information as to who in your organization might be involved in this? Or who Monica was with on your yacht? That is, if it really was Monica?"

Mark Conti was silent for a few moments. He seemed to be studying Adamo. "Does the name Luc Manzel mean anything to you?"

For a split second, Adamo couldn't breathe. Then he exhaled slowly and willed his hands to unclench. "It's not a name I'm likely to forget. He was the lawyer Monica found to defend me in the embezzlement case. He instructed me to plead guilty. When I refused, he more or less gave up on me. He didn't present much of a defense. In retrospect, I think he was convinced of my guilt from the beginning. When I asked him to file an appeal, he told me there were no grounds for it." Adamo looked sharply at Mark Conti. "Just what do you know about Luc Manzel?"

"Mr. Manzel is an employee of the Conti Corporation. He has been a member of our legal team for some years. One of our money men."

Adamo absorbed the shock. He sat forward in his chair, his body rigid, his mind trying to make sense out of what he'd just heard. His lawyer, the man who had effectively put him behind bars, had connections with the Conti Organization? The lawyer his wife had found for him? How could she ever have even met someone like that? Who could have suggested him to her?

Adamo took a deep breath. "So I had a Mafia lawyer?"

"If Luc Manzel is Mafia, I am unaware of it. He would not be working for me if I knew that for a certainty." Mark Conti sighed. "But yes, in view of the evidence, I must face the fact he could have ties to organized crime. And I'm no happier than you at the possibility someone in my employ may have such connections, and may have been independently involved in a scheme to put you behind bars."

"*Santista*," Adamo said. "Luc Manzel is a *Santista*. Uncle Valerio told me about men like that. Mafia lawyers dedicated to interfacing with the authorities and the world of business. He said they're members of Rotary Clubs, Masonic Lodges, business associations, and political parties. They're sort of outside the organization but inside it too. And above all, they appear legitimate."

"It's possible. We need more evidence to be certain."

Adamo grasped his hands tightly on the arms of the chair to keep them from shaking. He looked down and hesitated before speaking, weighing his words.

"So it appears a member of your organization was responsible for my jail sentence." His voice was flat, emotionless. "If Luc Manzel worked for you, why was he defending me in a criminal case? What did you or your business interests stand to gain through my conviction?"

"Nothing. Absolutely nothing. I would never have approved any of our associates taking on a court case outside the firm. For some reason Mr. Manzel considered the risk worth the taking. I wonder why that would be. Why did he interest himself in your case?"

Realization dawned. Adamo's hands clenched compulsively into fists. "Luc Manzel was the other man. The one my detective saw her with. Monica's lover. He has to have been."

"Yes, that was my own reluctant conjecture. We have no real evidence of anything, but it seems, not just possible, but probable. I've discovered Luc was one of the party on my yacht at Capri when you spotted your ex-wife."

"Monica's lover," Adamo said. "It all fits. He was the one behind the embezzlement. The one who got the money out of the country, and then arranged to get me conveniently out of the way for six years."

"It's all well within the range of possibility." Mark Conti chose his words carefully. "Through the firm, through our casino operations, he would have the necessary connections for transferring the money into off-shore accounts."

The two men sat in silence for a few moments. Finally Adamo said, "What do you propose we do about it?"

"You do realize this is all conjecture? And even if it were proven fact, I could not act on it in any public way. I'm in the middle of delicate negotiations with certain people in government right now. I cannot allow this…this unsavory affair…to spill over into my business."

Adamo looked down, weighing his response. Mark Conti had been incredibly forthcoming. But how could he expect the man to compromise his position in the search for a truth potentially harmful to him? A truth from which he had nothing to gain?

"I understand. You have been most helpful, sir." Adamo stood to leave. "We'll take it on our own from here."

"Sit down, son. I'm not through yet."

Puzzled, Adamo took his seat again.

The older man rubbed his jaw. "I must ask you about your priorities. What matters to you in this?"

"I don't understand."

"If you want me to help you prove your innocence, I must disappoint you. I can't do without dragging my firm into an unwanted spotlight. If, on the other hand, you could be satisfied with money returned to investors, with being safe from further harm, with those who matter to you knowing you to be innocent, then perhaps I might be able to help you."

Adamo looked at Mark Conti in astonishment. "You could do that? You could get the money back?"

"What remains of it. Yes, I believe I could possibly arrange it. You would need to supply a complete list of investors and amounts and their bank account numbers. And much depends on your being able to entice the elusive ex-Mrs. de Leone back onto American soil. I suspect Luc is too smart to have anything stashed away in his own name. Everything is probably in your ex-wife's name. Another reason we need her back here."

"Farrell. She goes by her maiden name, Farrell, now. The SEC will have the documents, and I believe Eve's sister's husband, Ed Richardson, can get most of the information we need on our former investors. He's already looking into the old files. As an IRS investigator he has considerable access."

"As long as he doesn't extend his probe into Conti Corporation matters…"

"He has no interest in your firm at this moment. And I believe he genuinely wants to see the money returned to the investors. He sees his sister-in-law's future is at stake."

"A wise man. You do realize this adventure, even if it works as planned, will not remove the 'felon' label that so seems to concern you. Were you hoping somehow to reinstate your business, to be recognized as not guilty?"

"Of course I'd like to be proven innocent. But I can live with the label, if I know we've done everything possible to right the wrong to our investors. I'll never again meddle in the world of high finance. The thought of it sickens me. I like my simple life…my life with Eve…in Positano. I'm not sure I ever knew what happiness was before."

"Ah. We're back to the lovely Eve. I look forward to seeing her again."

Adamo had the grace to laugh. "My life wouldn't be much worth living without her."

"Then you'll consider my earlier advice." It was a statement rather than a question.

The older man stood, signalling the interview was over. As Adamo stood to leave, Mark Conti gave one last directive. "You should take no action without conferring with me. I wish to be involved at all stages of the arrangements. When Mr. Richardson is ready to make contact with your ex-wife, I believe I can be of some service. You may call me at my personal number at any hour of the day or night."

He handed Adamo a plain white card with one number on it. "I have a plan of sorts. When you're ready to act, I will see to it Luc Manzel is out of the way, unable to contact Miss Farrell, until we want him on the scene. Above all, you are to leave Luc Manzel to me."

Adamo hesitated only briefly. "As you wish. Thank you, sir."

"My driver will return you to the place where you're staying. Silver Springs, you said?"

Adamo followed James Conroy down in the service elevator and out the basement entrance of the Willard to a waiting limo. All the way home his mind chewed on the new information he had received from Mark Conti. Luc Manzel, his lawyer, had been

Monica's lover, had deliberately engineered his guilty verdict. He owed to Luc Manzel and to Monica the six lost years of his life. His blood pounded in his ears. How he wished he had Luc Manzel in his sights at this moment. He didn't want to kill him. That would be too easy. He'd like to beat him to within an inch of his life and then throw him into a dungeon somewhere where he'd never see the light. He'd like Luc Manzel to suffer, as he had suffered.

But he had promised Mark Conti. However difficult it might be to let matters take their course, even if it meant letting Luc Manzel walk away scot free, he would have to agree to it. He owed Mark Conti that.

As they approached the tree-lined street where Bette and Ed lived, Adamo took a deep breath and consciously brought his anger under control. He couldn't let Eve see him like this.

Chapter Sixteen

Eve was baking a pancake supper for the assembled Richardson boys when Adamo entered. She took one look at his white face and called Bette to come downstairs.

"Can you take over here? I think I need to talk with Adamo."

"Of course. Go."

She followed Adamo up to the guest room. There, he threw his jacket over a chair and pulled off his tie. His actions were abrupt, almost violent.

"I need a shower." Adamo carelessly stripped off his remaining clothing and went into their ensuite bathroom.

Eve sat in the deep upholstered chair by the window and waited. She knew he'd tell her when he was ready.

Five minutes later he emerged from the bathroom, a towel loosely wrapped around his waist. He shook his head as if still not quite able to speak. He rubbed his hand across the back of his neck, tension in every line of his body.

Eve stood and walked over to him. She wrapped her arms around him and nestled her head against his broad chest. He drew in a sharp shuddering breath and she realized he was fighting tears.

"Six years." His voice was ragged. "I lost six years

of my life, our clients lost all their money, just so my ex-wife and her lover could live in luxury. And the joke? I was set up. Poor Emmett may have been the tool, but the mastermind was my own lawyer, Luc Manzel. A lawyer who most probably has connections to organized crime. My lawyer and my wife, working together to see I was out of the way while they moved eighty million dollars out of the country."

Eve drew back in shock. "Your lawyer? Are you quite certain?"

"As certain as can be without actually confronting them."

"What do we do now?"

Adamo sat in the arm chair and pulled Eve into his lap, his towel falling to the floor in the process. Eve snuggled against him as he nuzzled her hair.

His voice softened. "He said I should marry you."

"What? Who?"

"Mark Conti. I told him I loved you and he said I should marry you."

After the shock of actually hearing the word "love" on Adamo's lips, Eve couldn't resist teasing him. She pulled back and looked him directly in the eye. "You told Mark Conti you love me? You've never told me you love me. Don't you think I should have been the first to know? Before you started discussing me with strangers?"

Adamo tried to pull her back into his arms.

She pushed away. "No. If you love me, I think you should be able to say the words to me. Straight out. They're simple. Just, 'I love you.' Try it."

He shook his head, exasperated. "Of course I love you, Eve. How could you doubt it for a moment? But

199

marriage is something else. How can we contemplate marriage with all this hanging over our heads?"

"But Mark Conti said you should marry me. I think he must be a very wise man." Relenting, she snuggled back into Adamo's arms. "Now tell me about the rest of it. Everything that was said between you."

By the time Adamo finished his narrative, he was more relaxed. The lines of tension between his brows had smoothed, and his shoulders were no longer rigid. He took a deep breath.

"If our ploy works, I think we may see the bulk of the embezzled funds returned to our investors. But the downside is I'm unlikely ever to see my name cleared."

Eve stood and methodically picked up the clothes Adamo had discarded, putting them on hangers or in the clothes hamper. "I haven't noticed our life in Positano is in any way impacted by the fact you spent some time in a U.S. jail. It's a new life for both of us, Adamo. Don't let ancient history blight our future."

"I can't pretend it doesn't bother me that Luc Manzel may walk away from all this unscathed and my name may never be cleared. But if even a part of the money can be returned, and if we find out with certainty what happened to Emmett, I believe I can live with the rest." His shoulders drooped. "I feel deathly tired. As if I've run a marathon today. I think I'll lie down for a while." He stretched his long, lean body diagonally across the queen sized bed.

Eve pulled the covers up loosely over his nude form. He was asleep before she left the room.

Downstairs the boys had been fed and sent to do their homework. Bette and Ed were working together in the kitchen, preparing a simple supper for the four adults. Ed was seasoning the steaks for the barbeque while Bette assembled the ingredients for a tossed salad.

"I think we should just let Adamo sleep." Eve studied her sister. Bette no longer had the drawn look of the earlier days of her pregnancy. In fact she was blooming as her baby bump increased in size.

Bette looked up from tossing the salad. "She's kicking a lot today."

"She?"

"Well, we don't really know. I haven't done the ultrasound thing. I don't want to know. But I can't help but want a girl. I'm so outnumbered in this house." Bette gave her husband a playful punch.

"Hey, don't blame me." Ed laughed. "Can I help it if my little swimmers are all boys?"

How Eve envied their affectionate comradery. Would she and Adamo ever be able to live together in such ease? To have children, to create a real family, with all that entailed? Perhaps, if they could ever satisfactorily resolve this mess…

As she placed the knives and forks around the table, Eve recounted to the best of her recollection, Adamo's conversation with Mark Conti.

"He's a powerful ally," Ed commented. "Glad he's on our side in this. I'll get to work rounding up the information we need for restitution of the funds. I'm not sure how Conti's going to do it. It will be interesting to observe. That is, if he allows me anywhere near the process."

Bette took plates down from the cupboard. "How much longer do you think we should wait before we call Monica with instructions for the meet?"

"I think we could do it any time now." Eve poured their water and put the condiments on the table. "Adamo insisted Mark Conti had to be consulted first. Mr. Conti said he has plans as to where and how the meeting should take place."

Bette stopped what she was doing and looked directly at Eve. "I want to be there when it happens."

"Do you think that's wise in your condition?"

"I'm feeling fine, and I'm not due for another two months. I can get a note from my doctor if there's likely to be any problem with the airlines. I'm not about to miss this."

Eve knew better than to argue with her sister when her mind was made up, as it clearly was at this point.

When Eve went to bed, Adamo seemed to be still sleeping soundly. She tried to push him gently over to make room and found herself surrounded by a very awake man.

"Don't you want some dinner?"

"No. All I want is you. All I've ever wanted is you. God, I love you, Eve."

That night he made love to her sweetly, tenderly, with tormenting patience, smothering her cries with his kisses, prolonging her release until he could himself wait no longer. It was a new step in their relationship. Love had been admitted, accepted.

The next morning they called Emma to see if she was ready.

"Ready and chomping at the bit."

"We'll wait for instructions as to when and where," Eve said.

Adamo placed the call to Mark Conti.

"Tell Miss Farrell to check into a Miami hotel,"

Conti answered briskly. "May as well be one of ours, the Conti Miami Beach. From there we'll divert all the players on a carefully constructed schedule to my Key Biscayne home. A house party of sorts. How many of you will there be? I particularly want Miss Kenston and Miss Anderson to be there."

Adamo thought for a moment. "If it won't create problems, we'd all like to be there. Eve, of course. Emma Kenston if she's up for the travel, Ed Richardson, and his wife Bette. They've all been involved from the beginning of the investigation."

"An IRS agent in my home? That will be a first. Five of you, then. You are all invited to my Key Biscayne residence. Let's say Thursday, a week from today. I'll have my secretary send you directions. I'll want you in place and out of sight before our little drama begins, so arrange your travel so you arrive before noon."

Eve called Emma with the news they were ready to move. "Ed's going to make the call. He'll tell Monica to bring the money to the Hotel Conti Miami Beach. We're to say someone will contact her there with further instructions."

"That's all very good, but what then?"

"I think Mark Conti has some idea of how he wants this all to play out. He says he believes he can get the stolen funds back to the rightful owners. He wants us all there, and he's invited us to stay in his home in Key Biscayne."

"It sounds wonderful," Emma said, "but are you sure I'm included in this invitation?"

Eve laughed. "From what Adamo told me, I would say your presence is required, rather like when you receive a royal invitation."

Emma joined in Eve's laughter. "I know what you mean. That man has a way of making it difficult to say no. I'd love to join you in Florida." Her laughter ceased abruptly, and her tone when she continued was harsh and biting. "I want to come face to face with the woman who ruined my brother's life."

"Exactly what I expected you to say. I can come to Watertown and travel to Florida with you if you like," Eve offered.

"Certainly not. People travel in wheelchairs all the time. I can get as far as Washington on my own. You and Adamo and the others can join me there. Now exactly what do you think Ed should say to Miss Farrell when he speaks to her?"

"Mr. Conti said just to tell her where and when she must be in Miami. The Conti Miami Beach Hotel, one o'clock, next Thursday. She's to have the money with her. Ed's to tell her someone will contact her once she's there. Mr. Conti said to make it short and sweet. Ed isn't to wait for any response. He's to hang up after delivering the message."

****

Monica was nearly out of her mind with fear. She had read and reread the damning letter. Why now? Why after all this time was someone threatening her? And the worst of it was she hadn't been able to reach Luc. For five days he hadn't answered his cell phone. She'd gone so far as to call his home, something he'd told her never to do. They'd said something about Mr. Manzel being away. They'd asked if she'd like to speak to Mrs. Manzel. Not likely. Where could he be that he wasn't getting her messages to call?

The phone rang. Monica grabbed it. "Luc?"

There was silence for a moment on the other end of the line. Then, it was a man's voice, soft and menacing. "You have the money?"

"I…no, not yet. But I can get the money." Monica stood trembling. "I can get the money," she repeated more firmly. After all it was only a hundred thousand dollars. A drop in the bucket compared to what Luc had transferred to her accounts in Barbados and in various places in Europe.

"You will fly to Miami next Thursday. Bring the money. Stay in the Conti Miami Beach Hotel. You'll be contacted there with further instructions."

The line went dead.

Where was Luc? Why wasn't he answering his phone?

****

Luc Manzel swore under his breath. It was freezing here. What had his boss been thinking when he'd sent him to this distant northern mining camp to handle negotiations with the local native band? He'd been instructed to stonewall their demands. New housing, a new school, improved safety in the mines, all of it was to be haggled over endlessly, all of it to be only reluctantly and minimally acceded to. The negotiations had gone on long into the nights. Who knew the native chief had a degree in law from Harvard and was a personal friend of Mr. Conti's? Luc hadn't had a decent night's sleep or a hot shower in a week, and for the life of him he couldn't see what problem his boss had found so urgent that it required sending him off to this godforsaken outpost. Thank God the float plane would return for him tomorrow.

Wednesday evening, back in New York, after a hot shower and a meal that didn't include whale blubber in any form, Luc looked at his messages. Monica. Again Monica. Three, four times a day while he'd been gone. What was going on? He called her number.

"Baby. You've been trying to reach me?"

"Luc! Oh Luc!" Monica was crying and talking at the same time.

"Slow down. I can't understand a word you're saying. You're where? In Miami? What in God's name are you doing there? I thought we agreed you'd stay put. Or at least avoid the U.S. for the time being."

"But someone knows. Someone has a letter from Emmett to his sister. It incriminates us. And they've offered to sell it to me. They don't want a lot of money for it. I thought..."

"For God's sake, Monica, don't think. It's not something you do well. Stay put. I have to report to Mr. Conti first thing tomorrow morning, but afterwards I'll be on the first flight I can get to Miami. Just don't do anything stupid."

Luc disconnected and looked at his phone in annoyance. Who could be threatening Monica? And what so-called evidence could anyone threaten her with? She'd said the letter was written by Emmett to his sister? He hadn't even known Emmett had a sister. And another thing, why had the blackmailer waited so long to act? It seemed unlikely the blackmailer was de Leone. Luc learned enough about him when he was defending him in the embezzlement trial to know he'd never resort to anything illegal. Adamo had faith in the system, poor sap. If he'd come upon information that threw doubt on his conviction since his release from prison, he'd have gone to the authorities. He wouldn't be attempting blackmail. It just wasn't his style.

Luc shook his head in frustration. None of it made sense. He'd have to discover the identity of this blackmailer and get rid of him or her, before there was real trouble.

His mind flashed back to the night everything had fallen apart. It had all gone smooth as silk until Emmett caught him with Monica. They'd been careful, but that one time, at the Plaza…Emmett had caused quite a scene before he'd stormed out of the hotel.

Luc muttered to himself, "We'll meet with this fucking blackmailer and finish with it once and for all. And the payoff won't be what he's expecting."

His phone rang.

"I need to see you."

"Of course, Mr. Conti."

"Pack a bag and meet me at the hangar at ten tomorrow. We're taking the Cessna to Miami. Bring all the paperwork from the northern mine deal. We can work on the way."

Luc smiled. He was going to get to Miami even sooner than he had anticipated. He'd finish up with his boss and then take care of the situation with Monica.

Chapter Seventeen

Eve was conscious of people staring at them as they made their way through Miami Airport on their arrival at noon on Thursday morning. Emma, so strikingly beautiful, in her wheelchair, being pushed by Adamo, extraordinarily handsome with his towering height, his strong dark face, and burnished silver curls, Ed solicitous of his obviously pregnant wife and of course herself, rather inconspicuously taking up the rear. All traveling first class, courtesy of the Conti Corporation. A chauffeured stretch limousine awaited them at the curb.

"The Conti Party? Good morning. I'm Yasim, Mr. Conti's driver. Please allow me to help you." Deftly, the very large, very black man lifted Emma gently to her seat and then placed her wheelchair in the trunk. The rest of their small wheel-on bags he quickly stowed around it.

Eve peered with interest as, ten minutes later, they left traffic behind and crossed the Rickenbacker Causeway to enter the exclusive Key Biscayne area of Miami. Through the limousine window, she gazed with unabashed curiosity as they passed winding drives and pink and white houses sprawled along on both sides of the manicured roadside. Between the houses, she caught glimpses of the Atlantic Ocean. The car pulled up to an ornate wrought iron gate. The driver spoke into a box, and the gate swung wide to allow them to enter and then immediately closed behind them, as they wound their way down a palm-lined drive to a sprawling two story mansion.

A young man came down the wide marble steps to greet them.

Adamo leaned over to whisper to Eve, "I see James Conroy's exchanged his usual black suit for a tropical white one."

The man stepped forward to greet them. "Good morning, Miss Anderson, Miss Kenston, Mr. de Leone." To Ed and Bette, he said, "You must be the Richardsons. I'm James Conroy, Mr. Conti's personal assistant. Mr. Conti asks me to welcome you all to Bluewaters. He will be here shortly. I'll show you to your suite. He requests you stay there until he's had a chance to brief you. You shouldn't have too long to wait." He turned and walked back up the stairs, waiting at the entrance for them.

Adamo whispered to Eve, "That's the most words I've ever heard James Conroy utter."

Yasim ran quickly up the steps with Emma's wheelchair and opened it inside the entrance hall. Then he effortlessly lifted Emma out of the car, up the steps, and placed her in it. The others followed him.

Eve stood entranced. The wide black and white marble-floored hallway extended from the front of the mansion to the back. Art lined the walls. Double doors at the back stood open to admit a view of wide lawns and extensive gardens, and beyond them, the beach and the sea. A double curved staircase graced the end of the hallway, framing the view. "That anyone really lives this way..."

"I'll admit it has a certain appeal," Adamo said, sotto voce, "but I'll take our little inn in Positano over it any day."

"Maybe. But you must admit this is pretty impressive."

James Conroy interrupted their whispered commentary. "If the rest of you will take the stairs, I'll take Miss Kenston up in the lift and meet you to show you to your rooms."

Eve grasped Adamo tightly by the arm and nodded in the direction of the paintings. "Look at the art lining these walls. The Impressionists are not my particular field, but I could swear that Monet is an original."

"Very possibly," Adamo murmured. "Mark Conti has both taste and the money to indulge his taste."

At the top of the stairs they rejoined James, who was pushing Emma's wheelchair into a large, comfortably furnished sitting room. Eve walked over to examine the art on the walls. A Pissarro, for sure…and was this one really a Renoir? She was struck silent in awe at the collection.

French doors led to a balcony facing the sea. The others gravitated to the view.

"Your rooms are on either side of this sitting room." James opened a door. "Miss Kenston, this one is yours. It is fully wheelchair accessible."

"Thank you so much," Emma replied, her face breaking into a very genuine smile. "You've thought of everything."

"Not at all. Mr. Conti has a large circle of friends and he likes to be prepared for all eventualities."

"Mr. de Leone, Miss Anderson, your room is here, next to Miss Kenston's, and Mr. and Mrs. Richardson, yours is the front room on the other side of the sitting room."

The group moved to disperse to their assigned rooms.

"Just one other thing," James Conroy continued. "I'll turn on the television here in the sitting room. I think you may find it interesting."

They all turned to look at the large screen.

"Mr. Conti thought you might enjoy this channel," James said, his voice even more devoid of emotion than usual. The view was of an empty, book-lined room.

"Now if you'll excuse me, I have things to attend to. Lunch will be served to you here."

****

Luc had cooled his heels for three hours in Mark Conti's hangar at La Guardia Airport, waiting for his boss's arrival, trying unsuccessfully to reach Monica, to warn her about the delay.

Mark Conti finally arrived, with no explanation for his lateness. But then, Luc thought with annoyance, his boss was never given to explanations. On the plane, Conti was noncommunicative, retreating behind a newspaper rather than initiating work, as Luc had expected. Why had he been asked to accompany him on this trip if there was no legal work to do?

Finally they were in Miami, in Conti's fabled Key Biscayne house, in an oak paneled library. Luc had heard about this place, but he'd never seen it before. He looked around at the well-worn leather furniture, at the haphazardly filled bookcases and at the massive oak desk littered with papers. It all seemed rather shabby to him. If he had the kind of money Mark Conti had...

His employer walked behind his desk and began

rifling through papers. He had not spoken a word to Luc since they'd left New York.

Luc began, "If you don't need me this afternoon—"

Mark Conti answered firmly, "But I do need you. Why else would I have flown you down here with me? I'll see you get some lunch while I clean up a few details, then we must start in earnest on those mining negotiations. I've decided to accede to all their demands. We'll need to get engineers and construction crews up there immediately if we're to beat the snow."

"What?" Luc looked at his employer in confusion. "Why did you ask me to stall the negotiations if you intended to give in on every point?"

"I had my reasons. Now if you'll excuse me for a few minutes, I have something to attend to. Meanwhile you may begin drawing up the new agreements." Conti indicated a library table equipped with a computer, then turned his back on his employee and left the library.

As soon as he was alone Luc called Monica's number.

"Where are you?" she wailed. "You said you'd be here."

"I'm in Miami. I have a little business to finish up before I can see you. Just sit tight. I'll be there as soon as I can."

The door opened, and Luc severed the connection. It was just a man with a lunch tray.

When the man left, Luc tried to call Monica back. His phone was missing! How the hell had that happened? He'd put it beside his chair. He looked around on the floor to see if he'd accidentally dropped it. No. He went to the desk and searched. Not there.

There was no phone on the desk, not even a land line. What was going on? A first flash of fear slithered down his spine. Something was decidedly wrong. He needed to get to Monica. He crossed to the door and opened it.

James Conroy stood immediately outside the door. "Was there something you wanted?" he asked mildly. "Mr. Conti instructed me to be sure you had everything you needed."

"No. No. But my phone…"

"Sometimes the reception here isn't very good. May I help you place a call on a land line?"

The man stood firmly planted between Luc and escape.

"No. No, thank you." Luc backed into the library and closed the door.

For the first time he studied the room. There were no windows, just floor to ceiling bookcases. He was effectively a prisoner, stuck here until Mark Conti returned. He sat down at the library table and began rewriting the agreement on which he had obtained signatures less than twenty-four hours ago in a Godforsaken mining town. He had the uneasy feeling something had gone terribly wrong while he was up in that desolate northern community. What could have happened?

****

Adamo sat in a wide chair in front of the television, his eyes glued to the screen, as the others all retreated to their rooms to unpack and freshen up from the journey. At one o'clock, he was vaguely aware of lunch being served. Eve took a plate of lobster salad and a glass of iced tea over to him. He acknowledged the food with a brief nod, not taking his eyes off the screen.

213

He was eating absently when he heard voices in the lower hall, Mark Conti's, James's and a third, not quite identifiable. He put his plate on the side table and leaned forward. The conversation was cut short momentarily by a firmly closing door, only to continue again on the television screen in front of him. Adamo turned up the volume.

The library was fully visible on the large television screen, the camera focused on the figures of Mark Conti and another man. Adamo watched as they held a brief conversation, something about mines. Then Conti turned abruptly and left the library. The man tried to place a furtive phone call. He seemed frustrated by it. Finally he walked over to a computer table, and began silently working.

Adamo couldn't take his eyes off the scene. Unconsciously, he clenched and unclenched his fists. He stared at the man with the hypnotic fascination of a victim facing a python. This was the man who had cost him everything. His wealth, his career, his marriage, six years of his life. He studied Luc Manzel with a detachment he wouldn't have believed possible a few days ago. On a primitive level he'd still like to get his hands around Luc Manzel's neck, but somehow it didn't matter as much as it once had. He no longer longed for vengeance. He just wanted to see the stolen money returned to the people to whom it belonged. And then he wanted to get as far as possible from it all, the scheming, the casual affairs so common in his former set, the deification of money. He was sickened by it.

Eve walked over to stand behind his chair. "Who is he?"

"Luc Manzel." His voice was tight. He took her icy

hand in his. "Nervous?"

"A little," she admitted. "It's hard to believe we're almost at the end of this."

"That remains to be seen." Adamo's smile didn't quite reach his eyes. "Come sit beside me." He made room for her and put his arm around her, pulling her close. She was his reality. She was his future.

Adamo was aware of Emma wheeling her chair over closer to the screen, of Bette and Ed coming to stand behind her.

Ed put a hand on Adamo's shoulder. "The curtain goes up, the drama begins," he said. "Let's hope it's a farce, not a tragedy."

All had their eyes glued to the screen.

The library door burst open. Luc jumped up and strode swiftly toward the door. He was propelled back by a shapely, dark haired woman, who threw herself into his arms and burst volubly into hysterical speech as the door closed behind her.

"Monica," Adamo said in a neutral voice. He turned the volume up again.

"Luc, where have you been? I've been trying to get you for days, and then you said you'd meet me at the hotel, and you didn't come, and the blackmailer said they had a letter from Emmett, and it incriminated me and you too, and I didn't know what to do…"

"Shut up, Monica! This room may be wired. I thought I told you to stay put."

As if she hadn't either heard or comprehended his command she rushed on volubly. "But a man who brought me here said the letter was here. Do you have the letter, Luc? Is that why you're here? Because the letter says Emmett was in fear for his life and he was going to send a letter to the police and then commit suicide. But if he sent a letter to the police, what happened to it? Would he have committed suicide before mailing it? And how did it fall into the hands of a blackmailer?"

"For God's sake, Monica, be quiet." Luc looked wildly around the walls as if trying to assess whether they were being monitored.

"But…" Monica was crying. "You said we were safe. You said no one would ever know…"

Luc shook Monica violently, shouting, "There can't be any letter to the police or any suicide note, Monica. He didn't have time to write anything to anybody."

"Wha…what?"

"After he caught us together, and realized he'd been played for the fool, Emmett had an attack of conscience. He was going to spill everything to the authorities. I acted. There really was no alternative. The police put it down to suicide, so suicide it was. But I assure you there was no suicide note. There was no letter to the police. He didn't have time for either."

"But I don't understand."

Luc sighed. "No, I guess you don't, Monica. Intelligence was never your long suit."

The library door swung wide and Mark Conti entered. "Good afternoon, Luc. I see you have company. Please introduce me."

Luc stumbled over the name. "Miss…Miss Farrell, Monica Farrell."

"Ah yes. Miss Farrell. You would be the former Mrs. de Leone?" Mark Conti looked at Luc rather than at Monica.

"Yes." Luc mumbled the answer.

"Then I take it you're here to purchase a blackmail letter?" He spoke to Monica.

"Yes," she answered, her voice breathy. "Do you have it?"

"For God's sake, Monica! Don't you know who this is?" Luc was ashen faced, his hands visibly shaking.

"It's obvious, isn't it? He's the man with the letter. And he's willing to sell it to us for a hundred thousand dollars, and I've got the money." Monica turned to her lover. "I don't see why you're so jumpy. If you'd been here when I needed you…"

Luc collapsed into a chair, his head in his hands.

Mark Conti glanced at Luc with an expression of disgust. He turned to Monica. "I don't have the letter, but I'll send for the person who has."

He opened the library door. "James, would you please ask Miss Kenston to join us?"

"Kenston? Emmett's name?" Monica's face screwed up into a puzzled frown. "Emmett's sister? The one the letter was addressed to? Is she the blackmailer?"

Mark Conti moved to sit behind his desk, ignoring her question.

A few moments later the door opened again and Emma wheeled herself into the room. She nodded to the man behind the desk, then turned her full attention on Monica Farrell. She examined the other woman in stony silence for a few moments. When she spoke, her voice was brittle. "I believe you knew my brother… knew in the biblical sense."

"I…" Monica seemed flustered. "Yes, I knew your

brother. Do you have the suicide note? The money's all here. The other man counted it."

Luc's shoulders drooped in defeat.

"Here's what you want." Emma handed Monica the letter.

Monica glanced at it and handed it to Luc. "See? I told you."

Luc read the letter carefully. Then reread it. His voice was gravelly when he spoke. "There is no way Emmett Kenston could have written this letter."

"Why?" Mark Conti asked. "How can you be so certain Emmett Kenston didn't write a suicide note before he took his life?"

Nerves visibly jangling, Luc looked around him, as if seeking escape. He stood and reached to the small of his back. His head jerked up in astonishment.

"Surely you don't think James would have allowed you into my house carrying a gun? It's one of the advantages of having a personal assistant who was once, in his distant youth, a pickpocket." Mark Conti smiled a completely humorless smile and pushed a button on his desk.

James Conroy stepped inside the room and stood, large and intimidating, back to the door.

Turning to face Luc Manzel once more, Mark Conti continued. "You knew the note was false because you killed Emmett Kenston. Or you ordered him killed, which amounts to the same thing. Is that not so?"

Monica turned her lover and shrieked. "No! Luc wouldn't do such a thing. Tell them, Luc."

Luc answered the accusation with silence.

Mark Conti cleared his throat. "You have endangered the reputation of the Conti Corporation for personal gain. You have engaged in theft, and possibly in murder, while in my employ."

Luc seemed to shrivel in his seat.

"Perhaps the next of our guests could join us now?" Mark Conti signaled to James, who left the room.

Monica knelt on the floor at Luc's feet, holding tightly to his hands, frowning in total incomprehension. Emma stared at Monica as if she were a specimen under glass, Luc looked blindly at nothing, and Mark Conti sat, impassive, behind his desk.

Adamo opened the library door and strolled in.

Luc jumped to his feet.

Monica gave a little shriek and hid behind Luc for protection.

"Monica, Luc, I won't say it's nice to see you. But I've been waiting a long time for this. Six, going on seven years."

Adamo turned his icy gaze on his ex-wife. "You don't need to be afraid of me, Monica. I wouldn't dirty my hands by touching you. You, on the other hand"—Adamo's voice dripped venom as he glared at Luc—"it would give me the greatest pleasure to break every bone in your body, one at a time. You sent me to that hellhole. I expect you thought I wouldn't survive. Just one more victim of jailhouse violence. It wouldn't surprise me if the attack on me a month after I arrived wasn't orchestrated by you. But as you can see, I'm tougher than you realized."

Luc turned ashen. He staggered back a step and his knees buckled. "What do you want from me?"

"Maybe my former life back?" Adamo unclenched his hands. "No. I don't think so. I much prefer the life I have now to the one I had. So in a perverse sort of way, maybe I should thank you. What do I want?" His voice hardened to granite. "I want the money you stole returned to the clients who so mistakenly put their trust in me."

Luc gave a mirthless laugh. "Not going to happen. You may think you know about the money, but you've no proof of anything. A hysterical woman's outpourings? An unsubstantiated confession to a convicted embezzler? A phony letter?"

Adamo smiled. It wasn't a nice smile. "Actually, the confession you made a few moments ago was observed by quite a few people. Some of them of unimpeachable reputations."

Luc lifted his head. "What?"

James opened the door and Eve, Ed and Bette filed silently into the room.

Mark Conti spoke in tones more suitable to the host of a dinner party. "I've been remiss, Luc, Miss Farrell. You haven't met our other guests. They've been upstairs watching this drama unfold on closed-circuit television. I might mention it has also been videotaped. This is Eve Anderson. She's engaged to marry Adamo."

Eve shot him a look of disbelief.

"As for the other couple, Mrs. Richardson is Miss Anderson's sister. And her husband," Mark Conti paused, heightening the drama of the moment, "Edward Richardson, is your worst nightmare. He's with the Internal Revenue Service, in the Investigative Branch. Of course, I suppose it could be worse. I could have invited someone from Homicide. But one has to draw the line somewhere."

"I don't understand. What's going on, Luc?"

Monica looked at the three people who had just joined them, confusion in her eyes.

Luc looked vacantly at his mistress. "Game over. Game. Set. Match."

The moment stretched on in unbearable silence.

"What do you want of me?" Luc turned to Mark Conti, his voice strained with tension.

"Have you ever seen any of the old black and white gangster movies, the ones made in the thirties? 'Your money or your life' was the phrase they used, I believe. It seems appropriate to this situation. You may walk out of here now. James will accompany you and Yasim will see you to your final destination." Mark Conti placed very clear emphasis on the word "final."

Luc swiveled his head toward the large, impassive man standing at the door, then back to Mark Conti.

To Adamo's enjoyment, Luc looked like a fly caught in a web, staring at an advancing spider, frantically seeking some way out.

The silence in the room reverberated. The tension was palpable.

Adamo waited, sitting stiffly on the edge of his chair, every muscle taut, for Luc's response.

After a moment that felt like an hour, Luc spoke. "Or?"

Mark Conti's voice hardened. "The money you stole is to be returned. You may work on my computer. I have, as you may imagine, the very latest and best equipment. The sum, I believe, was eighty million dollars. Even Miss Farrell can't have made much of a dent in so large a sum. As you are well aware, the Conti Corporation owns ten hotels with casinos. I expect you to transfer roughly eight million dollars into each of those ten casino accounts. I'm sure you know how to make the transfers electronically. That's how you got the money out of the country in the first place, using my connections without my knowledge. When you've completed the task, and I've verified the deposits, we will discuss what is to become of you and Miss Farrell. Not much of a bargain, but perhaps you may escape with your lives."

Ed made a move to object, but Adamo restrained him with a hand on his arm. "Just wait."

Mark Conti pushed a button on his desk and a section of bookcases slid aside to show an electronic, interactive world map and a bank of electronic equipment. "I thought it might be interesting to follow the trail of the money you've hidden. I'm sure Mr. Richardson will find it instructive."

For a moment nothing happened. Adamo realized he was holding his breath. Would Luc capitulate?

Luc stalked over to the computer complex, flexed his fingers and hovered over the keyboard. He took a small black notebook out of his inner jacket pocket and studied the pages.

Ed stood behind Luc as he began entering codes, number sequence after number sequence. Occasionally Luc stopped and consulted his notebook. Barbados, Luxemburg, the Cayman Islands, Guernsey, Switzerland, one after the other they flashed on the map over the computer. A screen over his head showed each transaction as the money was transferred to Conti Casino accounts in Las Vegas, Atlantic City, Miami, New Orleans.

The room was silent. Adamo glanced at Monica. She seemed to have run out steam as she watched the money, her money, moved around in a way Adamo was sure she couldn't begin to understand.

It took three hours. Only three hours to reverse six years.

Luc pushed back his chair. "We're nine million dollars short. I can't help it. Monica's place in Barbados accounts for one point five million. Her expenses have been high."

For the first time since their brief interaction when he first entered the room, Adamo spoke directly to Luc. "Am I to understand you have never accessed any of this money for your own use?" He didn't even try to disguise the scepticism in his voice. "My ex-wife is solely responsible for the expenditure of some nine million dollars? Even Monica would have a hard time doing that."

Luc glared at Adamo. "I may have used a bit from time to time."

"It's of no consequence," Mark Conti interrupted. He turned to Adamo. "Your investors could easily have sustained those losses in the market in recent years. The money will be apportioned equitably. My accountants will see to it. Now, Mr. Richardson, if you have the information we need to disperse these funds—"

"Are we free to go now?" Luc's voice held a faint tremble.

"Certainly not. All the transactions must be complete. Only then will we discuss what is to happen with you. Meanwhile, you are my guests." Turning to James, he said, "Would you show Mr. Manzel and Miss Farrell to their rooms, please."

The tension in the room evaporated with their departure.

Adamo sat back, drained of emotion. "So now we know. Poor Emmett, poor misguided Emmett. What a waste of a life."

Emma wept softly. "I thought it might be so, but I tried not to believe it. What could Emmett, bright, clever Emmett, have seen in such a tawdry, stupid woman?" She paused and shook her head. "Sorry, Adamo, I forgot she was your wife."

"*Was* is the operative word. No need to apologise. I can't imagine what I ever saw in her myself." Adamo exhaled and then laughed. "We did it. I can't believe we did it! With absolutely no hard evidence, we did it!"

Eve put her arms around him. "We're free. It's over. We can go home."

Ed cautioned, "I'm not sure how safe you'll be from reprisals once Manzel recovers from the shock of what's happened."

"I can assure you Mr. Manzel will have more to worry about than reprisals. I think I can pretty well guarantee your safety." Mark Conti stood and stretched. "We'll leave the rest to the accountants. James will send them the names and amounts supplied by Mr. Richardson. This stage of the drama will all be over in six or seven hours. Meanwhile, perhaps you'd like to take a swim, or rest? We will reconvene for dinner at eight." Mark Conti turned to the library door.

Then he turned back to Bette, a frown on his face. "Are you all right, my dear? You look a trifle uncomfortable."

All eyes focused on Bette. She had been unnaturally quiet during the last several hours. She stood now, gripping the back of her chair, white faced.

"My water just broke. I think I'm having a baby."

For the first time in Adamo's experience of the man, Mark Conti fell apart. "No. Don't do that! James!" he shouted. "Do something!"

Chapter Eighteen

Ed moved quickly to his wife's side, putting his arm around her, supporting her. "The doctor said the baby wasn't due for another two months. I should never have let you come."

"I guess we miscounted. But I think we'd better get to a hospital sooner rather than later." Bette sucked in her breath and grimaced. "This one's in a hurry."

James was already on the telephone with emergency services. "Yes. The Conti residence on Key Biscayne." Next he placed a call to Mark Conti's personal physician in Miami. "The best obstetrician you can get on this short notice. Yes. Immediately. The ambulance is on its way here. She'll be at the hospital in twenty minutes. The doctor must be there to meet her. She is not to go through Emergency. Mr. Conti will take care of all expenses. Yes, the best of everything. A private room, of course."

Ed was remonstrating, "I will take care of my wife's hospital expenses. We're well insured."

Bette moaned and doubled over.

The ambulance pulled up to the entrance within moments and shortly thereafter Bette was placed gently on a stretcher by two paramedics. "You're going to be fine, ma'am. We'll have you in the hospital in no time."

Holding Bette's hands, Ed moved to join them in the ambulance.

"I'm sorry, sir. You'll have to follow by car. Regulations. There's no room for passengers in the ambulance."

The black Cadillac in which they had come from the airport pulled up behind the ambulance as the paramedic was closing the doors.

"My car and driver are at your disposal," Mark Conti offered.

"Thank you." Ed raced down the steps to the waiting car.

"You want us to come with you?" Adamo called after him.

"No." Ed turned back to them briefly. "It will be some hours, if past experience is anything to go by. I'll call you."

Emma sat in her wheelchair at the open front door. Mark stood behind her, his hand resting lightly on her shoulder. "You shouldn't have pushed yourself out here."

She reached up and covered his hand with hers. "I'm quite capable of pushing my chair around, Mark. I've had years of practice."

"Of course, my dear. I'm sorry if I've offended you."

"It's all right, Mark. I just hate being treated as an invalid."

"I can assure you, my dear, I don't think of you in that way."

"Is she going to be all right?" Emma's face was creased in worry.

"She's in good hands now, and her husband will be right behind the ambulance." Mark turned her chair and wheeled her into the house. "I assure you she'll be well looked after. I'll see to it someone keeps us informed as to how things are progressing."

Eve sighed as she walked back into the entrance hall. "I feel the need to decompress. Would a nap be out of order?"

Adamo put his arm around her shoulder. "It's been an eventful day, and I didn't sleep much last night either."

He turned to Emma. "We're going upstairs. Would you like us to take you to your room?"

"No, I don't think so." She looked up at their host. "I think I'd like to go down to the beach if it's not too much trouble."

A wide smile crossed Conti's face. It was the first time either Eve or Adamo had ever seen him smile.

"I assure you it would give me the greatest pleasure to take you down to the beach."

Wearily Eve and Adamo climbed the stairs to their rooms. When they opened the door to their suite, sunlight flooded in. Eve took Adamo's hand. "Let's go out on the balcony for a little while. The sun is glorious."

As they stood, Eve leaning against Adamo, admiring the view, they overheard voices drifting up from just below them, Mark and Emma.

"Do you have any use of your legs?" Mark asked.

"A bit. I can manage around my little house using a walker. But I can't stand or walk unsupported, no."

"How long have you been like this?"

"Since I was eight. I haven't known since then what it is to walk freely. I've never felt sand between my toes."

"You will now."

Eve and Adamo watched in amazement as Mark Conti took off his jacket and threw it carelessly on the grass, took off his shoes and rolled up his pants legs. He knelt in front of Emma and unfastened first one and then the other of her shoes. Gently he smoothed his hands over her feet.

"Can you stand if I support you from behind, with my arms under yours? I won't let you fall."

Emma's laughter shimmered like silver. "I can try."

A moment later they walked across the sand, Mark's legs supporting Emma's to the edge of the surf.

Their voices were muted now. Eve and Adamo couldn't hear what they were saying, but they saw Mark Conti lift Emma Kenston into his arms and carry her into the surf. He didn't release her until they were well past the breakers.

Emma's laughter floated back to them as with Mark's help she pulled off her outer clothes and paddled on the gentle swells, dressed only in her bra and underpants. Mark appeared to be stripping off his clothes as well.

Eve and Adamo continued to watch, not wanting to intrude on the scene, but unable to look away. After some twenty minutes Mark Conti rose from the sea like an ancient Greek God, carrying a nearly nude and laughing Emma Kenston in his arms, like precious cargo, back to her wheelchair. There he draped his jacket around her shoulders.

As they reached the house, Adamo and Eve could once again hear their voices.

"That was glorious. Thank you."

"You'll be here for another few days. You won't

want to leave before Mrs. Richardson is out of the hospital. We can do this again, every day, if you like, Emma. I'll see to it you have a proper bathing suit next time. And we'll need to replace the offering of clothing we've left to the sea."

****

"Well, well." Adamo grinned. "That man never ceases to amaze me. Who'd have thought it? Shy, quiet Emma."

"And strong, demanding Mark Conti. Didn't you say he was married?"

"He told me he was happily married for twenty-two years. I understand his wife died five years ago. Cancer. She was only forty-eight."

"They're a good match in intelligence," Eve mused. "I wonder if anything will come of it. It's too much to hope for...two people such dissimilar backgrounds..."

"Rather like the felon and the woman who majored in Renaissance art?"

Eve had the grace to laugh.

His voice roughened. "I need you, Eve. Now."

"I thought you were tired."

"I can be tired later."

Wordlessly he led her through to their bedroom. There he slowly undressed her. He gazed at her, standing before him, nude, defenseless, with a smile of utter trust. He touched her breasts, curving his hands under the weight of them, and gently rubbed her nipples with his thumbs. Eve's low moan ripped through him, singeing his soul. He shuddered in response. Stripping off his clothing he lay down on the bed and pulled her on top of him, fitting her body to his, feeling her warmth enclosing him, surrounding him. He lay still, not yet willing to begin the journey to oblivion, wanting to prolong this intense, almost painful anticipation, with its sense of belonging.

His voice was hoarse with the effort of self-control. "Do you have any notion of what you do to me?"

"I think so," she said. "I suspect it's pretty much what you do to me. In one way it's like coming home, in another, it's like striking a match to tinder." She gave in to the needs devouring her and started moving in the age-old dance of love.

Later as they were drifting off, Eve murmured, "How can two people fit so perfectly together?"

It was nearly seven-thirty in the evening when they awoke.

"Get up, Adamo. We're due downstairs for dinner at eight."

He groaned.

Eve headed for the shower. Reluctantly he followed her. As he stepped under the running water behind her, he said, "No fooling around this time, I promise."

Eve quickly stepped out and dried herself off.

"Don't you trust me?" came the disembodied voice from the shower.

"Not for a moment." She laughed and retreated to their bedroom and was sitting at the dressing table, fully dressed and brushing her hair when he emerged.

"I've put your clothes out to save time."

"Thanks," he said as he pulled on the blue dress shirt, the light tan slacks and the dark blue jacket. "Is the tie really necessary?"

"I think so. Dinner at eight sounds pretty formal to

me." Eve looked at her watch. "I wonder why Ed hasn't called. It's been more than four hours."

"He'll be with Bette. You told me he would be coaching her all the way. I imagine he's way too busy to call right now. And even with my limited experience, I know pushing a baby out usually takes more than four hours."

"I just wish…She's my only family, Adamo." Eve's lips trembled.

"I'm sure everything's all right. Ed would call if it weren't."

"Still…"

"Come on. We're due downstairs."

James Conroy, as always Mark Conti's shadow, met them at the foot of the stairs. "Mr. Conti is in the music room. He invites you to join him there." He led them to a room across from the library.

The strains of Cole Porter's "Night and Day" greeted them as they entered the room. On a grand piano in one corner, Mark Conti was very competently playing while Emma sang along in a soft sultry alto, a rapt expression on her face. They finished the piece and Mark looked at Emma, a long, intimate look. Then, with a quick glance at Eve and Adamo, his face resumed its usual careful neutrality.

"Ah, I see you've found us." He stood and stepped toward them, picking up a champagne bottle sitting in a bucket of ice on the way. Deftly he removed the cork. "I thought tonight we should celebrate." He poured the champagne into four tulip-shaped glasses and handed them around. "To a job well done!" he toasted.

"To a job well done," the others echoed.

It was only then Eve noticed how Emma was

dressed. She was wearing a long, blue evening dress. Her shoulders were bare and the neckline of her dress was low, displaying to advantage her full high breasts. The fabric clung to her figure provocatively. Gone was the blanket with which she usually covered her legs. She still wore her sensible tied shoes, but the long skirt did much to cover them.

"Emma!" Eve gasped.

Emma had the grace to blush. "Yes. Well, somehow I lost my clothes. Mark was kind enough to provide me with this lovely dress…" She took a deep breath. "…and with a few other things. He made some phone calls and next thing I knew…"

"You look lovely." Adamo raised her hand to his lips in admiration.

Mark Conti cleared his throat and refilled everyone's glasses. "All that remains is to hear from the hospital. My man on the scene assures me everything is proceeding quite normally. I'm afraid I have no personal experience with such events. My wife and I were childless."

Eve gave a deep sigh of relief. This was Mark Conti. Of course he would have a "man on the scene" at the hospital. He lived like some sort of Renaissance prince, controlling everything in his environment. Not a Borgia. Perhaps a Medici, imperious, but just.

"This is a beautiful house," Eve said. "Do you get here often?"

"Not as frequently as when my wife was alive, but I consider this to be my home. In New York I keep only a small flat on the floor above my offices in the Conti Building. My wife seldom traveled to New York with me. She loved it here. She was only happy when she could see the sea. She had a hand in designing this house and the gardens, and it was she who named it."

"Bluewaters," Emma mused. "It seems so appropriate."

Mark turned to Eve. "I noticed you admiring some of my art collection earlier. Would you like a personal tour after dinner?"

Eve grasped Adamo's hand. "Yes, I'd love to see all your paintings."

The dining room table was set with white linen, fine porcelain, and silver. Crystal goblets for red and white wine were arranged above the service plates. On the center of the table, in a bank of flowers, candelabra glowed softly, sputtering occasionally as the breeze from open French doors touched them.

Course after course arrived. Rich lobster bisque, followed by sea bass, then small lamb chops on a bed of spinach. Dessert was a rich dark chocolate soufflé. A young man they had not seen before waited on the table and served the wines.

"I wouldn't want you to think I dine like this every night," Mark Conti said. "This has been a very special day for me." His gaze lingered momentarily on Emma. "I haven't enjoyed myself so much in a very long time."

Color rose in Emma's cheeks, and she looked down at her plate.

At the end of the meal, fruit and cheese were offered to each of them. Adamo and Mark Conti helped themselves to some bleu cheese and pear. Eve declined, as did Emma.

"I believe we'll dispense with the antiquated custom of the gentlemen remaining behind with their port while the ladies retire to the parlor. My very English wife was quite insistent on observing traditional formality, but I always preferred the company of women. No offense intended," he said to Adamo, the only other man present at the table. "I propose we return to the parlor for our after-dinner coffee and perhaps some cognac. Then I'll give Miss Anderson, and any others who might be interested, a tour of my collection of Impressionists. I'm really quite proud of it. It has taken me many years to find and acquire these paintings."

In bed some three hours later, Eve said, "I've never seen such a collection outside of a museum. Mr. Conti clearly loves art, and he's knowledgeable about it. He's an intriguing man. Fortunately, he isn't one of those collectors who keeps paintings hidden away to enjoy in solitude or who collects art merely as an investment. He wants other people to see his collection. Did you hear him mention he has offered his complete collection to the National Gallery for four months next spring for a special exhibition?"

Adamo observed the glow on Eve's face as she spoke about art, a subject near and dear to her heart. He smoothed her hair. "Have I mentioned I love you?"

"Have I mentioned I'm too tired?"

Adamo laughed. "You have a headache?"

"No. I just need sleep."

"Then sleep it is. I must admit I'm tired too. It's been a long, eventful day." He pulled her close to him. "Come. Fit yourself against me. Just two spoons in a drawer. Sleep, love."

Chapter Nineteen

Eve's phone rang at five the next morning. Fumbling around the bedside table, she finally managed to bring it to her ear. "Hello?"

"It's a girl!" Ed's voice was jubilant.

Eve was suddenly wide awake. "A girl? Wonderful! How is Bette?"

"She's just fine. The baby was premature, but she came in sturdy and yowling at six pounds, and the doctor thinks we'll be able to take her home soon. Both mother and daughter are asleep now. I'm heading back to the house. I need food and a shower and some sleep, in that order. I'd like to be back at the hospital before noon. You can come with me then if you'd like. They're not going to release Eve until the baby's ready to come home, and the doctor doesn't think we should travel for a week. I hope my mother can survive another week with the boys. I guess I'll have to check into a hotel here. I certainly can't continue to impose on Mr. Conti's hospitality."

Eve was pretty sure Ed underestimated Mark Conti's consuming drive to micro-manage everything in his environment, but she said nothing. Ed would discover soon enough his daughter had a godfather.

Adamo had slept soundly through her conversation with her brother-in-law. She looked at his face. It had the innocence of a child's when he slept. His hair was tousled, and the shadow of a beard covered his cheeks and chin. Love for him welled up in her and, for a moment, she was perilously close to tears. Gently, she touched his face. "Wake up, Adamo."

"Wha…What's wrong?"

"Nothing's wrong. Everything's right. As right as can be." Eve slipped out of bed and danced around the room. "I have a niece. A little girl! Bette's fine and Ed's on his way here now. We need to see if we can find our way to the kitchen. I'll make him some scrambled eggs and toast. If I'm right about how these things go, he hasn't had any food or sleep since they went to the hospital."

Adamo stretched and got out of bed. "I suspect we'll find there's already somebody up and working in the kitchen. And he or she won't want an amateur mucking about."

"Amateur?" Eve stopped in her tracks.

Adamo was already slipping on jeans and a shirt. "No disrespect to your cooking. But your degree is in Fine Arts, not in Culinary Arts. I'll bet the chef in this household is from France and studied with some distant relative of Escoffier's. I've never had a dinner like last night's." He slipped his feet into his running shoes, quickly tying the laces. "I'll try not to wake the others, but I think I should give the kitchen a heads up. You go shower and dress."

Adamo stepped into the sitting room pulling the bedroom door closed behind him quietly, so as not to disturb Emma, who had the room next to theirs. He was almost across the room when Emma's door opened and a dishevelled Mark Conti stepped out. Seeing Adamo he retreated quickly back into the room.

Adamo grinned. So that was the way the wind blew. Good for Emma. Good for them both. Softly he whistled as he descended the stairs and headed toward the back of the house. The kitchen had to be somewhere back here.

He found it through the dining room and butler's pantry, the latter filled with floor-to-ceiling cabinets of china and glassware. A swinging door led to a kitchen which would have done any restaurant proud.

In the center of the room, a rotund woman wearing a black and white striped apron was rolling out dough on a marble-topped pastry table "May I help you?"

She didn't sound particularly helpful; the question had more the ring of "What are you doing in my kitchen?"

"I'm very sorry to disturb you, ma'am, but in about fifteen minutes a man will be here and he'll be famished. He's been at the hospital all night, since four o'clock yesterday afternoon. His wife has just delivered a baby girl. He's had no food and no sleep in the last twenty hours. We don't want to disturb your routine. Perhaps I could just make him some eggs and toast?"

As he spoke the woman's face lost its stony expression. "You'll do no such thing. I think I can handle some scrambled eggs. Will you be joining him?

"If it's not too much trouble. And my…my fiancée, as well."

"Very well. Meanwhile, if you want to make yourself useful, set the table in the dining room. Everything you need is in the butler's pantry. The kitchen staff won't be here before seven."

"Right. Thank you."

Adamo retreated to the butler's pantry and studied

the row upon row of possibilities. Finally he chose a rather breakfasty-looking set. The plates were sturdier than most of the others and had designs featuring people in old-fashioned clothes against rural backgrounds. He turned one over. Villeroy and Boch. He shrugged and took down enough place settings for five. Mark and Emma might be down for breakfast. He smiled to himself. Or they might not. He remembered times when he and Eve had missed meals.

When Ed arrived, unshaven and exhausted, he found a sideboard heaped with home-made biscuits and jams, and covered silver serving dishes filled with scrambled eggs, sausages and bacon.

He grinned at Adamo. "Thanks. You're a lifesaver."

"Not me. There's a witch in the kitchen who can work miracles."

Eve appeared in the doorway and went to hug Ed, who was too busy shoving food into his mouth to respond with proper enthusiasm.

"Tell all," Eve said as she helped herself to eggs and toast.

Ed sighed and shook his head. "You'd think I'd be used to it. This makes the fourth time I've been through this with Bette. But it's plain terrifying. I don't know how you women do it. And then she smiled when the baby was placed on her stomach. Women are so much stronger than we poor males."

"But Bette's all right?" Adamo couldn't keep the worry out of his voice.

"She's right as rain. She came through it like the trouper she is. And when the doctor told her it was a girl, she gave a whoop of sheer joy." He pushed his chair back from his now empty plate. "I must get some sleep. Can you wake me at eleven? If I'm not there by noon, Bette will worry."

"Sure, no problem," Eve said.

They were quiet for a while after Ed left.

Adamo spoke hesitantly. "I don't think I could do what Ed did. I'm not sure I could hold your hand and try to be encouraging while you were suffering the pangs of hell. I've seen childbirth. My sister...I don't think I could bear seeing you in such agony, knowing the dangers inherent in it, knowing I was responsible for it."

"I see." Eve was silent for a moment, digesting the full import of what Adamo had just revealed. "Do you mean I don't have any say in this? It's my body. It should be at least partially my choice. We've never discussed this, Adamo. Don't you want children, our children?"

Adamo was saved answering as Mark Conti entered the dining room pushing Emma's chair. He sent a wary glance to Adamo.

Adamo merely said, "Good morning. I hope we didn't wake you."

Eve broke in. "Bette's had her baby. It's a girl."

Emma clapped her hands. "That's wonderful, isn't it?" She looked up, her face glowing, at Mark Conti.

"Yes, it is. The miracle of life. May I get you some breakfast, my dear?"

"Absolutely. I'll have some of everything. I don't believe I've ever been so hungry."

Eve studied Emma's flushed, happy face. She was wearing rose this morning. A soft sweater and matching pants. Another of Mark Conti's choices? It suited her creamy skin and soft dark hair.

Adamo broke into Eve's musings. "Where are Monica and Luc Manzel?

Eve came back to earth with a thud. She hadn't even thought about them in the last twelve hours.

Conti's voice had an edge when he answered. "They're confined to a suite in the east wing. Meals have been taken to them, and they have every comfort and convenience they would in a hotel, save one. They can't leave until I'm ready for them to do so. And I must set a few things in motion first."

"I'd like to be present when you meet with them." Adamo made it as a request, but it was more in the nature of a demand.

"You've earned the right. Let's say at two this afternoon. But only you."

Eve was momentarily annoyed, but on reflection, she could see his point. It was Adamo who had suffered at Luc's hands, it should be Adamo in at the end. She looked across the table at the man she loved. They hadn't finished their conversation about whether he wanted children. Whether they could ever be a family was considerably more important to her than anything else at the moment.

She said, "I'd like a walk on the beach before we go to the hospital. Adamo?"

"I believe I'll just have another cup of coffee if it's okay with you."

Eve gave him a look that said *coward*. Chill dripped from her voice. "Very well."

She nodded briefly to the rest of the table and stalked out.

Adamo stood indecisively, looking after her.

Conti shook his head. "I don't know what that was about, Adamo, but I'd advise you to follow her and set it right. You'll regret it if you don't."

"You're right, as usual. I suspect I've been a fool." Adamo squared his shoulders and followed Eve.

He caught up with her striding through the garden toward the beach. He grabbed her arm. "Wait, Eve. Hold on. Talk to me."

She whirled on him, her words tumbling out. Words she'd been bottling up for too long. "My sister is younger than I am, Adamo and she has a husband who adores her and she has five children. Do you intend to marry me, Adamo? Do you want children? Do you even see us as a family? I've accepted the way things are between us because I was certain the day would come when you'd want more. Was I wrong?"

"Eve, you're reading too much into what I said. You know I love you." He sighed. "But marriage, children…"

She and drew up to her full height, her eyes blazing fire. "Let me see if I understand. Marriage is an unnecessary complication. Sex is fine as long as it doesn't lead to children?"

"I didn't mean it that way, Eve, I…"

"Admit it, Adamo. You don't really want me for anything except a bit of fun. You don't want children. Don't deny it."

"Eve, you're not being fair. You know that's not what I meant…"

Eve interrupted him, her tone scathing. "Don't worry. I won't trap you into marriage, Adamo. I promise you I could never allow myself to become pregnant by a man who isn't sure he wants marriage, or who is afraid of having children. You never even said you loved me until you were prompted by Mark Conti."

"But…"

She took a shuddering breath and continued in a calmer voice. "I'll be moving across the hall to the spare bedroom in our suite until we leave here. And I won't be coming back to Positano with you. Playtime's over."

"Eve, you misunderstand. I…"

She turned and ran back to the house, leaving him standing with his hand outstretched, his world crumbling around him. What had he said to instigate all this? What idiocy had come out of his mouth?

****

Bette's room was filled with flowers, courtesy of Mark Conti. Ed's dozen white roses held place of honor on her tray table. She sat up in bed, pillows fluffed around her, a blue silk robe covering her shoulders as she held the tiny, red, wrinkled infant to her breast, coaxing her to feed.

"Isn't she the most beautiful thing you've ever seen?" Bette cooed.

Eve agreed the baby was a thing of beauty. She knew, in a few days, when the trauma of birth had passed, the baby would indeed be beautiful. "What will you name her?"

"*Fini.*" The answer was quick and definitive.

Ed burst out laughing. "You wouldn't!"

"Feeney?" Eve queried. "It seems an odd name for a girl."

"It's not a name," Ed explained between bouts of laughter. "She means *fini.* As in 'the end.' I think she means she doesn't intend to go through this ever again, now she has her girl. And it's okay by me. Finding the wherewithal to send five kids to college will be enough of a challenge."

A nurse bustled into the room. She took Bette's temperature and checked her chart. "Are you comfortable?" she asked.

"Comfortable? Here I am in this huge room filled with flowers and I have the daughter I've been hoping for. I'm not comfortable, I'm ecstatic."

The nurse smiled. "I'm glad. Mr. Conti rarely asks us for anything, but when he does…"

Ed interrupted. "Why should Mark Conti's requests have any influence on the care my wife receives in this hospital?"

The nurse looked at him in surprise. "You don't know? His wife died in this hospital five years ago. That new wing?" She pointed out the window.

His eyes followed her hand and, for the first time, he noticed the impressive new building adjoining the original hospital.

"It's the Carolyn Conti Cancer Clinic, one of the best in the state, if not the country. Mr. Conti donated the funds for it." The nurse turned and left the room, leaving Ed and Eve and Bette looking at each other in astonishment.

Ed shook his head. "That man never ceases to amaze me."

Bette turned her blue eyes on her husband. "Ed, would you go down to the gift shop and get me a candy bar? One of those big Dutch ones? I'm famished."

"Of course, darling."

When Eve and Bette were alone, Bette said, "You want to talk about it. I can see it in your eyes, in the way you're looking at me. And you didn't want Ed around."

Eve sighed. "Was it awful?" Her curiosity was genuine. She wanted children, but a certain anxiety about childbirth lurked in the back of her mind. She knew a part of her anger with Adamo was founded in her own fear. She was used to him being fearless. This was the man who, with his bare hands, had attacked an armed thug who was threatening her. She needed him to be strong. Instead, he seemed panicked at the mere prospect of marriage and family.

Bette broke into her thoughts. "Childbirth is never easy, but I had Ed with me through all the hours of labor."

"I've read about 'natural childbirth,' how it isn't really pain, it's just work…labor."

"They lie." Bette laughed. "I had my first baby, Jonathan, without anything to dull the spasms except Ed's coaching and help. We attended natural childbirth classes together. I was sure with Ed beside me, I could pull it off, and I did. It's true, childbirth is a natural function. What they don't tell you is, even with all the huffing and puffing and counting, and changing positions and back rubs, it hurts like hell. It went on for eighteen hours. I remember toward the end, screaming until my throat was raw. Ed did everything we were taught to do. He held my hands, he breathed with me, he rubbed my back. He helped me to walk instead of just lying in bed waiting for the next wrenching pain. Anticipating the next pain is almost as bad as the pain itself. And then toward the end when you're too exhausted to think coherently, and the pain is almost unendurable, some idiot doctor keeps saying 'push.' "

Bette took a deep breath and touched the fuzz on her baby's head. "It's easier when you've been through it once. You know what to expect the next time, and you know it will end. And the doctor can help with moderating the pain these days, especially toward the end, if you ask."

Bette laughed. "The twins arrived so fast Ed barely had time to get me to the hospital. This one took a bit longer. That's a girl for you. She took her own sweet time. But when they put the little wet yowling creature on my belly, the sense of achievement, the euphoria I felt, defies description."

Eve studied her sister's face. "I must say you look very self-satisfied."

"I had some bad hours yesterday and this morning, hours I'd rather forget, but here I am. I'm fine and I have a little girl, and she is worth everything she put me through."

****

Adamo had hung back when the others entered Bette's room. He wasn't sure about facing Eve in front of Bette and Ed, trying to act as if nothing were wrong when there were so many unanswered questions between them. He watched from down the hall as Ed left. Bracing himself to go in, he stopped just outside the door, glued to the spot, as he heard Bette describing to Eve what her labor had been like. He stood frozen, eavesdropping in spite of himself, listening to Bette calmly describing the agony of childbirth. Feeling sick, his face bathed in sweat, he headed to the men's room, where he threw up his breakfast. He rinsed his mouth out and splashed cold water on his face. Then he stalked blindly down the hall to the elevator. He was pushing through the doors leading out of the hospital when he saw Ed coming out of the gift shop, laden down with candy and magazines.

"Adamo! Wait. What's wrong? Let's grab a coffee and go sit on one of those benches outside."

A few minutes later they sat in the sun sipping coffee out of paper cups.

"You look like hell. What gives with you and Eve? It's obvious something's wrong."

There was a long silence. Then Adamo said, "She wants children."

"Don't you want children, Adamo? Don't you think it's natural for a woman to want children with the man she loves? To create a family?"

"I'd love to have children, but the thought of putting Eve through childbirth…"

"I see."

"No. I don't think you do." Adamo sighed. "I was eleven years old. My older sister, Adele, was pregnant. She was just sixteen, and it was a home birth. It wasn't uncommon in Italy in those days. I could hear first moaning and then screams coming from her room. They seemed to go on forever. At the beginning I buried my head in my pillows, but still I could hear her, so I crept out of bed and slipped inside her doorway. My mother was there, gripping her shoulders. The doctor was there too, and they were both too busy to notice me huddling there. I heard Adela's cries rise to shrieks as her baby was delivered. There was blood. So much blood. Then suddenly there was silence. The silence was more terrifying than her screams had been. The doctor looked at my mother and shook his head. I slipped out the door and ran back to my room. I learned only the next day the baby was stillborn and my sister was dead. She hemorrhaged. They weren't able to save her. She just quietly bled to death."

Ed shook his head. "It must have been a terrifying experience for an eleven-year-old, Adamo, but it doesn't have to be like that. It isn't usually like that today. Childbirth is never without some risk, but it is safer today than at any time in the history of mankind. Women want children. And so do men. We all want family. It's unfair the burden and pain of producing children falls on women. But I suppose on some gut level it's built into our genes, the survival of the species."

"I overheard Bette telling Eve what it was like. I can't...I just won't put Eve through it."

Ed sighed. "You can't make that decision for Eve. It's not yours to make. Eve wants children. She wants them with you. Are you going to deny her? Are you going to allow her love for you to wither over this issue?"

Chapter Twenty

Back at the Conti residence, Adamo sat on a bench in the garden staring at nothing. How could his life have plummeted into the abyss with so little warning? Of course he wanted Eve. He wanted to grow old with her. He couldn't begin to imagine his life without her. His fear of losing her...

"Life can be a bitch, can't it?" Mark Conti's voice interrupted his thoughts.

Adamo sighed. "It seems in trying to hold on to Eve I've lost her."

"Loosen your grip." The older man sat down beside Adamo. "Stop trying to 'hold on' to her. You can't live Eve's life, or make Eve's decisions, no matter how much you may want to. Whatever has come between you, talk it out. Then give her what she wants. You will eventually, anyway. We're no match for them. Most women are smarter and stronger than we are in every way except physically. I find grovelling helps. And flowers, lots of flowers."

In spite of himself Adamo laughed. "Thank you, Mr. Conti. I needed to hear that. I may be frightened of life with Eve, but I'm terrified at the idea of life without her. I'll take your advice...if she'll even speak to me."

"It's Mark. Call me Mark. And I'll help you arrange for the flowers. You think of a suitable short note to accompany them. I suggest something along the lines of 'I've been an idiot.'"

They sat side by side in companionable silence for a few minutes gazing at the sea.

Mark sighed and stood. "Now on to business. I think it's time to speak to our guests. They've had sufficient time to worry. Are you ready, Adamo?"

In the library, Conti took his usual place behind his desk. Adamo chose a wing chair where he could observe without being intrusive. The door opened and James Conroy ushered a furious Monica into the library. "Miss Farrell," he announced.

Monica stormed over to Mark Conti and leaned over his desk, hissing out her words. "You can't keep me here. You can't prove anything against me. I demand you release me immediately!" Her voice rose hysterically on the last words.

"My dear lady, I have no intention of keeping you here any longer than I have to. Have you found your accommodation unsatisfactory? Your meals not to your taste?"

She took a step back. "Our rooms were locked and there was a guard outside. You've been holding us prisoner. What you're doing is against the law."

Adamo spoke from his chair in a dark corner in the room. "I wonder how that stacks up against murder and embezzlement?"

Monica whirled, seeing him for the first time. "You! You're behind all this."

"No." Conti's voice held a hard edge. "Let us be very clear about who is responsible and for what. You were involved in entrapment and embezzlement. I think a good case could be made you were involved in murder, even if only after the fact."

Monica collapsed into the chair in front of the desk and whispered, "What are you going to do?"

"I'm going to allow you to walk out of here. One of my men will put you on a plane for Barbados. Once you're there, you are on your own. You still have your house, but you'll find your money source has dried up. In a word, my dear, you are broke. And if you try to return to the U.S. you will be denied entry. You will be on the 'no fly' list. In fact, I think you'll find you are not welcome in a number of countries. I hope you like living in Barbados."

"You can do that?" Her voice was a whisper.

"My dear lady, I can do that and much more. I want you gone. You may be thankful I have chosen this way to make it happen. James, will you please ask Yasim to take Miss Farrell to the airport? I believe you've already arranged for her luggage, her travel documents, and her escort?"

"You mean leave? Right now? What about Luc?"

"Luc Manzel is the least of your worries. You will not see him again. If you choose not to accept my very generous offer, I will resort to the law. Let's see. You're forty now? You might be out of prison in time to apply for Social Security benefits. Oh. I forgot. You've never worked a day in your life. No Social Security benefits."

Monica turned to Adamo. "You did this to me."

"No." Adamo stood. "No," he said. "Your greed, your avarice did this to you. My jail was a prison cell. Yours is a mansion on a tropical island. You'll manage. You always do. You'll find some man to pay your bills." He turned his back on her as she was led out of the room.

When she was gone, he sat down again. He felt empty. He should feel vindicated, but all he could feel was sorrow. How could the woman he had known through all his college years, had married without much thought, have come to this? Was he in some part responsible?

He looked at Mark Conti. "I'm glad you decided not to pursue legal alternatives."

The other man sighed. "Don't give me too much credit. I've worked for thirty years to create the Conti Corporation as it is today. I grew up in Napoli, in an environment with which I believe you are familiar. But I was determined to take a different path when I emigrated. It hasn't always been easy, and I may have taken some shortcuts along the way, but the business I run today is legitimate. My problem is, Luc Manzel has been with me for a long time…"

"And he knows where the skeletons are hidden," Adamo completed his sentence.

"Just so. How to deal with Luc, there's the problem. In the old days, he'd simply have disappeared. But, in spite of what I implied to him earlier, it's no longer a viable solution."

"What will you do?"

"Have you ever played poker? He'll be here in a minute or two. We'll see whether my bluff will work."

They sat in silence.

The door opened. "Mr. Manzel." This time James Conroy followed Luc into the room and stood, back to the door.

Luc Manzel strutted to the chair in front of the desk. To Adamo, he appeared to have regained his assurance in the hours since the previous afternoon. He exuded confidence as he sat facing Mark Conti. "You have an offer to put on the table?"

"You will write a full and detailed confession of the embezzlement scheme. You will also confess to the murder of Emmett Kenston. This confession, in your handwriting, will remain in my possession. Of course if I were to die unexpectedly, or if any harm should come to Adamo de Leone or any of those closely associated with him, your confession will go to the police. So you'd better hope I live a long life."

"Why would I even consider such an action? You won't resort to the law. Your 'proof' would not hold up in any court. The murder, if murder could be proved, happened a long time ago. Evidence would be hard to come by."

Mark Conti stared at Luc before speaking. Then he sighed. "You are correct in all your assumptions. I have little faith in the courts to find you guilty, and I have no desire to drag the name of the Conti Corporation through the mud."

Luc frowned, clearly puzzled. "What am I missing here? What do you have to bargain with? What exactly is your offer?"

"I could, of course, see to it you never work again, anywhere. I don't have to resort to the law. I simply have to let it be known in certain circles you were caught with your hand in the till. Life, as you know it, would be over. I wonder how you would adapt to being poor, Luc? To being penniless and jobless?"

Luc jumped to his feet and banged his fist on the desk. "You wouldn't!"

"Sit down, Luc. I merely mention it as an alternative."

There was a long silence in the room.

"So what do you propose?"

"You will continue as a member of my staff. In fact, you will be promoted to vice president in charge of our mining interests. You'll draw a commensurate salary. You will have to travel frequently to fairly remote places. You will be my representative in all matters regarding our mines, answering directly to me."

"Why would you do such a thing?" Luc sounded genuinely puzzled. "What do you want in return?"

In a completely reasonable voice, Mark Conti said, "In return I expect only the insurance of your confessions in my safe."

Luc Manzel shook his head. "I'm supposed to trust you not to turn my written confession over to the law?"

"Have you ever known me to break my word? If you accept my terms, you may begin in your new position next Monday. If you agree, you may walk out of here now, a free man."

"Mines? Like that hell-hole I just got back from?"

"That one and others like it. They tend to be in primitive locations."

"And if I refuse to give you a written confession?"

Mark Conti's words were without inflection. "You may still walk out of here, a free man"—he paused—"but a man with perhaps a very brief future."

Luc sat on the edge of his chair. "Are you threatening me?"

"If you choose the second alternative, I will enlist my brother's help with my problem. It will take only one phone call."

Adamo intervened, his voice soft and measured. "I believe you know someone in the lower ranks of Don

Alfonso Conti's organization. Twice you had someone there try to kill me without the Don's knowledge or consent. He's already annoyed with you."

For the first time Luc realized Adamo was in the room. "You're behind this!" he spat out. "I knew you were trouble the minute you got out of jail."

"A jail I'd never have been in without your machinations," Adamo answered mildly.

Mark Conti interrupted. "Unfortunately for you, Luc, you didn't have access to Don Alfonso's full resources. I have. If you force me to enlist my brother's help, you can measure your life in days, if not hours."

Luc stood and paced. He stopped and glared at Adamo, then started pacing again.

Adamo sat quietly in his wing chair, his eyes following Luc, the clenching of his hands on the arms the only outward sign of his tension.

Mark Conti remained impassively waiting, his hands folded on his desk.

Luc came back to face his nemesis. "I'll be on salary? With a raise?"

"Yes."

"Vice president in charge of mining, you said?"

"Yes."

"No further threats against my life? No throwing me out on charges of theft?"

"Your life, worthless though I consider it, will not be forfeit. You will continue to work for the Conti Corporation, dealing with our mining operations."

Luc gave a sigh of resignation. "What do you want me to write?"

"A description of when and how you murdered Emmett Kenston, and a confession of your part in the embezzlement scheme. Keep it simple. One page should do it. A pen and paper are on the table over there."

****

An hour later, Luc Manzel walked out of the library, out of Mark Conti's house, and out of Adamo's life. The confession had been handed to James Conroy to be put in a safe in another part of the house.

Mark opened his desk drawer and pulled out a bottle of cognac and two glasses. He poured generous tot into each and handed one to Adamo.

They toasted silently and drank.

Adamo said, "I liked the one about firing him and making sure he never worked again. Why did you opt to keep him on instead?"

"I couldn't have gotten a confession out of him if I'd fired him. And my life and possibly yours would have been perpetually under threat. A man with nothing to lose is a dangerous man."

"But this way he's not only still in your organization, he's got a promotion."

"*Keep your friends close and your enemies closer.* A piece of good advice that's been around since the fifteen hundreds. Machiavelli said it in *The Prince.* You should read Machiavelli. His principles have guided men of power for centuries."

Mark walked over to a section of his book cases and pulled out a slim leather bound volume. "Here. You may keep it." He smiled "Even an innkeeper may find something of interest in Machiavelli."

"Thank you." Adamo accepted the book. "Would you really have had him killed?"

"No. It was a bluff. I'd never risk my business

empire in such a way. Besides, my brother isn't all-powerful these days. He's an old man who enjoys his influence in small ways. He's highly respected in Naples, but he has no arm in the United States. And his days of ordering people dead, if they ever existed, are no more."

Somehow that knowledge made Adamo feel better.

Mark took a sip of his drink. "Of course, those mines are dangerous places…"

Startled, Adamo stared at Mark Conti. The older man's expression was totally impassive.

Adamo stood. "I'd better see what I can do to get back in Eve's good graces."

"The flowers and note will have softened her up a bit."

"I hope so."

Adamo went up to their room and opened the door. No sign of Eve. He retreated to the living room. She had said she was moving across to the empty room. Had she? He crossed to the door and knocked.

There was no answer. He opened the door tentatively. The room was filled with flowers, but there was no Eve.

He went downstairs and out the back of the house. He found her there, on the bench, facing the sea. He sat down beside her, his arms resting on his legs, his head down, resisting the impulse to start babbling. What if she meant it? What if she wouldn't come back to him?

"It's over," he said. "Luc and Monica are both gone. Luc signed a confession. It's in Mark Conti's hands as insurance against further damage."

Eve sighed. "He did what he said he'd do. The money's back where it belongs and as for Luc and

Monica, I don't think they'll be causing us any further problems. Are you satisfied, Adamo? Your name hasn't been cleared. Legally you're still a felon."

Adamo took a moment before he answered. "It doesn't seem to matter. The guilt I had over all those people losing their life savings is gone. They have most of their money back. I'm happy in the life we've built together. But I need you, Eve. My life is nothing without you."

"Ed told me about your sister. What a terrible experience for a child."

"You know how careful I've always been. If I got you pregnant...the danger..." His voice caught, and he put his head in his hands. "I'm terrified of losing you, Eve."

Eve touched his hair. "Adamo, life carries no guarantees. I could be struck by lightning tomorrow. You could be run over by a bus. Or we could get married and have seven children and live to ninety-eight and die within a day of each other." Her lips turned up in a gentle smile. "We have to choose life, with all its untidiness and unpredictability. To retreat from life, to live in constant fear of the 'what if's'...I can't live that way, Adamo."

"Seven children?"

"It was just a number. A possibility."

"Can we begin with just one? And see how I survive pregnancy and delivery?"

Eve laughed out loud. "It's usual to start with just one. Unless I have twins. Twins run in my family."

"Now you tell me."

They sat without words. Adamo put his arm around Eve. She let her head rest on his shoulder.

Sometime later, they strolled, hand in hand, back toward the house.

"Mark suggested the flowers, didn't he?"

"I was planning on them anyway. But I had in mind more like a dozen, not a roomful."

"For future reference, a dozen roses would have done the job."

"Are we going to be all right, Eve?"

"I think we're going to be just fine, Adamo."

Chapter Twenty-One

The family were all there to greet them at the bus stop, just as they had been on the first time in Positano. Could it really have been only a few months ago? Now though, Eve was fully a part of their welcoming greeting and happy chatter, as they all wound their way down the hillside to the inn. Her Italian was almost as fluent as theirs.

"You won't believe how full we've been, even out of season!" Gianni said.

"I've been thinking," Zio Valerio said. "Signora Ghirando has decided to move to Rome to be with her daughter. She says she getting too old for all these steps."

"Nonsense," Graziella interrupted. "She's ten years younger than I. She's just lonely now with her husband gone, and her daughter, Maria, needs a baby sitter."

"Be that as it may, she's thinking of selling her house." Zio Valerio looked significantly at Adamo.

Adamo made a very Italian gesture that said, "And so…"

"It's right next to yours. It would give you another eight to ten rooms."

Adamo laughed. "We're barely keeping our heads above water now, uncle. I can't imagine how we'd manage another eight or ten rooms."

"We'll see. I have some money put aside, and Don

Alfonso might be interested in a little investment."

Eve shook her head. They were back in Italy. Things were done differently here. Or were they? She'd been reading Adamo's copy of *The Prince*. Men in power behaved in remarkably similar ways in every part of the world. Now if the world were run by women...

Her musings were interrupted as they arrived at the entrance to the Albergo de Leone, with its winged marble lion standing guard. Adamo fitted the key into the lock and opened the door.

"Home," Eve sighed.

"Your dinner is in the oven," Zia Graziella called back over her shoulder as the family trooped on down the path to their own residence.

Adamo and Eve walked through and dropped their bags in the bedroom.

"Leave the unpacking until morning," Adamo said. "Right now, let's just enjoy being here."

Eve went out on their balcony and breathed in the scent of the lemon blossoms. Adamo followed a few minutes later with two small glasses of limoncello in his hands. He handed one to Eve. "Welcome home, *cara mia*."

Eve lifted her glass to touch his.

Adamo put his arm around her and pulled her close as the setting sun settled into the sea, leaving the sky molten, throwing crimson ribbons across the water.

"I never tire of this beauty," Eve said. "It's unlike anyplace else in the world."

"Do you think you could live the rest of your life here? With me?"

"Is that a proposal?"

Adamo reached into his pocket and pulled out a worn velvet box.

"This was my grandmother's ring," he said, opening the box. "Will you wear it? Then the correct word would be *fidanzata*." Adamo slid the ring on Eve's finger. It was a perfect fit.

Eve studied it in wonder. The gold of the wide band was a rich dark color, almost rose rather than yellow. At the center of its old-fashioned setting was a small oval-cut sapphire.

"Oh Adamo, it's beautiful."

"The stone matches the blue of your eyes. I knew when I first looked into them. I tried to tell myself I had no right to think of you that way…"

"You have every right. I love you. And yes, I am honored to wear your ring."

Adamo sighed as if some great weight had been lifted from his shoulders.

"However…" Eve looked up at him.

"Yes?" The one word was filled with tension.

"I think I'd like the word *sposa* better. Perhaps tomorrow we could check to see when the little church in the square in Ravello has space for a wedding."

A triumphant laugh seemed to start someplace around Adamo's toes and work its way all the way up his long lean form.

"Tomorrow it is." He threw his arms around her and hugged her close.

****

It was April. The Amalfi Coast was a riot of blossoms. The fragrance of lemon trees hung heavy in the air, bougainvillea was in bloom, and wild roses tumbled over stone walls.

Eve stood in front of the full length mirror studying her reflection. Her dress was perfection, its antique lace over silk cut modestly in the bodice, swinging out to a full skirt, shorter in front, touching the floor in the back allowing just the briefest glimpse of her silk pumps. She wore a circlet of fresh flowers on her head, over the full lace and net veil worn by Zia Graziella at her wedding.

"Aren't you ready yet?" Her sister Bette rushed into the room. She gasped. "You look like a fairytale princess!"

"I feel like a fairytale princess." Eve hugged her sister. "You look pretty good yourself. She examined Bette's shorter pale blue version of her own dress. "Do we have the bouquets?"

"They're on the table by the door. We'll pick them up as we leave."

"I can't believe we're really doing this." Tears were close to the surface. "I love him so much, Bette. And I wasn't sure I'd ever get him to the altar. He has this ridiculous notion he's not good enough for me. I'm not sure he'll ever get over the fact he's been unable to clear his name."

"Give him something else to worry about. A house full of children should take his mind off an indictment long ago in another country, in another life. Everyone who counts knows Adamo was innocent of any wrong-doing. In any case, he's on his way to the church now. It was lovely of him to ask Ed to serve as best man."

"He thinks the world of Ed. Of course he wanted him as best man."

"Come on. Graziella and Alicia are waiting for us. You'll need help getting up all those steps in that dress."

Eve was silent on the drive to Ravello. Like the road to Ravello, the past had been a long and tortuous, filled with unexpected twists and turns. But this was their destination. She had never doubted it, even in Lisbon. This was her future, here with Adamo, surrounded by family she loved and who loved her.

The church was filled to overflowing with neighbors and friends. As she walked down the aisle on Zio Valerio's arm, to the strains of Purcell's Trumpet Voluntary played on an antique organ, she noticed the elderly man in the wheelchair. Don Alfonso was here. All these steps couldn't have been easy for him.

Her thoughts turned briefly to absent friends. Emma Kenston and Mark Conti weren't here. She'd so hoped they'd be able to come.

Then she was at the altar, beside Adamo. She lifted her eyes to his. He was impossibly handsome in his formal black suit with the sprig of lemon blossom on his lapel, the white of his shirt and tie stark against the darkness of his skin. And, as always, his riot of untameable silver curls. He took her hand and his eyes held hers for an intense moment before they knelt and the priest began the wedding mass.

Later, back in Positano for the reception at Leone's, Ed pulled Adamo aside for a moment. "Mark Conti asked me to give this to you after the ceremony. He said it was in the nature of a wedding present."

Adamo looked quizzically at the large envelope. Carefully he slid a finger under the flap and pulled out one single page with its cardboard backing. It seemed to be a document of some kind. He read it and sat down abruptly.

Ed gave him a worried look. "What's wrong?"

"Get Eve."

Ed was back a moment later with the bride in tow. "What is it, Adamo? You look in shock? What…?"

Without speaking, Adamo handed Eve the one-page document, Mark Conti's wedding present to them.

Eve read, and then reread the document. With a joyous laugh she flung herself down into Adamo's lap. "It's a full pardon," she explained to a bewildered Ed. "It's a full pardon from the governor of New York. It's as good as declaring Adamo innocent. He can no longer refer to himself as a felon."

"That was Mark Conti's wedding present to you?" Ed shook his head and laughed. "Is there nothing that man can't do?"

Adamo finally found his voice. "He knew how much it meant to me."

Eve took the large envelope out of Adamo's hand and shook it. "There's a smaller envelope in here."

She opened the envelope and withdrew a single sheet.

"My dear friends," she read aloud.

"We are so sorry to have missed your wedding, but we are presently on our honeymoon in Bermuda. We'll come to see you soon. All our best, Mark and Emma."

"They did it!" Adamo whooped.

Finally the last of the guests straggled out of Leone's.

"Ready to go home, Signora de Leone?" Adamo's eyes held the promise of passion.

"More than ready, Signore de Leone."

Hand in hand they strolled down the hundred and ten steps to their future.

A word about the author…

Blair McDowell's first career was as a musician and teacher. She studied in Europe and, during the course of her academic career, lived in Hungary, the United States, Australia, and Canada, teaching in universities in the latter three countries. She has always loved to write and has produced six widely used professional books in her field.

A voracious reader, Blair decided when she retired from university teaching to turn her talents to her first love, writing fiction. She moved to Canada's scenic west coast and, with a friend, opened a bed & breakfast. Mornings she makes omelets and chats with guests from far and near, and afternoons, she writes. From March through September, the world comes to her doorstep, bringing tales that are fodder for her rich imagination, but once the tourist season is over, she packs her bags and takes off for exotic ports. Europe in the fall, the Caribbean in the winter.

Where Lemons Bloom is set in one of her favorite destinations, the Amalfi Coast of Italy.

http://www.blairmcdowell.com

CPSIA information can be obtained
at www.ICGtesting.com
Printed in the USA
LVOW07s1132270917
550076LV00006B/20/P